A search along the forbidden
of sensual consciousness...

'In US I have explored ideas and energies
for which I have been seeking a means of
expression during my entire writing life.
Here, I know with the best part of me, I have
spoken the old and lovely truths of the
human heart, the honest language of love
penetrating to the secret parts of ourselves
that hold our most ardent – and therefore
our most immeasurable – meanings and
desires.'

Anonymous

US

A discovery of the erotic essence of the
human heart...

US

BY ANONYMOUS

ARROW BOOKS

Arrow Books Limited
17-21 Conway Street, London W1P 6JD

An imprint of the Hutchinson Publishing Group

London Melbourne Sydney Auckland
Johannesburg and agencies throughout
the world

First published in Great Britain 1983
Published by arrangement with Bantam Books

© Bantam Books, Inc., 1973

Made and printed in Great Britain
by The Anchor Press Ltd
Tiptree, Essex

ISBN 0 09 930800 2

Dedication
for *HER,*
once more—*with feeling*

Preface

First, Anonymous wrote *Her*. Then, Anonymous wrote *Him*. Now, Anonymous has written *Us*. The time has come to make a public confession: I am irretrievably entranced with the idea of appearing before the reading public in the guise of Anonymous, as well as under my own name.

In the Preface to *Her*, I wrote: *Under my true name, I have written many books, which have sold several million copies and have been translated into virtually every language of the world. . . . Why, then . . . do I choose to publish this novel,* Her, *under the ancient and honorable appellation of Anonymous? . . . I want* Her *to be read and known for* Her *sake alone. . . . Under Anonymous,* Her *stands apart from the personality and/or previous work of the author; it is a creation in its own wholeness, as woman is a woman.*

My entire consideration, you will note, was directed outward, toward the reader and critic, with no thought given to the impact of anonymity upon the author. However, when I came to write *Him*, I had begun to realize; for in that preface I said: *Had I, wrapped in the ancient and honorable cloak of Anonymous, only now achieved the utter abolition of author's personality that every truly serious writer seeks? . . . once having tasted such utter freedom from expectation and personality and ego, it was impossible not to return again—and perhaps again and again—to that primordial spring of inspiration. . . . There was, curiously enough, a definite reluctance to submerge myself so completely again—even while I longed to do so. So, almost against my will, and yet in accord with my most profound impulses, of artist and of person, I found myself writing again in "the best and truest tongue in the world, the language of love."*

With the completion of *Us,* I have come to realize that through such anonymity of authorship I have become two writers. I now live in twin houses of the mind, capable of passing at need, freely and without effort, from one to the other. The materials and meanings—yes, even the style—that is accessible to Anonymous is completely separate from the materials and meanings and style of the writer who publishes under my true name.

I am as proud of the books by Anonymous as of the others. In an odd sort of way, perhaps even prouder, for I can enjoy all the rewards of an enormous success without suffering any of the handicaps. As just one example, a known author of books being read at the rate achieved by *Her* and *Him* would be subject to a barrage of public and private attention—newspaper and television interviews, publicity trips, a flood of mail and phone calls—that inevitably results, in my experience, in a debilitation of the self that makes it extraordinarily difficult to get on with the work. Indeed, many good writers have been destroyed, or altered beyond recognition, by our modern cult of the personality.

As it is, I can pursue the even tenor of my ways

undisturbed, as I privately enjoy the awareness, so important to a writer, that millions of readers have come eagerly to these books. Not even my closest friends are aware of my identity as Anonymous; indeed, several have innocently recommended these novels to my attention!

But of course the greatest reward lies within the act of writing. In my new Anonymous self, there are available to me truths and meanings I could not otherwise unearth. In *Us*, I have explored ideas and energies for which I have been seeking a means of expression during my entire writing life. Here, I know with the best part of me, I have spoken the old and lovely truths of the human heart, the honest language of love penetrating to the secret parts of ourselves that hold our most ardent—and therefore our most immeasurable—meanings and desires.

And it is my best hope that this new author named Anonymous will remain alive and active, to discover in due time the form and meaning of a future book.

We shall see.

Anonymous
[The Author of HER and HIM]

us

Chapter 1

When the taxi left me at the mainland dock, the sun was slanting westward over No-Name Key a mile away across the bay. All I could see, except for the dense mass of mangroves guarding the approaches, was the variously slanted reaches of red-tile roof. Under that roof, I knew, dwelled the woman named Maria who had made a certain few of my days a vivid splash of time, like an abstract blob of paint smeared redly over a drab façade.

Once the taxi had gone spinning away up the sun-whitened shell road, I was very much alone. The dock, made of sun-weathered wood, was ancient, ramshackle, the pilings whitened with pelican droppings; like a thousand other deserted Florida docks, it rotted inexorably under the twin impacts of weather and salt until a hurricane should, one season, find it vulnerable to destruction. To all appearance, I was the only man to come this way for years. The only sign of anything currently useful was the concrete-block garage, large enough to hold four cars, standing whitely mute with its padlocked doors.

Hefting the suitcase, I walked out onto the dock, wondering if there had been a misunderstanding about the time of arrival. I saw the bell then, mounted low on a bracket, above it a weathered legend. RING

FOR BOAT. I put my hand on the lever that would toll my summons across the intervening water.

Then—I paused.

Did I truly wish to see Maria again after all these years? In this moment, really thinking about it for the first time, I felt strongly that it would be the better valor to leave us possessed of the old times only. Maria had called and, as I had promised, I had responded. In that last day of our life together, I had said, "Maria, if you ever need me, will you let me know?" She had answered softly, her head turned away; "Yes. Yes, Jerry. I will."

For a long time, much too long, I had kept hoping. Even married again, I had held a corner of my soul for Maria; and when the second marriage had ended so bitterly, I had had to fight myself to keep from calling her. Now, when I had long since given up all thought of the possibility, her summons had come desperately. In less than three hours after hearing her voice, I had been aboard a jetliner that was leaving California behind.

But, in this last moment in which I could still walk away, I remembered that, the first time I had laid my hand on her warm flesh, Maria had been nineteen, and I had been thirty. Now Maria was thirty, and I. . .

No. There was not the faintest justification for the green hope that had started growing inside me the instant I had recognized her voice. There was, I knew so well, no soil in which such dreams, compounded equally of memory and desire, might flourish. I had married again, and so had Maria, and though we had parted in sadness, not in anger, I had learned long since that there is no going back.

But, I argued, my hand on the bell-lever, I'm not

2

trying to go back. It isn't that way at all. I am here on this deserted Florida dock because I made a simple response to a simple summons. "Jerry?" she had said. "Thank goodness it's you, Jerry. I've been trying to find you for three days."

"But I told you—remember? . . . my New York agent always knows where I am."

She had laughed. "I couldn't remember his name, Jerry. Not until I got desperate."

Her voice was deeper than I remembered, throatier, with an underlying throb. I wondered if the pulse was there all the time, the beat of her blood, or only because she was speaking again to me.

"Maria?" I said.

"Can you come, Jerry?" she said, her voice pulsing quietly in my ear. "I've never asked . . . until now—but can you come?"

A bad time. Only this morning I had taken on a script assignment. I don't do many movie scripts, because I don't like what's involved . . . not the writing itself, but all the endless conferences about the writing. I don't like the kind of people you have to deal with, either. There's always somebody intent on taking the cheap shot, making a place in the Hollywood sun for himself at your expense. After a sober consultation with myself concerning how much free time I could see ahead, as represented by my bank balance, I had told my agent to accept the terms. Fifty thousand dollars, in my scale of values, works out to two more years I've got 'em fooled.

I didn't hesitate, though, for which I am grateful to the good part of myself that's so often so hard to live with. "Yes," I had said. "Where are you? I'll be there on the next plane."

That first time—though she had come to me, not

3

I to her—she had shivered with the innate fear of a girl who has not yet known a man.

"If you're frightened," I'd said. "You can leave."

She had bitten her lower lip under upper teeth, "I'm scared," she had said. "But I don't want to leave. Put it in me."

I had put it in her. And my life had never been the same; not only what had been lived before, but all that would have to be lived after. A gray façade of time, daubed with the bright smear of Maria.

She was not the Maria she had been, nor was I the Jerry Dorn. So the summons had not been simple, but complex. She had not even tried to tell me her reasons for needing me, nor had I found it necessary to ask.

It'll be a long walk back to that little grocery store where I can phone for a taxi, I thought. And, later on, I'll have to call her, tell Maria why I failed her. Surely, by then, I will understand well enough why it was all so impossible. How much does a man owe, anyway, to the established fact that his greedy cock was the first to probe her trembling flesh?

But it was so much more complicated than that. Or was it? I didn't know. I reached forth my hand and tolled three measured strokes across the water that separated me from No-Name Key.

On the instant, I heard the distant roar of a motorboat, saw it slicing swiftly toward the mainland. I sat down on my suitcase to wait. A pelican flapped clumsily down to stand on a piling, eyeing me hopefully for a fish. Sorry, fellow, I told him silently. No fish today. Behind me the palm trees were still, with no breeze to rustle dryly the harsh fronds.

I had expected Maria to come to meet me herself, so I had been holding an anticipatory tension. But

4

the boat brought only an old fellow, lean and tall, with a skin dark enough to be called bronze, a combination of heredity and years of sun.

When he cut the motor, gliding expertly alongside the dock, the sudden silence was so thick that his voice sliced through it loudly. "Mr. Jerry Dorn?" The words of my name lilted with the faint music of a nearly forgotten accent. Cajun? I thought, remembering the picture I had worked on in the Louisiana swamps five or six years ago.

"Yes," I said. "Jerry Dorn."

He smiled. "John Kershaw, me. You are most welcome."

He took my suitcase as I passed it over the side, then grasped the dock with one hand to steady the boat as I climbed in. It was a beautiful thing, about sixteen feet, with sleek lines. The brass shone in the sunlight, the decks gleamed with painstakingly rubbed varnish. I moved gratefully under the canopy out of the hot sun. He took the boat in a flat-out run as it curved away from the dock in a graceful arc. The motor was too loud for conversation, so I settled into my seat to enjoy the ride.

He had to slow the boat in order to thread the channel through the clusters of mangrove near the key. Once or twice we were close enough to reach out and touch the tough, gnarled roots. Bringing the boat to the bay-side dock, he leaped out with an agility remarkable in a man of his age and began tying up. I lifted out my suitcase, got out of the boat, and stood looking . . . at the dock, not at the house.

The dock was solid marble. Old stone now, stained and discolored, though scrupulously clean. There were iron rings along the water's edge, and rust from each ring had made indelible stains.

5

At the time of our marriage, I had not known that Maria was rich. A college is one place where money need not flaunt itself ostentatiously. Only later had I discovered that her grandfather, one of the Florida real-estate pioneers of the Twenties, had built a fortune so immense that it had continued to grow, of itself, during the bad years that had followed.

Maria had spoken of the house on No-Name Key where she had done much of her growing up. I was seeing it now for the first time, for we had never come here. It was ornate in the Spanish manner . . . even somewhat Moorish . . . with a red roof, and beautiful tiles set decoratively in the walls. In the space between the dock and the bay-side entrance was a scatter of statuary, weathered like the marble dock, and thick walls enclosing patios rich with greenery in tiled jugs, huge and ornate. The path was made of flagstones of variegated marbles, laid in an intricate pattern. Unlike most houses of this vintage, the establishment was not merely a shabby remnant of one-time glories; the greenery was trimmed and trained, and the flagstones had surely been polished this morning.

John Kershaw took my suitcase and motioned for me to follow. I was tight inside, once more, with the anticipation of Maria. She was here, so close . . . and waiting. My throat was dry, and I swallowed, hard, as we entered through enormous double doors. The reception room was cool, still, silent. The walls were covered with old tapestries and rugs, the only decorations large enough, vivid enough, to maintain identity in such grand surroundings. The furniture was sparse, massive; tall-backed black chairs, an enormous sofa, a huge oriental rug brilliantly covering the brilliant, cold floor-tiles.

The room was empty of Maria. The old Cajun set down my suitcase, crossed the floor to tug at a bell-pull at least a foot wide. It was as heavily embroidered as the suit-of-lights a bullfighter wears. In the deep reaches of the house, I heard the faraway sound of a bell.

"Constancia will show you to your room," John Kershaw told me in his musical accent.

So I was not to see Maria immediately. I watched the maid approaching down a long corridor. She was plump, matronly, her broad expanse frilled by a tiny white apron. Her face was mooned with comfortable fat, her legs were short, her breasts huge.

She greeted me, not as a servant, but as a friend of the family. "Mr. Jerry?" she said. "I have heard Miss Maria speak of you so often."

I took her outstretched hand, felt its plumpness, felt the strength beneath. The old man stooped for the suitcase, stopped, listening to a distant jangle of bell.

"There is the next one," he said to Constancia. "I will go now."

Constancia took charge of the suitcase, though I attempted to carry it myself. "No, no," she protested. "It is light as a feather."

I followed her and the featherweight suitcase up a broad sweep of stairs to the second floor, then a smaller staircase to the third. She opened a door and stood aside for me to enter.

"You will have the time for a small siesta, if you wish it, as well as a bath," she said. She smiled a friendly smile. "In this heat, a siesta is a most grateful thing. There will be cocktails at six. Beside the pool."

And Maria? I thought, wondering why she had

7

not greeted me herself. But I did not say anything. When I was alone, I sat down on the massive bed, wondering how old it could be. I needed something to occupy my mind, or else I would have to wonder why another arrival was expected. Is it a house party? I asked myself. Is that all she wanted of me . . . simply to make another guest? I had thought, without really thinking about it, that we would be alone.

I got off the bed and went to the tall windows. My room was on the west side of the house, facing toward the Gulf. The estate, I could see, had been modernized with a huge swimming pool, open to the air but shielded on each side by high screens of shrubbery. Modern tile here, lounge chairs and mats, a curved shape of bar. Beyond the elevated swimming-pool area, steps led down to a broad expanse of white-sand beach, showing sunwashed and empty in each direction as far as I could see. Two gardeners were on ladders, working on the hedge alongside the pool.

What an establishment, I thought, still occupying my mind with trivia. How much it must cost to maintain; especially on a key with no connections to the mainland except by boat. That meant its own power plant, its own sewage disposal, its own water supply. I knew, from what Maria had told me long ago, that her family owned the entire key, some four miles long, though narrow enough at this end for the house and its grounds to bridge from Gulf to bay. Now it belonged to Maria.

Subconsciously, I realized, I had been listening for the speedboat. I heard it now, the powerful roar diminishing as the Cajun boatman guided it into the twisting approach channel. Moving swiftly, I went out into the hallway, oriented myself, and entered another room on the other side where I could look down on the marble dock.

I gazed down from my secret vantage point at the man getting out of the boat. Foreshortened from this height, I saw him tall, slender—and much younger than I. He was wearing a white tee-shirt that showed off his arms and shoulders, and beautifully draped blue slacks. He was careful of the slacks, getting out of the boat, and he did not offer to help the boatman with the three large bags.

Lifting his head toward the house, he stood absolutely still for a long moment. I could see his profile. Not a handsome man...a beautiful man. Roman nose, a solid, unbroken line from forehead to tip; clean, chiseled features, with flat cheeks, and his mouth could have been shaped by a sculptor of the classical school.

So it is a house party, and I was a fool to come, I thought, an anger stirring that was surprising in its intensity. Had Maria become so frivolous, having come into maturity and money, that she would exploit my old solemn promise simply to secure one more guest? It had been so long, there could be no knowing how much she had changed. I hadn't thought about that, listening to her voice pleading on the telephone.

Back in my room, I drew the drapes against the westering sun and busied myself with the contents of my suitcase. Then, moving slowly, meticulously, blanked away from thought, I undressed. The bed was turned down. I folded back the sheet and the spread and got into it. The sheets, heavily starched, were smooth against my flesh. I turned over toward the blank wall, feeling the illicit comfort of being

9

abed in the afternoon. As Constancia had remarked, a small siesta would be a grateful thing.

I slid one hand into my warm crotch, holding myself. What had I expected, after all? Had I truly counted on being alone with a Maria made a stranger by time? Had I even wanted to begin again, where we had ended so long ago?

No, I assured myself. Not that. I had only expected to be needed. Since, by all signs and portents, she had no needs that I could satisfy, I would be most polite and easygoing—and tomorrow morning I could tell Maria that, since I had a job to do in Los Angeles on a screenplay, I must return immediately.

The huge old house was so quiet about me, the bed was so seductively comfortable, in spite of myself I slipped into a dreamless napping. Perhaps it was only another, more successful, way to avoid my own thoughts.

I was roused again, an indeterminable time later, by the sound of the boat arriving once again at the dockside. Getting up, I went to peep through the drapes, to see that the sun was low almost to setting. More guests, I suppose, I told myself, and denied the temptation to go again to my spy-window to see who it might be. Instead, I padded into the bathroom and started the bath water.

It was a big, old-fashioned tub, so that the water reached almost to my shoulders after I had sunk into its blissful warmth. I had plenty of time to luxuriate; I meant for the house party to be in full swing when I made my appearance.

I had determined to have as little to do with Maria as possible. But she was here, in this house; and, more importantly, she was also in my mind. I was disgusted with myself. All day I had been remembering how it had been with her. During sleep, old memory had touched the flesh unawares, so that ever since I had come awake I had been carrying a semi-hard that simply would not be ignored.

I sighed as I slipped my soaped hand down to clasp my cock. I had lived alone for a long time now without acquiring the habit of relief by masturbation. But in these circumstances, I told myself, it is a species of self-protection.

Already, my hand moving sensously in the warm, soapy water, there was rising in my mind, as vividly as yesterday, an image of her. Naked. Her skin dark, her abundant black hair worn long and straight, brushed to a high gloss. The patch of hair between her legs, black, too, and intensely curled, and how she had always bit her lower lip, hard, at the moment I went into her.

Caught up in the fantasy of memory, the orgasm came jarringly, so complete that my whole body was clenched like a fist. I slowed my soapy hand to a caressing movement, clasping it around the head of my cock now, and lay dreamily half-awake, half-asleep, stroking myself with a sensuousness almost forgotten.

I bathed, finally, with an enjoyment almost equal, and rejoiced that the towel was rich and thick, and big enough to wear as a toga. The masturbation seemed to have sensitized my flesh, rather than satiating it, so that I began to wonder if it had been such a good idea after all. But at least I had emptied my body of its urgent seed, accumulated through nine or ten months of recent celibacy.

I chose my outfit with care, putting on a sport coat and a blue shirt with a discreet tie. Black shoes, black socks. Very conservative, almost staid, and not at all the sort of thing for a Florida weekend. Which was exactly how I meant it. I sat down on the bed to wait until I had some clue as to the proper time to put in an appearance.

A knock sounded on my door. I opened it to Constancia's smiling face.

"I was afraid that you had overslept your siesta," she said, "But I see that you are ready."

"Yes," I said. "How many . . ."

She gave me no time for the question; she was already going away. I followed slowly. Coming down the wide stairs, I saw that the servants were gathered in the reception room: Constancia; the old Cajun; another woman who was probably the cook, a thin, severe Spanish type; and the two men, one young, one middle-aged, whom I had seen working in the grounds.

"Goodnight, Mr. Jerry," Constancia said with her familiar friendliness.

"Are you all leaving?" I asked.

She nodded. "We live on the mainland. But all is prepared—the bar at the pool, the dinner for when you are hungry, the bedrooms . . . all prepared."

"And Maria . . .?"

Her teeth flashed. "She will be down. Soon now. The others are . . ." She gestured toward the pool area.

That had not been my question. "But Maria . . . does she stay here at night by herself? Always?"

Constancia nodded soberly. "It is her wish." She smiled. "But tonight she has you. And the others."

I watched as they went together, at an impatient gesture from the boatman, out the bay-side entrance. Then, slowly, I turned toward the French doors that led into the pool area. Even as I went, I heard the departure of the boat, and knew that I, Maria, the other guests, were alone in the big old Spanish house on No-Name Key.

The two men had already taken their territory; the young man whose arrival I had spied on standing with one elbow elegantly propped on the bar, a drink in his hand, the other sitting—squatting, rather—on the corner of a long deck chair.

I glanced at him quickly as he stood up. A man of indeterminate age, his face was marked by the wrinkles and crowsfeet of a life outdoors. He was small, wiry, with large hands and strangely delicate feet, shaped into a pair of cowboy boots. Standing, he showed lean hips in a pair of tight pants, a slight belly-bulge over his large, silver belt buckle.

"Well, I see we're all here," the Italian boy said from the bar. He came forward, a broad smile on his face. "I'm Tony Two."

"I'm Jerry Dorn," I said. I turned toward the cowboy. "And you . . . you're Casey, of course."

I was beginning to see it now, even as Casey nodded without smiling and came forward to shake my hand.

"I don't suppose there's anyone else after all," I said slowly. "Just us . . . and Maria."

Tony Two laughed, his teeth gleaming as he tossed his head. "If Maria had another husband besides us, she certainly kept it a secret from me," he said. He made an intricate dance step, twirling prettily at the end of it, and half-sang, *"Just we three . . ."*

Seeing what I needed most, I went to the bar, picked up the open bottle of bourbon, and measured out a hefty shot. Without taking the time to add ice, I tilted my head and poured it down my throat. The others watched me.

"A good idea," Casey said. "I'll have some of that sour-mash myself." He ranged himself alongside me,

13

took the bottle, poured a drink. I watched his strong, long-fingered hand delicately select an ice cube, drop it into the liquid, before he drained the glass. Tony Two had twirled himself into another dance step, still humming the tune.

"Mr. Dorn ... Jerry," Casey said to me. "What is Maria's trouble? Do you know?"

I glanced at him, quickly away. "Don't ask me," I said. "I just ... "

He nodded, as though he had understood before hearing the first word of my answer. "So she didn't tell you either." He studied me appraisingly. "She just said, 'Come,' and you came."

"That's about the size of it."

Turning away, he called to Tony Two. Tony Two ceased his self-absorbed prancing and came to join us at the bar. I watched him, unbelieving that he, like me, like Casey, had been married to Maria.

"What did Maria say, exactly, when she called you?" Casey asked him.

Tony Two handed us the gift of his brilliant smile. "She just said, 'I need you, how soon can you get here?' And I told her, 'Darling, I'm halfway home already.'"

Casey regarded him sourly. "That's right. You lived here, didn't you, when you were married to her?"

Tony Two sighed, rolling soulful eyes. "The love-liest time of my life. I always *knew* I'd love living like rich people."

I poured another drink, taking time, now that I had survived the first shock of realization, to use ice cubes and a splash of water. As I sipped at the drink, I was wondering if he was really homosexual, or was it only an act put on for our benefit. Surely Maria ...

14

Tony Two had been her second husband; then had followed Casey. Though I had heard their names—Maria always wrote me at least one letter a year—I had not met either of them until tonight.

"I guess we can only wait until Maria is ready to tell us, then," Casey said. "I reckon she wanted us all together first. So it must be . . ."

He's as concerned as I am, I thought, watching his face. Tony Two, as well. For they must have loved her in their ways, as I had in mine. Else they wouldn't be here.

I wondered if they felt it as weirdly as I did, to be talking to two other men who had known Maria. Not simply the truth of her flesh—perhaps there were many men who had made those explorations since my time. I didn't know, didn't want to know. But these had shared her life, her thought, her feeling. . . .

They had lived with her early mornings, slow and mean before the first two cups of coffee. They had ridden her bright euphorias of singing and dancing and inventing wonderful new ways of making love—at least, with her, they had seemed wonderful and new. All the roller-coaster rides of her mercurial joys and sorrows, the deep depressions she had always called the Green Horrors and lasted, sometimes, for a gloomy week.

And . . . I had to make myself know this, too . . . their flesh had tasted her flesh. She had caressed their risen cocks with hand, with mouth, she had opened her legs to their deep plunges, as she had opened for mine. But me, I told myself fiercely. I was *first*. Me, with no other before me. And they can't make that claim, can they, either one of them. Because there was *me*.

Casey was studying me. "But I thought you were married again," he said, and I realized that it was the second time he had spoken the words.

"Not any more," I said. "Not for a long time."

"With a couple of kids?"

"A boy and a girl," I said. "I see them ... from time to time."

Casey glanced at Tony Two. "I don't suppose you've ever married again."

"Darling, I've been too *busy* to get *married*," Tony Two said, his eyes mocking Casey.

"Why did you marry Maria?" Casey said bluntly.

I expected Tony Two to really flip that question. But, surprisingly, he became sober, he answered quietly.

"Because I loved her," he said. "Because she loved me." He looked at me, looked at Casey again. "I wish it could have stayed that way. I wish she didn't have to need you guys at all."

He was showing us another side of himself, a side we could only respect, because it must have belonged to Maria. He had loved, as I had loved her. And Casey.

Tony Two came to the bar, picked up the martini pitcher and poured himself another drink.

"The fact is, we're all still hooked into her, aren't we?" he said. "Or we wouldn't be here. Right?"

Casey nodded, along with me.

"And maybe she still loves us—one of us, anyway —or she wouldn't have called us when she got into whatever trouble she's into right now." Tony Two's voice became belligerent. "Because what the hell else do we have in common except that we were, at one time in our lives, married to the same great woman?"

Casey gave me a small, tight smile. "Tony Two is right, Jerry. He's spread it out like a calf hogtied for

16

branding. We all came hoping. We all expected to be the man called."

"You think I didn't want to go away when that old man told me somebody else was already here?" Tony Two said. "And then I saw Casey coming, looking like he ought to be toting a saddle on his back instead of a suitcase in his hand...." He turned on Casey. "Why the hell would a woman like Maria marry a damned cowboy, anyway?"

"Why would she marry a fucking queer?" Casey shot back.

The words shook Tony Two out of his bravado. "That's not fair," he said angrily. "I was good with Maria. I was..."

"But it didn't last, did it?" I said. "Did it?"

He whirled on me. "*You* didn't last. *Casey* didn't last. *I* didn't last. So that makes it even-steven. Doesn't it?"

"Yes," Casey said. "We're starting dead level. And it's going to help a lot, isn't it, for Maria to find us fighting when she gets here."

His delicate mouth trembling, Tony Two turned abruptly and walked to the edge of the pool, where he stood staring down into the water.

Casey, with a troubled frown, watched him go. He took a cigarette out of his shirt pocket, lit it with quick movements of his hands. But his fingers, I saw, were trembling as he held the wooden match.

"I've got no business being in Florida," he said. "I found out one hell of a long time ago that every time I leave the home ranch I get into trouble as sure as shooting." His eyes were wistful. "It's a fine place, Jerry, up in a box canyon, and because there's plenty of water it's so lush and green you wouldn't believe it. There ain't all that much water in Nevada, you

17

know. Just a small spread, some cattle but mostly horses, one hand to help out during the busy season ... This is the first time I've been away from home in nearly three years. But when Maria called . . ."

"I had a screenplay to write," I said sympathetically. "I needed the money, too, needed it pretty bad if I intend to avoid honest work for the next couple of years. But ..."

"What the hell can it be, Jerry?" Casey said softly. "What the hell can it be?"

Tony Two came toward us, drawn by our voices. "It's got to be serious. Or else she wouldn't have ... "

"A long time ago, I made Maria the promise I'd come if she ever needed me," I said in agreement. "Never until now has she used that promise."

"My friend didn't understand," Tony Two said plaintively. "'A woman?' he said. 'I didn't think you'd cross the street for a *woman*.' 'But that woman was my wife,' I told him."

We stood looking at each other. There was nothing else to say. Nothing at all. They knew as much, as little, as I did. Their own complex feelings, their memories and desires, had transported them to No-Name Key. Now there was nothing we could do but wait until Maria should come to us and tell us the state of her soul.

Why didn't she greet us at the dock as one should greet guests? I asked myself. Why has she brought us together, then made us wait?

A sense of foreboding possessed me. I wished fervently that I had been the sort of man who wouldn't have cared about Maria after such a long parting. So long ago, when we had been two other people; certainly there was no longer any validity to the contract. I was not the same, nor was she. She had,

18

for one thing, married these two men after I had departed from her flesh. Or had she departed from my flesh? During all these years, I had not been able to answer even that simple question.

I poured another drink, left it on the bar without touching it. Tony Two was wandering moodily at the other end of the long pool, both hands crammed into his pockets. Casey had resumed his hunched seat on the edge of the lounge chair, his hands clasped before him, a cigarette burning between his fingers. A fierce puff of blue smoke rose above his head. There was a faint taint of insecticide in the sea air. The gardener must have sprayed the area for mosquitoes before leaving. I knew how vicious saltwater mosquitoes could be.

The truth is, I thought to myself, I possess a fragment of Maria, as they each possess a fragment. The Maria of their time, their place, their knowing. But—out of such fragments we can find no truth, no understanding, no intuition. With all the will in the world, there is no way we can put these fragments together to make a whole. And yet. . . .

"Casey," I said.

Casey raised his head. Tony Two, at the sound of my voice, quickened his returning steps.

"Casey," I said, "all we can do is the best we can."

He nodded, a quick, tight jerk of the head. "Yeah. The best we can. Because we owe her, don't we? We owe her."

"Tony Two?" I said.

"I heard you," he said. His mouth was quick and sensitive, almost frightened. The words came like fluttering birds. "I'm game. I'll go all the way for Maria, any direction she wants..."

I was still looking at him. So was Casey. Tony Two

19

stood facing the French doors that led into the house. It was in the widening of his eyes that I first realized that Maria had come among us. Casey stood up. Slowly, I turned. I saw Maria. As they were seeing her.

She stood very close, having come quietly into our midst. Having come, also, naked.

Chapter 2

Under the impact of our combined regard, she had paused. But she stood without a trace of self-consciousness. She might have greeted us in this manner a thousand times before.

My first reaction to her nakedness was shock, of course. But her remarkable beauty immediately invaded the shock, leavening it with an emotion esthetic rather than sexual.

Thirty years old now, I remembered. I had known her at 19, 20, 21. Lovely then, too—but a loveliness both enhanced and marred by an immature grace, like that of a filly. Time had taken away these youthful charms, granting her in their stead a marvelous maturity of line and form to make a man's throat ache with acute lust.

I had always considered—rather smugly, I suppose —that I had had the best of Maria. So many women of Spanish blood reach an early, perfect blooming, only to ripen too rapidly into a stocky heaviness of belly and thigh and leg . . . yes, even of face. But not Maria. Good God no, not Maria.

Facing us, she held her head high and proud, exactly as I remembered—and her lower lip was caught between her teeth. Her eyes were wide and lambent, jet-black, and her face was marked with slants and facets of experience that had entered into it since she had been my wife. It only enhanced her beauty, did not destroy it. She had always worn a certain sadness in her face, like so many beautiful women; now it had become a salient mark of her character.

As in my ancient time, she wore her black hair long and straight and brushed gleamingly. It flowed down each bare shoulder, lying on the slope of each breast, the ends teasing at her nipples. The bright flesh of her throat gleamed through only in glimpses. At 19, she had been short in the waist. No longer; her belly lines slanted with long, subtle shadowings into the abrupt black cave of pubic hair. Her thighs were strong, but slender, and though she stood unmoving there was a subtle play of muscle in them. She had always had slender hands and feet, and extraordinarily long legs.

She was, at 30, all of one piece, having grown out of coltishness into a remarkable concatenation of shapings and shadowings of flesh and hair and skin. And so, in such womanly perfection, she stood naked before us, three men who had owned, however briefly, this body, this spirit, this mind—as in the way that love owns the person loved without violating its entity. Her lower lip was caught and held between her teeth, as she had always done, in my experience, in the moment of a cock thrusting into her waiting pocket; and all with a great pride of grace, of bearing, for beauty is not simply of flesh and favor, but of the spirit as well.

It was only for a moment, in which I experienced her more totally, I do believe, than during the entire scope of our marriage. Then she came to me quickly, putting her arms around me and pressing her naked body against my clothed flesh. One hand went behind my head to press my mouth down to her mouth for the welcoming kiss. Automatically, my arms shaped her close, tight, and again I experienced the forgotten tininess of her body structure. It was like living through an episode of *deja vú*, for I had never got used to the sensation of her smallness. Somehow my mind perceived Maria as a woman greater than her actual size.

She took her mouth away. "Jerry, I knew you would come," she said warmly. She put her hand on my cheek. I could feel the warm silkiness of her palm. "Thank you, dear Jerry."

She turned to Tony Two. Her small flesh merged against his tallness, and her buttocks quivered. "And Tony Two," she said. "I was afraid you had gone so far away. . . ."

"No," he said huskily. He cleared his throat. "I had to. . . ."

"My sweet Tony Two," she said tenderly, and went to Casey.

Casey, who had not risen from his seat on the corner of the lounge chair, looked up at her. She clasped her arms around his head, pressing it against the naked curve of her belly. He did not resist, but laid his cheek against the sloping roundness. But his arms did not lift to encircle her waist.

"Casey," she said.

"Maria," he said in a shaky voice. "Maria." For a quick, involuntary instant, his hands, broad and work-hardened, clasped her buttocks, pressing her against his face. Then he pushed her away, to look up into her eyes. She stood gazing at him, their eyes locked.

He had been the last one, the nearest one; and so, perhaps, for her, the best. I had to look away, a jeal-

23

ous anger curling in my stomach. I pushed it away; my claim was the oldest, but it was also the most distant. I had no rights here beyond their rights, equal to mine.

As a means of breaking the spell, he kissed her belly with a pecking, birdlike movement. She wanted to clasp him close again, but he evaded her by standing up.

"There's a reason we're all here, Maria," he said. "But you'll have to tell us what it is."

She stood rigid, as though a chill had struck through her flesh. Recovering, she said, "Yes. I must tell you. I want to tell you. But . . ."

Turning away from Casey, she came back into the center of the group.

"But I can't tell you," she said. "Not yet. Not until . . ." She paused, absorbed so deeply into her emotion that she seemed unaware of her nakedness in the midst of our clothed state. She smiled, then; not a brilliant smile, but quiet, almost sad, the lines of her mouth betraying a deep and constant hurt she had lived with for a long time. I ached suddenly with a tenderness I had not known since the day I had taken her cherry. She was so vulnerable, so open, that my emotional response went far beyond the sexuality her available beauty had first aroused.

"When I called you, it was only a way of beginning," she said. "Even though I didn't know how to go on. I still don't know." She lifted her head. "But there is a way. There must be. Because, if we can't find it . . ."

The desperate, ending note was like the chime of a distant warning bell. Until now, I had entertained the possibility that a crisis did not really exist. After all, I no longer knew her; she could be playing a

24

game, or was simply lonely, or . . . But I knew now that she needed me—us—as she had never needed anything or anyone before.

"Tell us, dear," Tony Two said softly. "That's all you have to do. Just tell us."

She shook her head, her long hair in rhythm with the movement. "But that's the trouble. I can't. We're not close enough any more. We've gone so far away from each other . . ."

She paused, thinking about it.

"I have loved you," she said. "You have loved me. But all so long ago, on the far side of yesterday. Other people have happened to us in between, so many things you've done that I don't know about, thoughts you've thought and feelings you have felt. Me, too. And me, too."

She showed us the challenge of her eyes. "I've got to see you naked. We've got to be naked together." Coming to me, she lifted her hands to unknot my tie. Pulling it from around my neck, she threw it toward the pool in a sudden angry gesture. The tie fluttered in the air, dropped to the ledge, one end lapping into the water. She caught the lapels of my coat, going halfway behind me to slip it down my arms. Sheer, social horror struck at me as vividly as a dream of being naked in the midst of strangers. I spun away, clutching at my coat and my dignity.

"Maria!" I said.

She was not smiling when she looked at me. "We've been naked together, Jerry. So many times. Three years of being naked together."

"Yes," I said. "But . . ." I gestured helplessly toward the others.

She did not seem to understand. "But I've been

naked with them, Jerry. I've fucked them, like I've fucked you. So why shouldn't we . . ."

Stopping, she stood solemnly gazing into Tony Two's face, then Casey's. They wore expressions, I think, essentially similar to mine. She burst into sudden laughter.

"For God's sake," she said. "You men! You're all prudes!"

Her laughter, as much as her words, offended me. The idea that she was over the edge flicked at me like a stinging whiplash. "I don't know what kind of game you're playing, Maria," I said stiffly. "But I don't want any part of it."

Her voice was suddenly frantic. "Game? You call it a game? When I . . . ?"

Tears glistened suddenly in her eyes. With the heel of her hand she made a fierce dash at her cheek.

"I loved you, all of you," she said. "One after the other. But I . . . but it didn't last, did it? Three times it came, three times it went, leaving me holding nothing. Nothing. And not even knowing why."

She stopped, not as though she had run out of words, but as though she could not make herself say them.

"Not even a baby. I couldn't even keep a seed, and make it grow. So I've got to find . . . something, find . . ."

Turning, she went abruptly against Tony Two, one arm encircling his waist, the other hand tugging at his zipper.

"My old friend, Tony Two," she said in a bitten voice. "Show me my old friend. Please, Tony."

His face flamed red as she groped for his cock. But he did nothing to stop her. She brought out his penis into the nakedness of our gaze, held it swelling in her hand. I was outraged, embarrassed, as much by the

26

flamboyant size of his instrument as by Maria's actions.

Far down under all the turmoil was the acute awareness that she had had it before, though how any woman could take such an enormous organ I didn't know. An acid taste in my mouth, I watched as Maria went to her knees, to press her lips against the great ruby-red glans.

"My dear friend," she said, crooning. "My old friend. He never knew whether he liked me or not. But he did, really, didn't he? He learned how to like me."

Tony Two orgasmed, the tight wad of sperm shooting an enormous distance, spraying white puddles on the tiled floor. In an agony of shame, Tony twisted away from her touch, from our sight. I felt sorry for the boy. I would have been dying of shame, too. Any man.

Maria was still kneeling. Her face was sad, bruised by the event. "I'm sorry, Tony," she said. "I just wanted you to fuck me. All three of you, one after the other. For the old times—and, maybe, for the new." She got slowly to her feet. "But it's no use, is it? Oh, you'd all fuck me in private, out of the sight of the others. But not this way, all together, all sharing it, all feeling it. So there's no way to tell you what I mean. We're all just strangers here on No-Name Key. Like I've always been a stranger to myself."

I did not move, did not speak. I was so lost inside of myself I knew that any action, any words, of mine would be dead wrong. At least, I had sense enough to know it. Casey was looking at Maria with a strange expression on his face, equally compounded of the shock that I felt, the bewilderment—and yet with a compassion I had not reached. And something more,

27

I knew suddenly, deep and dangerous . . . there was a gathering of violence in him. Tony Two had withdrawn to the side of the pool, hunched over himself as though he had the stone ache.

Maria had found, in her nakedness of body and of spirit, a certain dignity. "So I apologize," she said. "Not just to Tony, but to all of you. For believing that you could come to me truly, that you could give me . . . us . . ."

Casey moved. I was astonished by the explosive speed with which he grabbed Maria's arms, turned her, pushed her down on the padded lounge chair.

"If you want to get fucked, I'll oblige you," he said. His words were harsh and panting. "Oh yes, ma'am, I'll do that."

He was leaning over her, holding her pressed down with one hand to her shoulder. The other hand fumbled at his fly. Maria, without resistance, stared into his violent face. There was fear in her. Fear— and arousal. Her lip was bitten between her teeth, though her face was blanched white.

He found his ready cock. He straddled her, not getting between her legs but putting down his knees outside her thighs. With a quick, ruthless thrust, he plunged his cock raping into her unprepared pocket. I heard the loud rasp of breath gushing out of her lungs as she took him.

I couldn't look. I couldn't not look. I counted myself a reasonably sophisticated man; but the fact was, I had never seen a man and a woman fucking. To me, as to most people, sex had ever been a private matter. Oh, I had read all about wife-swapping, group sex, the encounter groups . . . all those things. But these were legends from a distant people, whom I had never visited.

28

My first reaction was, How grotesque, how vul-
gar! It was like watching two animals coupling, driven
by the instinct of oestrus, unaware, uncaring, of
the public nature of the act. Indeed, Casey was fucking her like an animal, crouched on her like a jockey
on a horse, thrusting with a rapid, continuous drive
devoid of human tenderness, human love. And there
was in her face a taut, ugly grimace of strain as she
raised herself to take again and again and again the
dripping wet redness of his ruthless cock.

I swiveled my head as I felt Tony Two drawn
near, saw his ghastly fascination. The only sound was
the thump and smack of the hips, the whistling of
their breathing.

But then the grotesque ugliness turned into a kind
of agonizing beauty. Violent, ruthless, un-tender
though it was—there was yet a rhythm established, an
intricate blending, not just as cock and cunt, but of
their entire bodies, complex and subtle, and ever-
changing as they shaped themselves through the
quickening phases of their fucking. It was so quick,
so angry, so violent, so animal—and yet so utterly
and beautifully human; for when Casey groaned and
launched into the finality of come he leaned to lay
his mouth on hers, and brought her along with him
into the ending, as though he knew there was violence
in her, now, to match his own, and if he should leave
her unfinished she would kill him for the neglect.

When it was done, I felt as wrung out as though I
had fucked, and been fucked, myself. For a long minute, he remained crouched over her, staring down
into her face. She was looking up at him, panting in
a slowly ebbing rhythm, and there was a soft, used
look to her mouth, her eyes. How many times, I
thought, has he taken her so violently, so completely

29

without manifest love? And why were they remembering it so tenderly?

Casey rose from her. With no vestige of shame, he wrapped his fist around his cock and stripped it dry. He wiped the palm of his hand on his pants, looking directly at me. I could not help the thought that leaped into my mind. We had all three—all four, counting Maria—had an orgasm tonight; only mine had been secretly arrived at.

"I've done my part," Casey said. "Now you do yours."

I felt the urge almost irresistibly. I have to admit it. I could taste as real as reality the next moment when I would invade her sweet flesh . . . ready, so ready, for Casey had warmed it, moistened it with his sperm, quickened her lust. Yes. Maria had turned her head toward me, her lower lip was caught waiting between her teeth. If I had not masturbated so secretly, I believe I would have broken through the barriers of myself.

As it was, I turned to the bar and poured a drink with trembling hand.

"Jerry," Maria said softly. "Please, Jerry."

But I could not let myself hear her call.

"Tony?" Casey said. "Maybe you've got something left."

Tony's reply pranced like a light-footed mare. "Darling, if I took off my clothes, I might go for you instead of Maria. Because that's the way I'm built. I'd love for you to ride me, cowboy."

Tony, I thought, had retreated into his private refuge—as I into mine. Again I felt a flash of understanding for a kind of man I had never been able to understand. He had his standards, as I had mine. I wondered, suddenly, how he had come to be

30

married to Maria. It must have been a strange marriage.

"Listen," Casey said in a hard voice that forced me to turn. He was sitting beside Maria, one hand resting on her naked belly.

"It's like we said before. Maria needs us. Not Casey. Not Jerry. Not Tony. But Us. All three."

I had no answer. I could only stare at him, wondering, as I had wondered about Tony. What had Maria found in him to love? Certainly, something. I felt a flush of shame. Maybe more than there was in me. He was dealing with the situation better than I had, up until now. I was supposed to be the articulate one, good with words and ideas. He was a cowboy—yet he had spoken so much more to the effect of the occasion than any of us. And acted.

"Did you think it would be something easy?" Casey said, his voice quiet, no longer edged with hardness. He turned his head to look at Maria. "I knew it had to be a tough row to hoe. Else she wouldn't have had to call on us."

Maria, swinging her legs around Casey, sat up. I noted, with a lingering jealousy, that her hand rested familiarly on his still-clothed shoulder. But they've just fucked, haven't they? a voice whispered deep inside. While you haven't touched the woman in years.

"I'll try to say how it is with me," Maria said. Her voice trembled. "In spite of it not working like I thought . . ." Maria took her hand from Casey's shoulder. She stared at the two hands clasped on her naked thighs. Her face was shadowed by the fall of her hair.

"The truth is, I'm a failure," she said. "As a person. As a woman."

"Maria!" Tony Two said.

31

Maria glanced up, hid her face again. "Tony, it's true." She moved one hand in a sudden, fierce gesture. "I had three good men, one after the other. And I lost them all."

She lifted her face, baring the indelible lines of a long-suffered sadness. So many hours spent here alone on No-Name Key, I thought. Hours of fruitless thinking and deep despair.

"I ought to be the happiest woman in the world. I've had what every woman wants. I'm not bad-looking, there's more money than I know what to do with, I've read the books that count, I've thought the thoughts. And—I've had you three. But none of it has been enough."

A long silence followed. I yearned to comfort her. But, having been inadequate once, I feared—I knew—that I would not be enough now.

Maria took a deep, calming breath. "After Casey, I came home to No-Name Key, believing that in solitude I could discover the fault that lay so deeply in me. But no matter how hard I tried, how deeply I probed, I couldn't find it."

"I turned, then, to you. Individually, I mean, believing, needing to believe, that Jerry or Casey or Tony Two must have been the key to my life. If only I could discover which one, I could repossess that key which could unlock the secret door of myself."

She made a faint smile. "But I wasn't on the right track yet. If the answer had dwelled with one of you, surely instinct, instead of driving me away, would have held me close to my salvation. Because I have come to believe this one thing, at least, through these tedious, painful years. If I hadn't been able to believe it, I'd have gone crazy or killed myself, become a drunk or a drug-user. There is something in us that seeks for wholeness. That's what life is all about; finding our total selves, becoming a person in tune with ourselves as with the universe. Without this completeness, we are only fragments of humanity, bleeding and hurting and dying like untamed animals crowded in cages. Oh, I've thought about these things, *felt* about these things, a million times over during so many nights alone on No-Name Key!"

"Maria, dear, you *always* tore yourself up with too much thinking," Tony Two said. "Remember how I used to tell you . . . *Don't think, darling, let yourself feel. Riding the merry-go-round of sensation, you can't go far wrong.*"

Maria smiled faintly. "That might be right for you, Tony. But not for me. I have to think. I have to *know.*"

Yes. She had been so young, then, in my time of her life. But not content with youth, with love and sex. She had eternally poked and pried at herself and at me. Wanting to know Why. So often I had been amused by her youthful earnestness, knowing in my smug maturity that, like all the rest of us, she would grow out of it. I was not amused now. I was deeply moved.

For had I not had the first and best chance, when she had been young and pliable? And I had failed. I had enjoyed her lovely flesh, but I had not nurtured her beautiful spirit. So, in the end, she had gone away from me, restlessly seeking. Or, sensing that I was incapable of satisfying her deepest needs, I had driven her away. Perhaps I had, after all these years, refused to let myself understand the truth of our parting.

"When I had got that far, I went sort of crazy, I guess." Maria said. Her voice was trembling with the confession. Bravely, she firmed it. "I went away from

33

No-Name Key, to New York and London and Biarritz, all the places where people are supposed to be gay and happy and successful." She gazed down at her hands, a wry smile showing faintly on her face.

"I tasted men. I tasted women. I tasted all the things that a person can taste."

She looked up directly into my eyes.

"Yes, Jerry. Tasting. Like you taste food in one restaurant after another, searching for the perfect dish. I became a wanton of people, rich men and poor men, dull and brilliant and methodical. Of women, too, in all the enormous variety of women. And all the ways that people find to live with each other, happy and unhappy, success or failure or accepted compromise." She sighed. "But there wasn't a solid meal among them. I discovered it very quickly, too, though I kept on sampling far past the point of good sense.

"When I came home once more to No-Name Key, it was for the purpose of dying. Oh, nothing as dramatic as suicide. Suicide would not be necessary; time could do the job, killing me with the slow, inevitable incompleteness of reality. It was in this state of unconditional surrender that the key—the only possible answer—was put into my hand."

She rose and came into the center of the group, standing with a naked and unconscious beauty. We were gripped by her intensity.

"It just came to me suddenly one night, without any warning. In one second of time I was empty of it, in the next I was filled with it. As simply and directly as that—after all the agony of a slow, failure-ridden groping, of being so lost in the sea of myself I could never hope to reach safety again.

"And so true that not for one instant could I ques-

34

tion its rightness. For it was the truth, you see. And the truth was Us. Not me. Not you. Us. Together."

Our eyes were on her face, deep and brooding and sad—and yet happy, too, lighted by the illumination of her hardly received revelation.

"Us, in our collective memory and experience of each other," she said in a low, husky voice. "I saw it in the way you see meanings in a dream, chalked white on black, like an equation on the blackboard at school. Jerry, do you remember the first time you ever understood fractions? They keep giving them to you, giving them to you, and they don't mean anything. But suddenly a fire blazes in your gut and there is the complete and eternal *feeling* of fractions. Or maybe it was long division with you, or how to scan a poem. But it's knowledge, any knowledge, that arrives in one thrust, like a man going for the first time into a woman."

She was panting now, her rib cage moving lightly with the thrust and pull of her breathing. "An equation. Three plus one. One and one didn't do it, even three times repeated. But three plus one, that makes four, too, doesn't it? Me. You. And you. And you. *Us.*"

She rushed on through her meaning, like a train through a tunnel.

"If we can come together. If we can know each other. If we can let go of our little egos, tell it, put it together; everything we've thought and said and done, every last truth of feeling, good and bad. All of it. The mind. The spirit. The flesh. Three plus one, making four—and all one. Us."

"Maria. There's no way."

My own voice, speaking quietly. The sound of it surprised me.

Maria looked at me.

35

"I didn't think so, either. Not at first. I knew I had found the answer—and the answer was impossible." She leaned toward me. "But it isn't impossible, Jerry. Not if we've got the guts to start it, to keep on with it, one step at a time. Not if we yield ourselves to Us."

Another long pause. I glanced toward Casey. A worried frown showed on his lean, weathered face. I looked at Tony Two. He was puzzled by these things Maria had said. Maria was making him think, after a grasshopper-existence dedicated to the avoidance of thinking. It was obviously a painful process.

I thought I could see a faint darkling of her meaning. What I saw frightened me. People can't open themselves the way Maria is talking about, I thought. It would destroy your whole sense of yourself. Such unbearable honesty as she demands cannot be sustained; why else have people always closed themselves off into essential solitude, if not for protection from others?

"We will know each other again," Maria was saying, her voice going on quietly, fatally, with the fatal words. "Not in a single line from me to Jerry, from me to Tony, from me to Casey, like it was before. No—multiple lines, spinning a complete web, between us all. For we shall know our flesh, and as the flesh becomes known we will spin out the stories of ourselves that no one ever tells to another human being. And the telling won't end until it encompasses us all."

She had been lifted into a euphoria, as though we were already launched successfully into the project she had outlined. But now a shadow darkened her face.

"That's what came to me, in one great flash of how

36

it could be. But—I've failed again, haven't I, just as I failed with each one of you individually. Because it can happen only if it happens in the flesh, and you won't let it. Only Casey had the courage of himself. Jerry wouldn't follow him, nor Tony. And so . . ."

"It wasn't exactly courage," Casey said painfully. "I was mad, that's all. And I was horny, I'll admit that, from seeing you walk around here naked. The way I was feeling, I'd have fucked you at high noon on the main drag of Dallas."

He's trying, I told myself. He's reaching for the honesty and the truth that Maria is asking from us all.

Maria was smiling. "*Why* doesn't matter, Casey. What matters is that, in taking me, you brought us together again. Just as though there had never been an ending."

She looked at me, a pity—it could only be pity—showing in her lambent eyes. "Jerry, I know it was painful for you. Not to refuse me; but to watch me with Casey. But I hoped . . . I thought . . ." She sighed again. "I guess it's too much to ask, to think of Casey as yourself, of yourself as Casey."

I couldn't help it; I had to go to her. I put an arm around her shoulders. The other hand I cupped against the curve and weight of her breast, not lustfully, but with a tender affection.

"Maria, listen to me. It doesn't have to be mixed up with sex and nakedness. We're intelligent people, after all. We can talk of these things."

She shook her head. "No, Jerry. Talking alone won't do it. It must go deep, so deeply, beyond the mind. We've got to *know* Us. . . ." She turned her head toward Casey. "It will have to hurt, in so many painful ways. I understand the hurt, I have accepted the necessity of it. But you, each of you, will have to accept it, too. It hurt you to watch Casey fucking me. Now Casey will have to hurt, watching me going down on you, because he never did like for me to do it to him."

She had put her hand into my fly even as she spoke the words, and now she went down on her knees humbly before me. She took my limp cock wholly into the warm moistness of her mouth. I was staring at Casey, I saw his eyes flinch. As I knew mine had flinched when he had plunged his cock into her hungry maw.

Her soft lips hardened my prick, bringing me to a stand. Reluctant though I was to do it, I had to take myself away from her. Not for my sake, or for hers, but for the sake of Casey's suffering.

She let me go without protest. Still kneeling, she said, "You see, Jerry? Casey has as much to overcome as you have. We all have. But we can make ourselves keep on through the hurting places if we can only help each other."

"I'll take you in the ass, next time," Casey said in a strangled voice. "You hear me, Maria? In the ass, by God."

She smiled, a tender smile, and rose to go to him. She laid her head against his breast. "If you want to," she said. "I never would let you, before, remember? But if you want to."

He stood with his arms half around her, staring at me over her head. "Jerry," he said, "what are we going to do with this woman?"

"Love her," Maria said, whispering. "Cherish her. But, above all else, let her know the truth."

Silence again, a long spell of silence as of magic. I knew now, in its totality, what Maria meant. I could see our days and nights laid out ahead of us as plainly as a treasure map. And I could not do it. There is in me, I know well, a Germanic rigidity of soul that forbids these easinesses of flesh and mind . . . and of spirit. You should have chosen another Adam, Maria, I told myself silently. I was wrong then. I am wrong now.

I knew that I could not leave No-Name Key tonight. But I could, at least, retreat from the presence of Us into the solitary fortress of my room. Early in the morning I could flee the island, in this definitive gesture showing Maria how completely she had failed.

But, incredibly, I could not make myself walk away. Tony Two rescued us from the stasis of the moment.

"Well, the least we can do is take off our clothes," he said, tossing his head and laughing suddenly.

We turned to stare at him. Humming loudly, *A Pretty Girl Is Like a Melody*, he was launched into a strut of elaborate body movement, suddenly self-absorbed as he slowly unbuttoned his shirt, removed it, let it dangle on a fingertip before dropping to the floor. Twirling coyly, eyes over one shoulder, he unbuckled his belt and, turning slowly again to us, shifted his pants low on his hips.

He gave us, I must admit, an enthralling spectacle. He was not simply handsome, but beautiful; his arrogant Roman profile was enhanced and elaborated by the smooth, gleaming muscles of his torso, flowing down into rippling thighs and calves. His movement was graceful, narcissistic, enticing. The marvelous performance was, at once, wholly serious and a satire of itself. Maria was delighted, applauding as each garment dropped away, cheering him on into a greater and greater frenzy of revealed flesh.

At last, he stood before us clad only in discreet

39

jockey shorts. His sex bulged the restraining fabric and I remembered, from my previous view, its enormous size. I had never had, to be as honest as it's possible to be, a homosexual impulse that I could remember. But my breath was locked in my throat as, slowly, he hooked his thumbs into the fabric and inched the garment teasingly down to reveal the magnificent apparatus.

No longer laughing now; and he had abandoned the campy, flitting movements of truth and satire with which he had started. He was, quite simply, beautiful in his maleness as he stepped out of the garment and posed naked before us.

Maria put both hands to her mouth, her breath coming with a gasp. "Beautiful, Tony! Beautiful."

With an abrupt shift, Tony twisted sideways and sliced into the pool. The water closed over him like a liquid blanket. Maria watched the underwater arrow of his body down the length of the pool. She turned her head, then, to look inquiringly at Casey.

Casey made a wry grin. "I'm not going to try to top that, Maria."

She did not look at me; she simply said, "Jerry. Get naked."

I yearned to obey. My clothes were smothering me; instead of concealing my nakedness, they only revealed my narrow, twisted self.

But it is hard to give up accustomed mores. "Sorry, Maria," I heard myself saying. "I think I need another drink.

I went to the bar, Maria following my movement toward escape.

"Mix me one, too?" she said coaxingly. "Bourbon?"

Casey had joined us; I poured drinks all around.

We turned, simultaneously, to see that Tony Two was swimming industriously, lap after lap.

"It doesn't matter," Maria said softly. "We're all trying." She made a brave smile. "I suppose everyone's hungry by now. After dinner . . ." Her voice faltered, became firm again. "After dinner, I'll begin. I'll tell Us how I first learned about sex."

Chapter 3

We were a strange group at dinner—
but strangely companionable. We ate in a formal dining room, furnished with a long, black, Spanish table
surrounded by tall black wooden chairs. However,
dinner was buffet style; along the short side of the
room, next the kitchen, was a steam table where
everything was laid out: beef tournedos for a main
dish, Spanish rice, mushrooms, a chef's salad, small
green peas, delicate and tasty, and even *flan* for
dessert. We served ourselves, chose our own places
at table. Maria sat at the head, me on her left and
Casey on her right. Tony Two went down the length
of the table to sit facing Maria from the other end.

Maria, on leaving the pool area, had picked up a
filmy white garment, slightly longer than thigh-length,
that floated about her body as gossamer as a spider
web. Presiding at the head of the table, her breasts,
small and perfect, with large, dark-ringed nipples,
showed enticingly through the shadowy half-conceal-
ment. So many times, so long ago, I had fed my lust
at those breasts . . . They still shaped themselves
youthfully, without sign of an incipient sagging,
widely spaced, the nipples pointing left and right at
an enchanting angle.

Tony Two had resumed only his jockey shorts, so

that, sitting at the far end, his bare, hairless torso, muscular, yet lithe and graceful, gleamed with the faint bronze of a carefully—nurtured tan. Casey and I remained fully clothed, except that I was no longer wearing my tie.

Ravenously hungry, we ate and talked with enormous gusto. Maria had brought a bottle of Spanish wine from the kitchen, asking me to do the honors. It was a rough, dry red, almost like a Chianti but slightly more delicate than even the best Chiantis, and it sharpened the palate marvelously for the Spanish food.

Our conversation was inconsequential. First, Maria wanted to know from each of us what we had been doing, where we were living, how happy we had been with our recent lives. Casey told about buying two very expensive bulls at a Dallas auction in an effort to upgrade his herd; as a result, considerable belt-tightening had been necessary these last two years. Soon now, though, he would see daylight; he expected to recover his initial investment through sale of five yearling bulls, next year, as breeding stock.

Maria asked about my next novel. I had to tell her I had a couple of ideas kicking around, but nothing firm. I was surprised that she knew it had been four years since my last book, and wanted to know why there hadn't been a movie. I said I didn't know myself, but movie money had been tough lately. Or maybe my connections were breaking down. I didn't mention the screenplay I had abandoned to come to No-Name Key.

"I've always thought it was really bad luck that your grandfather left you that annuity," Maria said. "You'd have worked so much harder without it."

I shook my head. "Without that few thousand a

43

year, I'd probably have been holding down a steady job. I'm not the kind of fellow who has a brand-new inspiration every Tuesday morning. My demon-angel works a leisurely schedule, I assure you. I don't think hunger would change his habits all that much."

Tony Two unblushingly bragged about his new friend, who had enough money for travel. "We go on cruises all the time," he said. "Don't you see my lovely tan? He's a bit long in the tooth, I must admit, but he's really very nice ... and then, I manage to slip ashore, from time to time, in the most *exotic* ports."

He was so shameless, we simply laughed with him.

All so light, so easy; and withal a strange sense of family feeling, as though we were linked by blood instead of marriage. The memory of the recent meeting, so harrowing and frenetic and communal, clothed in such ominous implications, surely dwelled in the forefront of their minds, as in mine. However, we were able, for this short time, to step aside into a genuine friendliness.

I held reserved still the decision that, as soon as the boat returned in the morning, I would leave Maria's house. Nothing had happened to change that. I accepted both the reality of Maria's crisis, and the sincerity of her effort to resolve it. But I knew that it was not in me to surrender myself to a new mode of being, as she demanded.

I could have, alone, cherished her again, with heart and with flesh. Even now, I realized as I watched her lovely breasts revealing themselves darkly through the sheer white garment, I was aching to fuck her. In my scrotum, not to be denied, was a mindless anticipation of an event that, I knew well, I could not allow to happen. For Maria believed, and perhaps

44

rightly, that she and I alone could not cure this ill-
ness of her soul.

After all, as I had guiltily realized tonight, her
sense of a personal failure had seeded itself in our
time together. Repeating ourselves, we would only
repeat those old mistakes and failures that had
driven us apart. Only in the community of Us, an
entirely new structure of love and passion and meaning, rested a possibility of hope for Maria's future.

I could accept the idea intellectually—but something in me revolted against participation. Let Casey
do it, I thought. Let Tony Two. I did not possess the
strength, the inner resources, the initiative, to con-
struct a new Jerry Dorn capable of rescuing Maria
from the dragons that dwelled hot-bellied in her soul.
I had told her that my demon-angel worked a leisurely schedule. In so much more than in the writing
of books.

Casey will stay, I told myself, watching him. Out
of instinct and animality, anger and love, he will
strive to become what Maria needs and wants. I
turned my head to gaze down the length of the table.
Maybe Tony Two also, I thought with a strange taste
of bitterness. After all, he's very versatile, he can not
only bat from both sides of the plate, but run the base
paths backward if need be. So where, I thought, rec-
ognizing the self-serving self-pity in the thinking,
where is there a need for me?

We were drinking coffee, after the crisp, burned-
vanilla taste of the *flan*, when Maria, laying her hand
on my arm, said, "I used to want to tell you, Jerry,
what I'm going to tell tonight. But—I never could.
I kept hoping that the right time would come along,
a moment when it would simply pour out of me. I
believed, because you were so much older and more

45

experienced—and a writer of books—that you would be able to explain it to me. But—the time never came in which I could begin saying it."

I had thought her transparent, in those days—so young, so passionate, so totally on the surface of herself. Instead, I knew now, she had been opaque. I never knew her, I thought sadly. And she never knew me. We fucked, believing that fucking was all.

My mind shied like a skittish mare. It was, I realized abruptly, a pattern I had sunk into long before coming to No-Name Key. I had formed the compulsive habit of abstaining from life one day at a time, as a reformed alcoholic abstains from liquor. Any day I could get through without needing to think, having to feel, without being . . . Maybe I needed help far more than Maria.

"If you couldn't tell me then," I said, my voice harsh in my throat, "Why can you tell me now?"

Maria's eyes were fearful, her mouth strained. "I'm not sure that I can," she said. "I'm only . . . going to . . . I must try." She stood up, raising her voice. "Let's take our coffee to the pool."

Casey, Tony Two—I—did not move. Perhaps, I thought, they are as reluctant as I am. Perhaps they, too, were reserving the intent of departure tomorrow morning.

She watched us, as we watched her, a tension creeping into her face. It was a moment of crisis, though obscure in its outlines. If any one of us meant to deny her, now was the time. Before the beginning. And, I realized with a great clarity, just one denial would destroy the tenuous structure she had succeeded in erecting at a great expense of spirit that showed plainly in her face.

Standing, the rich black delta of her loins was shadowed forth through the gossamer whiteness of fabric. She had the prettiest mount I have ever seen on a woman—thicketed with black hair, yet shaping forward prominently with seductive slants of muscle masses from her belly and thighs.

I stood up. "I'll bring the coffeepot," I said. "We can plug it in out there."

As we passed through the French doors, Maria shrugged out of the filmy robe, tossing it on a bench beside the door. Walking ahead of us, she led us to a cluster of chairs around a low table. I busied myself plugging up the coffeepot. When I looked around, I saw that Tony Two had removed his shorts.

Maria smiled at him as she sat down. "Thank you, Tony," she said softly.

Tony Two pranced and smirked, his big cock dangling. "I'm not ashamed of *my* body," he said. "In fact, I think it's rather nice. I *sweat*, darlings, to keep these pretty muscles. I'm not going to be anybody's fat old queen."

In spite of his defensiveness, he had made a brave commitment to Us that I could not even contemplate.

Maria turned to Casey, in the chair beside her. "Casey, could you take off your clothes, too?" she asked wistfully. She glanced at me. "I know Jerry's not ready yet. But you . . ."

Casey looked belligerent. "What's all this nakedness about, anyway? It reminds me of that old joke, *Take off your clothes, I want to talk to you.*"

Maria leaned forward earnestly. "That's exactly it. It's hard to explain, but . . . well, it seems to me it would be so much more difficult to avoid the truth, even unconsciously, when you're naked. And we *can't* lie. We *must* tell the truth. Do you understand what I mean?"

47

"What's all this truth you keep talking about, darling?" Tony Two said. "I've never lied to you about myself. Have I?"

Maria looked down at her hands. "Maybe you—all of us—have been lying to yourself. That's what we want to find out. The truth before we met, and the truth of being together. And then—the truth of what lies ahead. If we know the real past, we can know the real future."

"These encounter groups, made up of total strangers, take off their clothes during a session," I said helpfully. "At least, some of the California groups do, I understand. Is that what you had in mind, Maria? A sort of encounter group?"

She shook her head. "I don't know about that sort of thing. Oh, I've thought about psychoanalysis; I even went to one analyst, three or four times, but it didn't seem to work. We seemed to keep talking about somebody that wasn't me."

"I only get naked when I aim to fuck," Casey said. His voice was not harsh with anger, simply calm and matter-of-fact. "So I'd be likely to show you folks a hard cock. Now if you don't mind me walking around with a hard-on . . .?"

Maria looked at him. "If you want to fuck first, Casey, I'll fuck you. All of you, for that matter, one after the other or all together. Because that's part of our truth, too. Only . . . it can't be apart. There can't be any secrets of any kind between us."

"All right," Casey said. "If Tony can do it, I reckon I can, too."

Slowly, meticulously, he took off his boots. Standing up, he undid the big silver buckle of his belt and slid the tight pants down his legs. With equal deliberateness, he unbuttoned his body-fitted shirt,

48

laid it aside. Unlike Tony, he was wearing a short-sleeved undershirt. Last of all, he took off the wildly striped boxer shorts.

Again, I couldn't look, and I couldn't look away. I suppose, like most men, I possess a mild curiosity about other men's sexual equipment, though, again like most men, at public urinals I keep my eyes carefully level and straight ahead. In actual experience, I couldn't remember the last time, before tonight, I had seen another man's cock and balls.

Tony Two's nakedness was extraordinarily shocking in the context of homosexuality and his huge penis. Casey was not so much of a surprise; he was strangely built, almost deformed, so thickened about the waist, with a slightly sagging belly, yet showing a horseman's lean hips and strong, corded, slightly bowed legs. His body hair, rather sparse, was reddish. His balls were snugged up into a tight scrotum, the left hanging lower than the right. His cock was long, but thin, and as it came to erection under the warming weight of our combined gazes, it showed a left-handed curve. He was uncircumcised, so that the head emerged slowly, red and glistening with moisture, as the erection grew.

"I told you," he said shamefacedly. "I knew I'd have a hard the minute I dropped my britches."

Maria reached out one hand to touch his penis, not pruriently but with a gentle gratitude. "Thank you, Casey," she said. "Thank you for doing it for me."

"Well, Jerry darling, that makes you odd man out." Tony Two, his voice slightly mocking. "Doesn't it feel strange to have your clothes on while everybody else is naked?"

I was beginning to feel strange. I got up, slowly,

49

and walked away to the edge of the pool. The lights hidden in the shrubbery, apparently controlled by a timed rheostat, were dimmer than when we had gone in to dinner. I could see the stars now. No moon tonight, so they were very bright. I stood for a long two minutes, gazing up at them. About me was the warmth of a Florida night, and I could hear the gentle lapping of an incoming tide. We're all alone here on No-Name Key, I thought savagely. So why don't we all go skinny-dipping in the Gulf, and then we can all gangbang our darling Maria, and so to bed with consciences clear and balls empty. Maybe that's all she needs after all, a good tandem fucking, one, two, three.

So unjust, unfair; I was astonished to discover such anger stored inside me. I had always prided myself on being the thinking man, governed by mind and not by emotion.

Turning, I went back to the three seated nudes, Maria between the two men, each hand resting on their nearest knee.

I forced my voice into quiet statement. "I'll go on upstairs. You can get on with it then."

"Oh, Jerry," Maria said, the words a throb of disappointment.

"You don't need me," I said.

Maria, rising in one swift movement, came to me. "But we do. I can't tell it to Casey, or to Tony. I can only tell it to Us."

"I can't take off my clothes," I said. "Don't you understand that?"

"Then don't," she said. "Just sit down and listen. At least, Jerry, do that. For me."

I knew I was deceiving her by staying. But I had to give her a chance. I'll wait until tomorrow, I thought. I will tell her then that I am leaving. At least, that way, I won't ruin tonight. Maybe, even with me gone, she can find a way still, if a start is made tonight. I sat down in the remaining chair.

The night was still about us, very warm. Above, the lambent stars shone down, and the ocean, so tremendous and inevitable in its enormousness, lapped gently against our near shore. Three naked and one clothed, three plus one—though not as Maria had seen the equation of Us—like the pilgrims on the road to Canterbury, we began our tellings.

MARIA'S TALE

Because Daddy's wealth was so widely known, he was always afraid of kidnapers. That was one reason we lived here much of the time, because No-Name Key is so easily guarded. But of course I had to go to school—and Daddy thought I ought to go to public school, until time to go away to a girl's school, to give me a chance to learn how most people live. So we had a house in Miami, too, where we lived during school term. School was only a few blocks away, and Daddy allowed me to walk alone —though with the chauffeur-bodyguard following at a discreet distance, on foot.

One day, during the year I was ten years old, it happened, just as Daddy had feared. I was walking along, thinking the things a ten-year-old girl thinks on her way home from school, when a car drove up beside me, the door opening, and before I knew what was happening I was inside the car, my head smothered in a sack, and a needle pricking into my buttock.

I woke up in bed, in a dimly lighted room. I've

51

never forgotten that room. It was like something you'd dream about, it was so completely featureless; no windows, only two doors, and the walls were painted gray, with absolutely nothing on them for decoration. The room was furnished with a bed, like those you see in motels, and one chair. I think the room must have been soundproofed, for I couldn't hear anything from outside. I could well have been a million miles away, or just around the corner, from where I lived.

The stuff they had shot me with had made me sick at my stomach, so first I staggered out of bed looking for the john. I threw up, when I got there, but I still felt sick. My stomach was not only upset, but I was feverish and dizzy. I remember that I tried the outside door. When I discovered that it was locked, I climbed back into bed, huddled under the sheet, and went back to sleep.

When I woke up the second time, a man was sitting in the chair watching me. For the first second, I thought it was morning, and I must get ready for school; but, seeing the man, the whole thing flooded back on me, so that I scrounched up against the head of the bed and said, "Who are you?"

He smiled. Then he said, "I'm George. And you're Maria."

I could only stare. There had never been anybody like him in my life. He was so big, and so ugly. He simply bulged the suit he wore all out of shape. His arms were short and thick, his hands were huge. He had heavy eyebrows, just one straight line all the way across, his ears were thick and laid tight to his head. There was a scar on his lower lip, twisting one side of his mouth into an ugly snarl. In fact, he looked like

52

he'd got hurt all over his face, it was so lumpy. His skin, I remember, was very pale and yellow, like he had never been in the sun.

"What are you doing here?" I said. "I don't know you."

With the smile, his face was uglier than ever, so I wished he would quit smiling. "But I know you," he said. "Don't that make it all right?"

"No!" I said. "I want to go home."

Shaking his head, he said seriously, "I'm afraid that'll take a while, Maria. But don't you worry . . . you'll get to go home. Don't you worry about it one minute."

"Why can't I go now, then?" I asked. I was beginning to cry, and I felt like I was going to throw up right there in the bed if my stomach didn't quit churning.

"My partners have to talk to your daddy first," he said. "They'll just talk to your daddy, and then you'll go home. There's absolutely nothing for you to worry about, because your daddy loves you, doesn't he?"

I haven't mentioned his voice, so strange for a man of his size. It was high and thin, where you expected it to be deep and gruff. There was a growly edge to it, though, like his throat had got hurt sometime or other.

"I want to go home now," I said, jerking the words out one by one like they were on a string crammed down into my throat.

He leaned forward in the chair and patted me on the leg. "Don't get into a fit," he said. "I'm going to take care of you, Maria. Old George won't let anything happen to you."

53

I jerked away from his hand, though I was under the sheet and his hand was outside. His china-blue eyes clouded, as though I'd hurt his feelings.

"Are you hungry?" he asked anxiously, his voice going even higher in pitch. "I'll make you a hamburger if you're hungry. Wouldn't you like a nice hamburger with onion and ketchup and everything?"

"No!" I said. "My stomach hurts."

"I can even make you a cheeseburger." His voice coaxed me. "I'll bet you're a cheeseburger person, just like me."

My stomach retched. "No," I said. "I hate cheeseburgers." I turned over with my back to him. I was trembling all over, and I felt like I had the time I had been sick with the flu. My teeth were chattering, but at the same time I was flushed and sweating.

He was standing over me. "I know what you need," he said. "I'll be right back."

He left me alone, and I heard him lock the door after him. I lay there shivering until my stomach clenched suddenly. I threw back the sheet and ran for the bathroom. I nearly didn't make it. I clapped myself on the john and felt it go in one great big stinging rush, leaning over my arms folded into my stomach. Now I had it at both ends.

Only after I was eased did I notice how I was dressed. I was wearing a lightweight cotton night-gown that went all the way to my feet. No wonder I'm sick, I thought wretchedly. I'm cold, and I miss my daddy, and my bowels are loose. And this is all George has given me to wear in this cold room. The gown had little blue flowers all over it.

I looked up, hearing a small sound, and saw George standing in the doorway, holding a glass of milk. I pulled the gown down and held my legs tightly together. I was shivering again, afraid of him, yet embarrassed that he had caught me on the john.

"That's all right," he said. "I'm not looking. I just brought you a glass of warm milk. That'll settle your stomach. Just see if it don't."

"Go away," I said. "Go away."

He went away. But, knowing he hadn't left the room, I tried to outwait him. Finally, when I couldn't sit on the john any longer, I crept to the door. He was sitting patiently in the chair, holding the glass in one great paw.

"Now get into bed and drink your warm milk," he said gently when he saw me peering at him. "Then you'll feel all better."

So I wouldn't have to go near him, I slid into the bed from the opposite side. I was feeling so weak, I obediently drank the milk when he handed the glass to me.

"Now just go back to sleep, and you'll feel like a million dollars when you wake up," he said cheerfully. "Maybe it'll even be time to go home by then. How about that?"

I tried. I tried very hard, because sleep was the only hiding place I knew from the terror lurking just around the blank corner of my mind. I did the thing I had learned to do when a nightmare had waked me up. I used to have nightmares something awful. I curled in on myself, lying very quiet, very still, and thought about beautiful horses. But I couldn't keep still long enough, so I'd jar around on my other side and try it again. Once or twice I dozed off, but woke up sitting straight up in bed, wanting to scream. Once, I think, I did scream.

I didn't know whether it was the middle of the

55

night, or early in the morning, because I had been knocked out by the needle. I had a feeling of being suspended in time, lost completely from the nice, happy girl I had been yesterday. Or was it the day before, or last week? In this limbo, I couldn't believe, in spite of George's reassurance, that I'd ever again see Daddy. Indeed, all of a sudden, I couldn't remember him at all clearly, as though I had already been away for years and years. Daddy was in my mind exactly like Mother was, who had died when I was 5 years old and had never come back. Maybe I had died, too. Maybe I never would come back, either.

It went on like that for hours, even after I was so tired I could hardly bear it. My eyes simply refused to close. George, getting more and more worried, was in and out every few minutes. Once, with another glass of warm milk, he gave me a pill to swallow. I knew what it was, a tranquilizer, so I took it eagerly, wanting to sleep, by now, as desperately as George wished it for me.

When the tranquilizer didn't seem to work, George didn't go away any more, but began talking to me, not saying anything in particular, his voice going on and on and on and on. I knew he was trying to comfort me, soothe my ragged nerves. Once, he even started telling a silly story I remembered from one of my childhood books, about the little red hen that wanted to bake bread. But he couldn't remember how it went, and when he asked me what happened next, I wouldn't tell him.

The room was completely dark, because he had turned out the light in the ceiling that was the only fixture. I was lying on my back, staring gritty-eyed into the darkness, waiting for my stomach to roil *again, when I felt his hand under the sheet. I tensed. It groped, found my leg, slid toward my crotch.*

I jerked away. "You can't touch me," I said, my voice shaking.

"I won't hurt you," he said. "Don't be afraid Maria. I wouldn't hurt you for anything in this world."

I was trembling all over.

"Daddy always said, Don't let anybody touch you. Especially there." I said it in a miserable, hopeless voice, knowing there was no way to stop George if he didn't want to be stopped.

"Your daddy was right," George said. He had got up out of the chair, his hand resting its heavy weight on my leg again, and the bed sagged as he sat down on the edge. "But you need to go to sleep now, or else you're going to be an awfully sick little girl. So I'm just going to make you nice and soft and comfy and ready to go beddy-bye."

I was ten years old, remember. All I knew about myself was that you didn't touch yourself there, and you sure didn't let a stranger touch you. That's the first thing a little girl is taught, I guess.

But I was interested. I knew he meant to touch me right between the legs, in the place grown people are so funny about. I couldn't understand, though, how it could make you nice and soft and comfy—especially when you were as scared and lonely and sick as I felt right then.

I could feel my legs clamped tightly against each other, as rigid and straight as sticks—and the weight of the huge, heavy hand, above my knee now, cupped around my leg, not tightly, and he could reach around the girth of my thigh.

He was silent. It was dark, and I could not see him. I could only feel his hand as it crept up my thigh inch by inch, as though he were trying to catch a frightened rabbit trembling there between my legs.

Then: his finger found my little slit, pressed with a gentle pressure, slid inside. I shivered. In the darkness, I made myself blank him out, the big, ugly man named George, allowing myself to know only the finger. For the finger was a gentle kindness. It didn't poke or prod or hurt, it simply rubbed and rubbed and rubbed, barely touching, until my legs were relaxed from their stiffness. I settled down into the bed, spreading myself so that the hand could cup my crotch warmly, the middle finger still lightly inserted.

"Now isn't that nice?" George's reedy voice said, half-whispering. "Isn't that nice, to be so cozy and comfy and sleepy in your little bed?"

He kept on talking, the voice fitting itself to the rhythm of the finger, and it was just like he had said, so warm, so tender, so soothing. A warmth was spreading itself through my whole body, giving me a steady strength I had lost so long ago I had forgotten what it was like. My eyelids were growing heavy, too, heavier by the minute, and I wanted to say, "Thank you, George," but I was so sleepy I couldn't, and then I was gone over the edge.

I have no idea how long I slept, nor what time of the day or night it was when I woke up. But even after realizing that I was still in the strange, dream-like room, that terrible things were still happening to keep me away from Daddy, I felt quite my usual self.

I needed to go to the bathroom but before I could move George stuck his head in at the door. He always seemed to know when I was awake; maybe he had a peephole to spy on me.

"I'll bet you're starving," he said cheerfully.

I thought about it, and I was. I looked at him eagerly, and then, remembering what I had let him do last night, I looked away.

He was still grinning, even though I had so obviously flinched. "You just wait one minute, little girl," he said. "I'll fix you up with the best breakfast you ever put in your mouth."

He disappeared, and I leaped for the bathroom. My stomach was all right now—although terribly empty and clamorous—and this was just the needful sort of everyday thing. I finished my devotions, washed my face and hands and dried them on the small towel—and then, on sudden impulse, I lifted my gown, bowed my legs, and leaned over to look at myself.

I hadn't ever played with myself, had seldom even looked at that part of my body, because my governess had always been stern about any sort of self-curiosity. As far as I could tell, with my scant knowledge, George's finger had not altered me in any way, even though I had thought there would surely be a visible difference.

I was safely back in bed when he shouldered the door open and entered, bearing my breakfast tray. "Now, how about that?" he said, positioning it across my legs.

There was a huge bowl of corn flakes. There was a platter with three eggs and bacon, and a stack of toast as high as pancakes. There was a glass of milk.

George was watching me anxiously. "Now, if you're used to coffee or tea, I have that, too," he said. "But a growing girl like you, I figure you need milk."

I was so ravenous, I didn't take the time to answer him before I began spooning in the corn flakes. It tasted marvelous—crisper and better than any corn

*flakes I could remember. George, who had taken
the chair, watched with satisfaction as I plowed steadily through the breakfast. I left only one small bite
of toast.*

*He took the tray. "Now, that's the girl!" he said ap-
provingly. "I figured all you needed was a good
night's sleep to get you straightened out."*

*I looked up into his face. "Can I . . ." I said hesi-
tantly. "George, can I go home now?"*

*His china-blue eyes slid from me. "Not yet a while,"
he said. "There's been . . . some difficulties." He gave
me a reproachful smile. "Aren't you happy here with
old George? Ain't I been treating you nice?"*

*I was still watching him. "Yes," I said. "But every-
body always told me it was nasty to do that."*

*George became immediately serious, regarding me
with a frown for a long, still minute. Watching his
eyes, I thought suddenly, He's scared. He's scareder
now than I was, before . . .*

*"That's what my governess told me, I guess a thou-
sand times," I said severely. "A girl should never,
never, never let anybody touch her between the legs.
Especially a stranger. It's nasty, she said. So nasty a
person just couldn't want anybody to touch them."*

*Slowly, George put the tray on the floor. He sat
down in the chair, his arms braced on the chair arms.
He was so big he filled it completely, his thighs bulging out the sides.*

*"Maria, your governess is right." He hesitated. "At
least—halfway right. It can be nasty. Whether it's
nasty or not depends on how a fellow does it. Now,
you take me. I was worried about you feeling so
feverish and upset, and not being able to go to sleep.
You'd missed an awful lot of sleep, Maria. You were
pretty scared, too, you'll have to admit that."*

60

"Well, she was wrong. It was nice," I said firmly. "So nice, and I went right to sleep, didn't I?"

The trouble cleared out of his face like a magic wand had whisked it away.

"You see? It all depends. Done nice, it is nice. And that's how I meant to do it, nice and easy and so you'd settle down and get some rest."

"Is that what it's for, then, when you want to go to sleep?"

Grinning, he shook his head. Then he looked embarrassed. "Not exactly," he said. "It's just a . . . a nice thing between two people that like one another. You do like old George, don't you? Because George likes you."

"I'm beginning to," I said. "Even if you are keeping me from going home. You are a very nice person, George. You worry a lot about a person when that person isn't feeling well." I wriggled in the bed, wanting to say it. Then I could say it. "Will you do it again, George. Right now?"

He stared. He was flustered, and his face was red. "Now?" he said. "But . . . you don't need to sleep now. You're not scared any more, either."

"But you said it wasn't just for sleeping."

Moving faster than I had thought a huge man like him could move, he was out of the chair and stooping to pick up the tray.

"I've got to wash these dishes," he said.

He was gone before I could say another word. Alone again, I stared about the room, wondering why he had left so suddenly. Tentatively, I slipped my hand down into my crotch, put my finger into the slit. As George had done last night, I rubbed it, kept on rubbing, trying to recall what it had felt like.

It felt good. But I couldn't make it have the sweet,

wonderful quality of when George's finger had been in me, so pretty soon I quit. I was alone for a long, long time, thinking about it. So shut off from the world, there was nothing to do but think. Even time did not dwell there; the clock of my appetites for food and sleep had been put out of order. The world consisted of me and George; everything and everybody I had known before waking up in this room had faded into unimportance.

When George appeared again at last, I sat up eagerly.

"Hungry again?" he asked.

I thought about it, then nodded. He grinned. "I thought so. I'm all ready for you."

This time, George ate with me. My tray bore a hamburger steak, French fried potatoes, small green peas. For himself, George had fixed three cheeseburgers, along with a massive pile of French fries. Like me, he drank milk. Halfway through the companionable meal, I asked him for a bite of cheeseburger. He gave me a whole one. I had not lied to him; I had never liked cheeseburgers. But this one was extraordinarily good.

"Tomorrow," I told him, "I'll have cheeseburgers, too."

He was pleased. "Like I told you, there's nothing better. Cheeseburgers for lunch, then. That's a promise."

"George, why can't I have a television set?" I said then. "I'm so lonesome when you stay away so long."

George frowned. "Maria, I can't do that," he said. "You might . . . hear things . . . that would get you all upset again."

"You mean about myself?" I asked.

George was very uncomfortable. "You see, you're

a famous little girl right now. Your daddy didn't do like he was supposed to, and let the newspapers find out that you were missing."

I experienced a stab of pain, thinking how Daddy must feel with me gone. But it was faint and far away, like Daddy himself.

"But you'll let me go home when the time comes, won't you?" I said comfortably. "So Daddy doesn't need to worry at all."

"Just as soon as he pays . . ." George stopped suddenly.

I sat up straighter, nearly dumping the tray. "Pays?" I said. "Does Daddy have to pay to get me back?"

George was upset with himself. "Well, Maria, that's what it's all about," he said finally. "We wanted to get a lot of money from your daddy, and we decided this was the best way." He smiled painfully. "As soon as my partners have the money, I'll take you home. O.K.?"

"Well, Daddy has plenty of money," I said. "I don't guess there'll be any problem about that."

He took the trays and left the room. I was afraid he'd stay gone, but he returned almost immediately. I was down in the bed now, my legs not rigid and aching like before, but spread loose and easy and waiting. I watched him while he sat down in the chair.

"Want me to stay with you a while?" he said.

I wriggled in the bed. "Yes," I said. "Please, George."

"Want me to tell you a story?"

I laughed. "George, you're just about the worst storyteller in the world. You can't remember how they come out at the end."

He chuckled. "I guess you're right. So—do you want to tell me a story instead?"

I slid deeper into the bed. "No. I'm sort of sleepy." I waited. But he only sat there. I began to feel impatient. "George," I said. "I'm sleepy, I said. Aren't you going to . . ."

He tried to act like he didn't know what I was talking about. But he knew, all right.

"Then go to sleep," he said. "I'll stay with you until you drop off."

"George!" I said.

He sat still for a long minute that seemed like an hour instead. Then he said very seriously, "Maria, you don't need it this time."

"But I want it."

He shook his head firmly. "I don't want to hurt you, Maria. I wouldn't hurt a hair on your head." He stopped for another minute. "Not even if your daddy won't pay the money."

I was impatient with his stupidness. "But it doesn't hurt. It feels good. Come on, George. Please."

He didn't move. Gazing into his ugly face, I knew, somehow, that he wanted to and, because he did want to, he was afraid. I didn't understand it. After all, he had thought of it first himself.

I couldn't stand any more of the waiting. I threw back the sheet with one hand and pulled up my gown with the other. Then I took his inert hand from where it rested on his knee and laid it between my legs.

"Now, George," I said. "Now."

First, I could feel only the trembling of his hand. Then it turned over, his middle finger searching for the slit. I shivered all over, lifting my knees to open myself for him.

"Oh, George," I said. *"I love you, George. Did you know that I love you?"*

I said those words because I was looking into his face—he hadn't put the room into darkness this time —and I could tell how much he liked touching me there. I lay back on the pillow, soothed and dreamy. I could feel a wetness in me, a slow, deep secretion, and somewhere far back along my spine a gathering of tension. He was watching me now, like I had watched him, and that made it even better, until finally I couldn't stand to hold still any longer, so that suddenly I squirmed my whole body to press harder against his pressure. There was a tiny explosion, and the sensation spread all through me, like warm syrup over pancakes. I lay still, then, relaxed and warm and feeling so good.

He had stopped, but his hand had not left me. I gazed lovingly on his ugly, gentle face.

"Do you think I'm pretty, George?"

"You are a beautiful child, Maria," he said. His voice was so husky and growly the words were almost smothered. "The most beautiful child I've ever seen."

"You're ugly, George," I said gaily. "The ugliest man I've ever seen. But the nicest, too."

His hand still rested on me, as though reluctant to go away. "Are you ready to go to sleep now?"

"I'm wide awake!" I protested. "Don't you dare leave me."

We sat still together for a while. I was alert and so inquisitive, I wanted to talk about it as a means of prolonging this good time. But I didn't know what to say. Finally, a fragment of something I had once heard at school coming to the surface of my mind, I said, "George, is that how babies are made?"

He was startled. "Babies?" he said. "Don't you know about babies?"

I shook my head. "Not really."

It was true. A rich man's daughter, I had lived a sheltered life; certainly my prim governess had never told me anything. My information on the subject consisted of misinformation picked up at school. I hadn't been very interested, until now, so I hadn't paid much attention to the little I had heard.

"I don't know anything, I guess, about how babies are made," I said in a burst of honesty. "A girl told me once that a man does something to a woman to make it happen, so I thought . . ."

"That's a darned shame," George said. "A smart little girl like you, growing up ignorant of the facts of life."

He shifted to take away his hand. I laid one hand on top of his to keep it there.

"So I guess I'll have your baby now," I said. "I won't mind if he's as ugly as you are, George, if he's as nice."

George threw back his head, laughing a hearty, free laugh. Then he became serious again. "Maria, in the first place, what we've done wouldn't make a baby in a million years. In the second place, you'll have to be a grown woman before you can do your part of the job. So you're safe enough."

"Then how do people become fathers and mothers?" I said. "Will you explain it to me, George?"

He watched me for a still moment. "You're not kidding me? You really don't know?"

"I wish I did," I said indignantly. "After all, I wouldn't want to make a baby without knowing it, would I? When I'm old enough, I mean."

He chuckled. "No. I guess you wouldn't."

He told me all about it then, very slowly and very carefully, taking his hand away and leaning back in the chair and talking with exact detail, in words I could understand. I listened avidly, aware of areas opening up in my mind that had been closed off until now by the hushings and forbiddances of the grown people around me. It was astonishing how much I had actually known about it; I just hadn't put it all together. When he had finished, I lay staring at the ceiling, my mind sorting the new knowledge into clear patterns of awareness.

"It's just wonderful," I said at last. "Isn't it wonderful, George?"

"It's pretty nice, all right," George said. "At least, for most people."

"So why do people have to act so funny about it, making you feel ashamed?" I sat up in the bed. "George," I said. "Let me see yours."

He was shocked. "See . . . ?" he said, stuttering over the very idea. "Maria, I can't do that."

I glared at him. "You've seen mine. So why can't I see yours?"

"It's . . . it's not the same thing. Not the same thing at all."

I flopped down into the bed. "It's not fair," I said. "You told me all about it, and how nice it was, and everything. But now you won't show me."

"Maria . . ." he said uncertainly.

Tears surged up in me. Suddenly I was bereft—of me, of George, of my life-before-George. "I want to go home," I wailed. "I'm tired of staying here with you. I want my daddy. I want . . ."

His great weight sank down the side of the mattress. He reached over me, pressing his warm hand into my belly, turning me to face him.

67

"Maria," he said urgently. "Maria, honey. Please don't cry."

Because of the tears in my eyes, he was rainbowed with a halo. "Will you please show me then? Please?"

He stared, a tight, grim look to his face. "Kid," he said. "You're playing with fire and you don't even know it. But ... all right."

I sat up eagerly, the recent tears forgotten completely. He stood up and turned his back. His hands moved, hidden ... and then, slowly, very slowly, he revealed himself to my eyes.

I simply stared. I had never seen a boy's cock, much less a man's. It stood up out of his fly like a great club, the head red and glistening. I could trace a blue vein, gorged and snaky-looking, down the length of the shaft, to where it disappeared into his thick, curly hair.

"Can I ... can I touch?" I whispered breathlessly.

He didn't forbid me, so, tentatively, I reached out my hand to put the tip of my finger in the fascinating little eye. I felt the tiny drop of moisture that stood there break with my touch. He shuddered, as I had shuddered, and I gazed up into his face.

"Does that feel good?" I asked innocently. "Like when you touched me?"

"Yes," he said in his growliest voice. "My God, yes."

I cupped the body of his cock with my whole hand. It was warm and strong, so huge and wonderful in my fist. He made one step toward me, then a second step, pushing himself against my fist so that the loose skin slid back, my fist going with it, and the great head strained out bulging from my grip, like I was holding a snake. He was over me, now, so close that I was staring up, seeing the hairy bulk of his balls.

68

He pulled his hips back, so that my fist slid forward. Understanding suddenly, I pumped my hand, backward again and then forward, watching the great head as it glowed redder, larger. Far beyond it, I saw, out of focus, his tense face.

I stopped, struck by another idea. "George. Show me exactly what you do to make a baby."

He stared down at me. His mouth was open. I could hear his breathing in the still room. With an abrupt twist, he took his cock away from me.

"We can't do that," he said. "You're not big enough."

I sat up, excited. "But that's just it, George. You said I had to be grown up before I could actually make a baby. So you can show me how it's done without running any risk at all. Don't you see?"

Moving awkwardly, he sat down on the side of the bed. He braced one hand over on the other side of my body, so that he was leaning close, very close.

"The thing is, Maria, I'd hurt you," he said. "It would hurt terribly, more than you can imagine. It has to go all the way in, not just rubbing on top like with the finger, and you're not big enough, down there."

"That's all right, George," I said bravely. "I know you'd stop if it began to hurt too much."

He shook his head. "But I couldn't, Maria, once I got started." He paused, watching my face. "You see, I'm bigger than most men, so big that sometimes I hurt grown women." His face was suddenly sad and old, lined with the old hurts of his life. "Women won't have much to do with me for that reason. Even women I've paid, they take just one look and . . ."

His expression made me ache inside, so that I sat up and kissed him on the mouth. His lips were soft and warm and it was such a nice kiss I did it all

69

over again while his arms went tight around me, holding me close.

"But you're such a nice person, George. Women ought to like you, the way I do."

His mouth twisted. "Well, they like the idea... until they try it on for size. They say I get too wild, too, Maria, that I just go crazy and then they begin to hurt and bleed and try to get away from me." His breath was coming hard. "So I don't try any more. I don't even try."

I lay in his arms, thinking about it. I was disappointed. But I certainly didn't want to get hurt, not down there. I tried to imagine what it would be like to have that big old thing bulging hard into me. But I couldn't, not really.

"But I wanted to see the stuff that makes the babies," I said. "That white stuff you told me about."

He laid me down on the bed, then remained close, gazing into my eyes. I felt his breath catch. "Well, you can see that. If you want to. Are you sure you want to?"

I sat up, all excited again. "I can?"

"Yes," he said. "But you'll have to ... touch it again, like you did before. And keep on without stopping, until ... You understand?"

"Yes, I understand," I said. "And it'll be nice for you, won't it, like your finger was for me."

It was curious that he hadn't needed to explain in more detail. He stood over me, his hips clenched tightly forward. I wrapped my hand around his cock and began pumping it, faster and faster and faster, hearing his breath rasping in rhythm, louder and louder, until suddenly the white stuff came, some of it boiling over my hand, the rest shooting far out and raining down into my face. I could feel the

70

muscles pulsing in my fisted grip as the stuff kept coming and coming.

We stopped, then, and I looked at it smeared on my hand. "And that makes babies," I said wonderingly.

"Yes," George said. "Except, like I told you, the woman must have an egg ready. There's thousands of little fellows in there called sperm, just wriggling away, and one of them finds the egg, and then they grow together . . ."

With one finger of the other hand, I touched the puddle of semen in my palm; then, not knowing why I did it, I put the finger to my mouth. It had a strange, wild taste, reminding me somehow of the ocean, when the tide is out, you know, and you can smell the bottom of the sea.

He had put his limp cock back into his pants. "Now, that's enough," he said. "Go wash your hand."

"But I like to feel it," I said. "I want to sleep with it on . . ."

"Do like I said. Go on, now."

Hearing the tone of his voice, I hurried into the bathroom. When I came back, George was sitting again in the chair. I could tell he felt as good, now, as I did.

"Was it nice?" I asked fondly. "Like when you did me?"

He smiled. "You don't know how good."

"We'll do it again, won't we?" I said confidently. "Hundreds and hundreds of times, first you doing me and then . . . " I stopped, seeing that he was worried again. "What's the matter?"

He looked down at his hands so he wouldn't have to see me. "Maria," he said "I . . . " His voice choked, but he tried again. "Maria, I didn't plan to get into all this. It's not right, you just a little girl and all . . . "

71

"But it's nice," I said. "I like it. You like it. And there's no television or anything."

He made a wry smile. "Maybe I should have got you a TV. The thing is, Maria, if people found out I had touched you, let you touch me—well, it would be about a hundred times as bad as you could imagine."

"Nobody knows, though, but you and me."

"But when you get home, and they ask you all those quesions they'll be asking, about how you were treated and all . . . "

"I won't tell," I said passionately. "I promise, George. Cross my heart and hope to die." I watched him anxiously. "So we won't have to quit, will we? If I promise not to tell?"

He regarded me, the trouble still in his face. "You're just a child, Maria. I never thought I'd turn out to be the kind of fellow who messes with little girls. God knows, grown women are trouble enough." He stopped himself. "But you're such a strange little girl, Maria. So innocent, so beautiful, yet so . . . " He was leaning forward. "You liked it, didn't you? It didn't hurt you or scare you, or anything, when I put my hand there. Did it?"

I had to do something about the way he was feeling. I got out of bed and climbed up into his lap, where I put my arms tightly around his neck. I laid my face against his rough-skinned cheek. He had his arms around me so tight and close that it was hard to breathe, so I slid down to stand between his legs. I leaned into his crotch, knowing, without knowing how I knew, that if I got close enough I would feel his great thing hard against my legs. I did feel it, too, all the way through the cloth of his pants and my thin gown.

"You see, George?" I breathed. "Do you see now?"

"I see," he said huskily. He kissed me. On the mouth. But so gently, so carefully.

"You won't quit?" I whispered. "You won't make us stop?"

He pulled away to look into my eyes. "We'll have to think about it," he said. "We'll just have to think about that."

"Of course," I said, considering I was being intelligent about the whole thing, "we'll have to be careful about your partners. We don't want them to find out, do we?"

"No need to worry about them," George said. "You see, it's my part of the job to take care of you. They don't even know where we are, I fixed this place myself, all they know is a phone number to call when they've got the money." He was talking fast, under his breath. Then, slowly, watching me, he went on. "So there's just you and me, Maria. Out of the whole world. You. And me."

The way he said it scared me just a little bit. No, not scared; excited would be a better word. Because somehow, somehow, I knew . . .

He stirred, pushed me away to stand up. Then he lifted me, holding me for a minute in his great arms, my legs dangling, before he put me into the bed.

"Time to go to sleep," he said firmly.

I gazed up at him. "George. It's so lonely all by myself in this awful room. Where do you sleep?"

He gestured. "In there. I'm close . . . close enough, even, to hear if you have a bad dream."

I hesitated, afraid that he would refuse. I knew I was trying to make a big step. "Will you . . . George, sleep in here with me. Please."

He regarded me. "There's just the one bed."

I smiled at him. "That's what I mean. If we sleep together neither one of us will be lonely, will we?"

"No!" he said. "No!" Abruptly, he was gone. He could disappear so quickly whenever I reached a point he didn't want to think about.

I thought I had ruined it, this time. But when he brought breakfast—and I had slept well, even though alone—George was his usual gentle self. And we went on from there.

We didn't wait for the sleeping time, either. As soon as he had taken away the breakfast trays, he sat on the edge of the bed and put his hand on me without waiting to be asked. It was then that I got the next big idea, and begged him to take off his clothes.

He hesitated to do it, but he wasn't hard to persuade. He looked twice as big, both him and his cock, without the clothes on. I hadn't seen his balls, the time before, and so it was necessary to examine them closely, and find out what part they played. While he told me, we were side by side, me touching him and him touching me. Then I made him come again, with my hand, and I got the burny, warm, wonderful wriggles again, watching him do it.

I was so totally absorbed in George now, I didn't care if I ever went home. What more could a girl want? I had this huge, wonderful, marvelous man at my beck and call, playing with him, sitting naked on his great belly, laughing and talking and teasing. I could, and did, spend hours at it, his great hands all over me as my hands were on him. Yet there remained a small core of discontent. I couldn't stop thinking about how it must feel to have his cock inside me, like you had to do to make babies.

But this was one place where he absolutely refused to yield to my blandishments. "I won't do anything

74

to hurt you," he said every time I brought it up again. "So you might as well shut up about it."

Reluctantly, I tried to put it out of my mind. But the lust was still there, driving me to the sly invention of a near substitute. I persuaded him to let me sit with his great cock thrusting between my legs while I rubbed up and down, my legs clamped, until he reached orgasm. The second time I had his cock so close to where I wanted it, I waited until he was in the throes, then raised myself, shoving his rigid, pumping tool underneath with my hand, trying to sit down with it inside my pussy. He snatched me away, though, before I could discover whether or not the capture would work.

He was not angry, however, as I had feared. He was laughing instead. "You're a little devil, you know that?" he said. "If you were a grown woman, I'll bet you could handle him. And like it, too."

I sprawled along his length, close against his body, basking in his great warmth. "I know I could," I said. "And when I'm grown, I'll prove it."

He hugged me. "Will you, now?" he said tenderly. "Will you, my sweet little girl?"

"I promise," I said passionately. "I promise."

So we were together, in our own marvelous way of being together, and we went to sleep with my feet tucked between his thighs, his great arms holding me close, and I could feel his breathing body all along the length of my body.

When I woke up, George was still asleep. I went to the bathroom, and when I returned he had rolled onto his back, his arms and legs sprawled. I sat in the chair, gazing at the half-erection he carried even in his sleep. I loved his cock, the way it would rise and subside and then rise again, seemingly forever.

I loved the look of him, the smell of him, the feel of him.

I sat there for a while, thinking that, when the time came, I wished he could go home with me. Feeling so tender and warm, watching him in his naked sleeping, I crept quietly onto the bed, wanting to take the heavy balls fondling into my hand. It was such a nice, tender place. I moved very gently, not wishing to wake him. He stirred when I touched him, but only smiled and settled down again.

Sitting with his balls weighted into my palm, I was fascinated, as always, by the sight of his prick lifting slowly into gorged rigidity. It was so marvelous, that simply by the touching of my hand I could do this to him. Even if he was asleep. It was my first inkling of the power nature has given to the woman.

I realized, then, that my mouth wanted to taste him. I had tasted his come, once, but I had never tasted his cock. Leaning close, I blew warm breath on the great, red, moist head. When he groaned with a deep and sleeping pleasure, I ducked my head and took his cock into my mouth.

So strange. So marvelous. And I seemed to know exactly what to do. I pushed my mouth down on him, hard, until I gagged. I eased up, then, sliding my hard-edged lips lightly over the head, feeling it muscular and slippery against the tissues of my mouth. So much of him, so greatly much. But I felt as though I could swallow him whole.

Sensing that he was coming awake, I edged my teeth lightly across the groove just under the head. A deep groan traveled through his flesh. Fearful that he would try to escape as soon as he was awake enough to know it was not a dream, I climbed on top, like riding a bucking horse, and I still had him in my

76

mouth. But rather than trying to get away, he was fucking my mouth with hard, short thrusts and I was strangling, I was drowning in his come. But I wouldn't give it up, I wouldn't let go, and it was like I had imagined it would be inside my pussy, where babies would someday be made.

I stayed with him, taking it all, until he became quiet. Then I raised up, sitting straddled on his belly, and twisted around to grin at him. "Good morning!" I said. "Wasn't it nice? I just thought of it, all by myself."

"Good God, girl," he said. "Good God."

He reached for me, turning my unresisting body. I lay waiting, gazing avidly into his tight, hard face, feeling his huge hands clamped on my shoulders. His hips worked, thrusting his cock, rigid again so soon, against my naked thigh. I could feel its hungry need to enter into me.

I wanted it to enter. I struggled to turn on my side, wriggling frantically to put my pussy against the lusty head, knowing that if George touched me with his rod he was wild enough now to plunge in, heedless of how much it might hurt.

But it was my shoulders that took the hurting, because he squeezed them with his hands, making himself stop. He was groaning, as though he were hurting as much as I was. But I had not cried out, though his gripping hands were terrible on my flesh. I wanted to prove that I could take anything.

His eyes glared at me, showing the whites of the eyeballs. Then the eyes were gone, and I thought for a delirious second that he had put himself into me and it didn't hurt at all, it felt just wonderful. But then, seeing his head crammed between my thighs, I knew that it was his tongue I was feeling.

77

Oh yes! I thought, putting my hands on his head, pushing his tongue harder into me as I raised myself against his mouth. And I moved with him, as he moved with me, hoping that it would never end.

But of course it did end, it had to, and George sat up on the side of the bed. I looked at his cock. He must have come again, because it was limp.

His voice was as withdrawn as his body. "I've got to get you out of here," he said. "Now. Today. Before something terrible happens."

"George!" I said.

He turned his head to look at me. Slowly the terrible, strained look went away, and his big hand reached out to touch my cheek.

"Girl, you don't know what you're doing," he said. "But me . . . I ought to know better."

"The money isn't paid yet, is it?" I said fearfully. "You can't let me go until the money's paid, can you?"

"I'm not worrying about the money, not any more, I'm worrying . . ." He stopped himself. "Maria," he said gently, "I can't take away what I've already let happen. But I can at least see to it that you leave here a virgin, just like you came." His face became almost angry. But not at me. "Maria, damn it, I could cause you to bleed to death." He shuddered and put both hands over his face.

"I just want him in me," I said gently. "Just one time. That's all."

"No," he said in a fatal, still voice. "It can't be, Maria. It just can't be."

I put my hand on his shoulder. "But didn't you like me doing it with my mouth?"

"Yes," he said. "God, yes. That's just the trouble. One thing leads to another, and there's no going back . . ."

78

"I liked you doing me with your mouth," I said. *I put my arms around his head. "My sweet George. Nobody has ever been as nice to me."*

"When you know better, Maria, you'll hate me. I don't want you to hate me, ever."

I got down off the bed, put my hands on his wrists, trying to pull his hands away from his face. When I couldn't, I dropped down between his knees and put both hands on his cock instead. I held it warmly.

"I'll never hate you, George. Never."

Something inside me was exulting, even in the midst of tenderness, because his cock was stirring again, lifting its ever-eager head. I leaned to kiss it, knowing with a secret smugness that I could make George do anything I wanted.

And, beginning with that simple cock-kiss, I coaxed him step by grudging step, wholly against his will, until he was kneeling between my spread knees, holding his rod poised, one hand guarding all but the bulbous head, while I lifted my loins against it.

It was a great strain, holding himself back; I could see it in his face, his eyes, in the tensions of his body. I knew I was being cruel. But I had to have it once, at least this much, I had to know it truly. I craned my neck to see the beautiful, wet thing parting gently the lips of my hairless pussy, to rest against the place where only his finger and his tongue had been before.

I made the rhythm while, with a total effort, he held himself still. I watched my cunt lapping around the throbbing, swelling head, his big fist guarding still the mighty shaft, and I wished I could take it all, I yearned to taste its great length in my juvenile depths. Indeed, I pressed, and kept pressing, until a stab of pain shot through me. He flinched, and I stopped, for I had promised to be governed by his caution.

"Now you do it, George," I said.

This part was even more difficult for him. But he did what he knew I wanted, moving his hips, with tremendous control, a fraction of an inch backward and forward.

He was fucking me. I could feel the enormous, bulbous head embedded between the lips, could feel the pulse and beat of its fucking. I knew that I was demanding the impossible, risking an uncontrollable wildness that would rip me terribly if it slipped out of George's control. I knew. And I did not care.

Or, perhaps, I knew my dear George. For he did not hurt me. He constrained himself to this small fucking even as the lips of my unviolated pussy swelled and warmed him, clutching like a tiny, greedy hand around the beautiful head of his great cock; until, in that strained, incomplete posture, still gripping the shaft with one hand, he began to come; and for the first time, ten years old, I felt a man's semen spurting at me even as I posted into my own tiny orgasm.

With an effort, he tilted himself back on his heels. "Are you all right, Maria?" he asked anxiously.

I sat up, leaning to put both arms around his thick waist. "Yes, George," I said. "It was marvelous." I laid my cheek against his sweaty belly. "But it hurt you, didn't it? It hurt you instead of me."

"That's all right," he said. "That's the way it ought to be." His voice sounded very tired.

"George," I said. "When I'm big enough . . . will you do it all the way?"

"Yes," he said hoarsely. He laughed a small laugh, patting my cheek. "Yes, of course. If I ever have the chance."

80

I went to sleep again, so completely used up, and didn't wake until time for dinner. I sat straight up in bed when George opened the door, startled by his appearance. He was fully dressed.

"What's the matter?" I said.

He wouldn't look at me. "Well, little girl, I guess it's time to go home."

My heart plummeted. "You mean . . . the money's been paid?"

"Yes," he said. He still wouldn't look at me.

"George, I don't want to go," I said, bursting suddenly into a flood of tears. "I want to stay with you."

He gave me his gentle smile, then, and his eyes were loving. "You have to go home, you know," he said. "The money's been paid, and that's the bargain. It wouldn't do for us to break our word, would it? So we'll eat cheeseburgers together again for one last time, and then . . ."

My heart was broken. George, putting the trays aside, tried to comfort me, but I would not be comforted. I knew, deep down, that no matter how bitterly I wept, I would have to go home to Daddy. Still, I couldn't face the thought of leaving the great, gentle man whom I loved as I had never loved anyone before.

I was so miserable I couldn't think about eating, so George brought the dress I had worn on that day that seemed forever ago, the shoes I hadn't had on since waking up in this room, and helped me get dressed. At the last minute, I clung to him.

"George, one more time. Just once."

He held me tightly. "No time, girl. There just isn't enough time." He was trembling all over, as I was trembling.

I pulled back, to gaze despairingly into his face. "Let me do it with my mouth, then," I said. I began opening his fly. "It won't take but a minute. Daddy can wait one more minute."

I had believed I could make George do anything I asked. But George had come to the stopping place.

"There's no time," he said. "We've got to go."

As he opened the door, stood aside for me to walk before him, there was a strange, empty look to his face. He put one hand to my shoulder. "I won't forget you, Maria. Not ever. Will you try not to forget me?"

I was crying again. I put my hand on his hand. "I can't," I said. "I won't."

He took his hand away, found a handkerchief, wiped clumsily at my cheek. "Then don't cry," he said. "You don't have to cry, not if we're always going to remember."

So it was over. He had to blindfold me, so I wouldn't know where we had been during these beautiful days, and then he drove for a very long time. When he took off the blindfold, I saw that it was late at night, and we were in the big, empty parking lot of a shopping center. Right beside the car was a telephone booth.

"Here's a dime," he said. "Go call your daddy and tell him to pick you up." His voice became anxious. "Do you know the number?"

I looked at him, without moving, for a long minute. "Will I ever see you again, George?" I asked. "Really?"

He took a deep breath. "No," he said. "That's not likely to happen, Maria."

I nodded. I had known it for myself. I had only

needed to hear him say it. I opened the door, stepped out.

"Goodbye, George," I said.

"I'll wait until you reach your daddy," he said. He was having to make an effort to hold his voice quiet and firm. "But . . . when I go, I'll have to go fast. So . . . goodbye, Maria."

I regarded him steadfastly. "You're a criminal, aren't you, George?"

He looked away. "Yes. In more ways than you know."

"Goodbye, George," I said.

"Goodbye, little girl Maria," he said, and when he put his hand to his face, I saw that he was crying. "Goodbye."

Turning my back, I marched to the phone booth. I couldn't cry any more. My legs felt stiff and strange, as though they didn't know how to move in walking. I put in the dime and dialed the number. Daddy came on, saying, "Hello?"

"Daddy?" I said. "It's Maria. Come get me."

I turned to look, hearing Daddy's voice clamoring at my ear but not hearing the words. George was going away. The car was moving very fast.

. . . I did see George again, after all. It was in the courtroom, with George on trial for my kidnaping, along with another man, a woman, and the chauffeur-bodyguard who had been supposed to guard me. I sat in the big chair beside the judge, the lawyer leaning carefully toward me.

"Maria, you have told us that you saw only one of the kidnappers, who took care of you while they were holding you for ransom," he said. "If you see

*that man in this courtroom, please point him out for
the jury."*

I looked at George, sitting in handcuffs at one of
the tables. I knew by now that the ransom had never
been paid, that George had released me just before the arrangements were completed.

"I don't see him," I said. "He's not here at all."

Maria rose, went to the bar, mixed a drink. She
took a hard slug, then a second one. When she put
the glass down, she was looking at me.

"Jerry," she said. "You don't look at all like him, in
any way that I can think of. But there's something in
you that reminded me so strongly of my gentle George.
That's why you were my first lover."

Chapter 4

Early the next morning, I was walking the beach alone. Troubled by erotic dreams, I had not slept well. In my dreaming, Maria had been a ten-year-old child, with a woman's face and mature sexual organs. I had been George, with the rampant cock of a stallion. The woman-child screamed every time I thrust at her with the great red cock. Yet, even as she screamed, her head back and her mouth open, her loins were writhing up to engulf me greedily, the vagina gaping to reveal a clitoris as large and rigid as an ordinary-sized penis. It had shown a head like a penis, moist and engorged; at the same time, it had worn a human face—my own—with its small mouth open and screaming, too.

A Florida beach before sunrise is one of the beautiful experiences of the human soul. I needed a beautiful experience after such dreamings. Here on No-Name Key, the white sand, so incredibly fine-grained, was unmarked by the footprints of strangers. The tide was at low ebb, leaving a strand of hard-packed terrain, gray with moisture, and the musky smell of the ocean, loin-penetrating like the scent of a lusting woman, came to my nostrils. Seagulls clustered, standing with hunched shoulders, looking like plump, solemn, well-dressed men with their hands in their

85

pockets. Flocks of tiny sanderlings ran like clockwork toys keyed to the gentle wash of waves. To the east, over the mainland, the sky was faintly pink with the still-remote promise of sunrise. What I saw there, in dark-green banks of jungle, was the wilderness of the Everglades. I remembered that the Everglades, unable to sustain the steady encroachment of man, are supposed to be dying slowly year by year.

We are all being encroached upon, I thought to myself. We are all dying slowly.

Perhaps that was the secret of Maria's crisis; beginning when she was only ten, life had encroached steadily upon her private territory. In that young time when life was supposed to be starting, she had started dying instead. And then me, I thought. And Tony Two. And Casey. And now she is 30 years old.

I stopped, standing like a seagull with my hands in my pockets and my shoulders hunched, gazing toward the horizon where the Gulf waters seemed to rise, like a distant slope of hill, to touch the rim of sky.

But Maria, to George, had not been simply a warm hole. Obviously, he had accepted her in her total complexity, such acceptance placing on him a burden of denial and responsibility almost impossible to sustain. What he must have felt, watching Maria take the witness stand! Not simply beholding his beloved child-woman once more; but waiting for her to point a finger, singling him out in his enormous guilt, telling in child-earnest detail the evil things he had taught her.

Maria had never been, to any of the males who had counted in her life, simply a warm hole. Each in our various ways, we had cherished her during the mutual journey through the erotic maze of an unfolding experience. Why, then, should I now feel that Maria had been a territory inviolate unto herself, as the Everglades had once been inviolate, suffering the successive exploitations of our male-cock encroachments?

I could not deny it, even in the privacy of myself; Maria's telling had disturbed me. Not in the detailed facts; I knew, intellectually at least, that a child possesses an enormous erotic potential, protected and sheltered only by the wise taboos of society. In the low-sensory-stimulation environment of the featureless room where she had been held, isolated from all she had ever known, with George the only factor within her sensory ambience, the rapidly flowering sensuality was not at all remarkable.

Perhaps it had been the manner of her telling, as much as the substance. Sitting in the dimly lighted pool area, three naked and one clothed, she had talked quietly, almost abstractly, as though the events she was relating had happened to someone else. Yet there had been emotion in her voice—a certain joy, a certain sadness. It was as though she herself, for the first time, perceived the truth of her telling.

At the very end, she had looked at me, her eyes moist and luminous in the dim light, her breasts gleaming richly except where shadows deepened and enhanced their structure, telling me that she had chosen Jerry Dorn for her first fucking because I was, in certain secret ways, very much like George.

Walking again now, head down, hands thrust deep into pockets. A pre-dawn coolness, though the sun would bring tropical heat. Soon now the servants would return to the island. I could escape from these three people who were now naked together while I remained clothed.

The other two men possessed a flamboyance, of mind and of body, that I did not have. Casey, the cowboy, could be triggered into action by an explosive violence of spirit. Tony Two, living, like all his ambivalent kind, inside a shell of narcissism, had an ingrown exhibitionism that, once tapped, could lead him into extravagant commitment.

Jerry Dorn—I was quite an ordinary fellow, introspective rather than self-assertive, not the kind to have exciting experiences. My story would be drab, conventional, in comparison to theirs. After all, the biggest event of my life had been Maria.

Even at the time I had wondered, in the classic phrase, what she saw in me. A journeyman writer, after the publication of two novels that had made less than ten thousand dollars between them, I had accepted a spring-term appointment as writer-in-residence at one of the better Florida junior colleges. The pay had been extraordinarily good and my duties light, consisting only of teaching a course in creative writing and another in modern American literature.

Having arranged my schedule so that I could continue writing, I had cagily ensconced myself in a one-bedroom-and-kitchenette apartment a mile or so off campus, keeping its location, even the phone number, a secret from everyone but the head of the department. I intended, when walking away from the campus, to walk away from all obligations and pressures of college life.

The arrangement was ideal. In my office, in the seminars, I was totally available to the eager young literary ambitions. Leaving the campus, I entered again into my solitary existence as a practicing

writer, a solitude that held no terrors for me, for I
had shaped it myself.

Maria had enrolled in the creative writing class.
That first session, I noticed her; not because she
was so beautiful, but because she seemed to be unaware of the beauty. This, in my experience, is rare
in women. In no way whatsoever did she flaunt
her lovely face, her enchanting body. Quiet, self-
possessed, almost withdrawn, she listened along with
the others to my opening remarks.

Eleven years ago, college girls had not yet discovered the simplicities of dress and hairdo they
practice now. It was the era of the beehive hairdo,
of conservative dresses and a belief in the essential
rightness of the world as they experienced it. Don't
take the meaning that Maria was a rebel; she was,
very simply, neat and clean and tidy, her blue-black
hair worn long and straightly brushed, wearing a
sun-yellow shift that covered her body as naturally
and perfectly as an Indian girl's costume. She was
so marvelous in the midst of youthful self-consciousness; I thought to myself, It would be too much if
she were talented, too.

I never found out about her talent; after the second
session, she dropped out of the class. I was somewhat
piqued—after all, the other students seemed ade-
quately fascinated by what I had to tell them about
the art and craft of writing. A couple of the girls,
indeed, manifested, with the tentative manner of
young females toward older men, a certain sexual
interest—though I was careful to quash that sort of
thing rather quickly. I didn't need that kind of chancy
involvement.

Occasionally, going about my campus activities, I

would see Maria. Somehow, even at a distance, I was immediately aware of her. I was rather amused at myself to realize that, passing her on a walkway or in a corridor, I anticipated her speaking to me. But she never did . . . until less than three weeks before the end of the semester, the event that would signal my departure.

It was one of my days off-campus. I was returning, after sleeping late and working leisurely, from dinner at one of the local restaurants. She was sitting on the steps that led up to my apartment door.

Maria rose when she recognized me, and moved hesitantly aside, saying, "Mr. Dorn?"

Surprised, I paused in the act of passing her on the steps. "Did you want to see me?"

"Yes," she said.

After the direct, one-word reply, she stopped. There was no flurried attempt at explanation or excuse. I hesitated, rather at a loss. Given the immemorial reputation of writers-in-residence, it would not be prudent to invite a college girl into my bachelor apartment. But we couldn't stand here in the darkness and talk about her problem, whatever it might be.

"Come on in," I said at last, opening the door and standing aside. I flicked on the light, watching her as she silently surveyed my private domain.

One entered the apartment through the kitchenette, marked off from the combination livingroom-bedroom by a two-seated dining nook. The furniture was motel-room modern, flimsy and featureless; in one corner a sofa that, by the removal of two long back cushions, converted into a bed; an armchair; and, in the other corner, a straight chair and a table.

The only signatures of my habitation were a few books and my IBM typewriter, surrounded by a clutter of paper, on the writing table.

"How did you find out where I lived, anyway?" I said. "I thought it was a deep, dark secret."

She looked at me, her black eyes unfathomable. She was wearing the same yellow shift she had worn on the first day of class. Her legs were bare. Her hair was bright and shining in the artificial light.

"I followed you, one day when you left the campus," she said.

It was the way she said it, as much as what she revealed, that pulsed a stroke of excitement—and fear, too—through my web of nerves.

"Well," I said. I tried to laugh. "I hope you haven't told the whole campus. I'm trying to write a book."

"I haven't told anyone."

I regarded her, thinking about asking why she had dropped out of the creative writing class. Instead, I said, "How can I help you?"

She hesitated again, looking away from me toward the expanse of glass across the outside end of the room. Beyond the glass doors was a terrace, too narrow for usefulness, facing on the parking lot. The drapes were open and for anyone in the parking lot, I realized suddenly, we might as well be standing on a stage.

"Do you want me to close those drapes?" I said. "I wish you would."

I crossed the room to draw the drapes. We were suddenly shut off together into the featureless, impersonal apartment. I returned to her, saying again, "What did you want to see me about?"

"I'm not sure," she said. She looked about carefully, sat down on the bed-sofa. Her hands folded over each other in her lap. She lifted her eyes to my face. "I think I want you to fuck me."

I was startled, to say the least. By the frank statement . . . and because, at that time of my life, I had never heard a woman use the word.

Not knowing how to handle it, I retreated into social banality. "Would you like some tea?" I asked, and fled into the kitchenette before she could respond.

Busily, I filled the electric kettle, plugged it in. I rinsed out the tin teapot and dumped in two measured spoonfuls. I was using this time of the small tasks to think about what the girl had said.

First of all, her manner of saying it precluded a light dismissal; her seriousness demanded an equal seriousness from me. I studied her surreptitiously while I waited for the water to boil. Still seated on the sofa, she held herself erect, gazing with lowered eyes at her hands folded quietly on her lap. A beautiful girl—I had never made love to a woman as beautiful as she. And she was a gift, delivered through the front door like an unexpected Christmas package. I sternly repressed the knee-weakening thought.

"Do you think that's such a good idea?" I said from the safety of the kitchenette.

She did not raise her head to look at me. "I don't know."

The water boiled. I unplugged the kettle and poured into the teapot. I got out two cups and saucers.

"But why me?" I said reasonably. "I'm not only a good deal older than you are, I'm a college professor . . . temporarily, at least. I'm sure there are boys your own age . . ."

Realizing that she was not listening to me, I stopped. In the silence, she rose from the sofa, walked the length of the room until she stood with her forehead touching the drapes.

"I spent two hours in the parking lot last night, watching you at work," she said. "I didn't go back to the campus until you pulled the drapes and put out the lights."

There was no immediately available response to the confession—if it could be called a confession.

"Do you take milk?" I said.

"Plain," she said.

I poured the tea, added milk to mine, brought the cups into the living room. She came to accept the tea; our fingers touched for the first time, sending an electric tingle all the way up my arm. I couldn't tell if she had felt it too.

She resumed her seat on the sofa. I didn't dare sit beside her. After a momentary hesitation, I brought the straight chair I used for typing and sat down facing her. I watched as she drank the tea, not in delicate sips but with two hearty gulps that emptied the cup.

"Want another?" I said. She shook her head.

"If anyone should discover that you had been in my apartment, it would be a major scandal on campus," I told her.

"I know," she said. She gazed at me with her deep, black eyes. "I was careful, Mr. Dorn. Very careful."

"I might want to be offered another appointment sometime," I said. "This is a pretty good deal for a struggling writer." I tried to smile.

She smiled faintly. I finished my cup, went to the kitchenette to replenish it. I had never encountered such a situation. Waiting so quietly on the sofa, she seemed prepared to stay as long as necessary.

I sat down again. Forcing my voice toward lightness, I said, "Are you in the habit of this sort of thing, Maria?"

She gazed limpidly at me. Her answer was serious, and devastating. "I . . . haven't had . . . a man yet."

My laugh was rather forced. "I'm sorry, Maria. I don't want to be the one to . . ."

"But it's time," she said. "And you *are* the one."

She leaned sideways to place her cup on the shelf that became the head of the bed when the sofa was made down. Moving slowly, she stood up, reached behind her, and pulled a zipper. With a rippling movement, she shrugged out of the shift.

She was not wearing annything else. But the first shock was not her sudden nakedness; it was the thought that, all this time we had been talking, she had been secretly naked under the dress.

She remained still, revealed to my gaze, for only a moment before she stooped to lift the two back bolsters. She dropped them to the floor, then lay down on the bed. Her head was turned toward me.

"Please," she said. "Fuck me."

I had come to a stand. Any man would have. But still I denied her. "No," I said. "I'm sorry, Maria, truly sorry. But no."

She lay naked, open. Her eyes were suddenly perplexed. "Did I make a mistake then?" she said. "Are you queer? Some of the girls on campus think you're queer. But I . . ."

The statement angered me. I got up, went to sit on the side of the bed so I could gaze down into her eyes.

"I like women," I said. "I'm just not in the habit of deflowering virgins, that's all. I'm not in the habit of making love to girls ten years younger than I am, either. Girls too young to know ..."

She took my hand, placed it on her belly. "Then fuck me," she said. "Please."

I tried to pull my hand away. She held it clasped to her stomach with both hands. In my palm, I could feel the warmth of her flesh. She lay gazing up at me pleadingly, so beautiful, so filled with need. For me. I could no longer resist. I had gone over the brink of need myself when she had forced my hand to touch her.

"All right," I said hoarsely. "If that's the way it's got to be."

She smiled, a brilliant, luminous smile. She moved her body in one voluptuous wriggle. I was shaken by a gust of passion, so that my hand trembled as it shifted down to shape itself around her black-haired mount.

Some caution, however, remained to me. "It won't be much," I said. "Remember that. It can't be, if it's your first."

"But you'll know, won't you?" she said, with a trustingness I couldn't believe. "You'll know exactly how to go about it."

Her explicit surrender chilled me with the responsibility it imposed. I could not ravish her gift heedlessly; I must take her along step by easy step. For, though she believed herself ready, no girl can be truly prepared for the profound shock of a penis inside her body for the first time.

Rising, I began to take off my clothes. I moved slowly so that she could watch and anticipate. I wanted her to see my standing cock before she experienced it. Naked before her eyes, I sat beside her once again and placed my splayed hand on her belly. I slid it upward until my fingers found the erect nipple of her left breast. Taking it tenderly between thumb and forefinger, I massaged it gently, watching her eyes as they deepened and glowed.

Slowly, very slowly, I leaned to flatten my tongue against the nipple, then inhaled it wholly. She quivered violently, her hand reaching around behind my head to hold my mouth crushed against her breast.

It was, actually, a marvelous thing to proceed under such restraint. My own sensitivity was heightened remarkably during the long period I concentrated on the one breast. When I had exhausted my tongue's repertoire, I proceeded to the right breast and gave it the same intense attention.

Shifting around on my hip, I reached down to put my hand between her legs, opening them slightly. When I found her clitoris with my middle finger, she was, incredibly, still quite dry. Immediately, however, I felt the slickness of her beginning lubrication. A knowledgeable woman, able to rely on experience as well as imagination, would have been ready by now, so she had told the truth about being virgin. Slowly, slowly, I cautioned myself; even as deep inside I could feel the increasing need to assault her savagely, mindlessly, with my male weapon.

As my finger had penetrated the warm slit, she had rolled toward me. Now her hips thrust against my hand, withdrew, thrust again. We were face to face, gazing into each other's eyes. I looked at her mouth. She was not ready yet for kissing; there remained a hard lip-line still instead of a soft, hot readiness.

She put her flat palm on my waist. It was warm, damp with her light sweating. I wanted her to enfold my cock with the deliciously sensate palm. But she is a virgin, I reminded myself, she is still shy of such generous participation.

We remained so for a time, my finger stroking her while, to gauge her readiness, I watched her mouth. Almost imperceptibly it softened and warmed, the lips blooming, her tongue showing between her teeth. I leaned my weight against her, moving her onto her back, and laid my mouth on her mouth. The time was ripe; her tongue thrust deeply and she groaned as she suddenly mashed her lips hard against mine. her arms holding my head with a fierce, smothering grasp.

When the kiss was finished, I drew completely away. I was not touching her with hand or mouth, not even with the skin of my body, as I said, "Now?"

"Yes," she said. "Yes!"

I proceeded still in a teasing slow motion. I shaped her into an open position, pillow under her head, knees up, legs parted. I poised between her knees. She was gazing raptly at my cock, her chin held down so she could see.

"Now," I said again. This time I was not asking.

In that instant before irrevocable connection, she manifested a curious reaction. She did not try to fight it, as I had expected. Instead, lying beneath me, her body open, my cock ready, she turned her head, gazing about the apartment.

What could she find in this featureless, drab place to distract her from my rampant imminence? I did not know. I do not know now. But, whatever it was, it vanished as quickly as it had come. Her eyes returned to my cock, lingered for a suffused moment, then stared deeply, clearly, into my eyes.

"Fuck me," she said breathlessly. "Oh, God, Mr. Dorn, fuck me deep."

Even with the invitation, I knew that I must not hurt her in this important moment. I leaned slowly into her, guiding with my hand until the lips of her pussy had enfolded the head of my cock. A shiver rippled down my backbone as her scalding wetness registered on the seismograph of sensuous flesh. I held against the clitoris, massaging it with the mere tip until her lower body began to reach upward, demanding a deeper penetration. Slowly then, slowly, holding my breath while I listened to her panting body begin to rage against my continued denial, I came down on her with a full, violating thrust of my spear.

Her body tightened. I could feel her cunt begin to resist my forced passage. Her mouth opened and a harsh sound, as much of surprise as of outrage, erupted like a fart. I pushed hard against the resistance, and then harder, not pumping with ruthless thrusts but using a steadily increasing pressure. She gasped, the sound low and hurtful in her throat, as I tore through the shield into the hot dryness of recoiling vagina. I pulled out, thrust again and then again. With each full move her body jerked, her breath whistling raggedly as she made the hurting sound. I stopped, pegged hilt deep in her, knowing she could feel in her bruised flesh every pulsing inch.

"Does it hurt too much?" I said.

Her head was turned to one side, her lower lip caught between her teeth. "Yes," she gasped. "Yes. It hurts. But don't stop."

She was braced against me with every atom of her

body. But I moved in her most gently, a tiny thrust back and forth, until her vagina had softened and warmed and lubricated itself. When the tube of her flesh tightened on my cock, I knew without looking that the harsh pain was gone out of her face. Her flesh was listening to my flesh again, and it was all right now. I began to fuck her.

Until now, I had been trying her, but from here on I could let myself go. And I did—by the fifth stroke, her body was moving with my body, her pussy was tight and warm and smooth, and suddenly, having had to hold back for so long, I began to stride into orgasm. Though she had never experienced it before, she sensed my implacable rush and began hurrying her pace in frantic effort to match my stride. I felt her tighten and clench and then I exploded into an irresistible crescendo, no longer caring whether I hurt her or not, whether she came with me or not.

I did not stop fucking with the ebb of the first orgasm, but built with scarcely a pause into a new erection. She was slack under me now, in her deprivation no longer striving, simply taking my deep thrusts. I hastened, more frantic for the second coming than I had been for the first. For a tragic moment, I feared that I had failed; but then it was a ripping, scalding sensation, running like molten lead down my backbone, and I collapsed upon her.

We lay tangled. But, somehow, she was far away. I knew, in the sanity of self-accomplishment, that I had hurt her more than I should have. I rolled away, looking not at her face but at her mount. The black hairs were tangled and wet. A streak of blood showed on the inside of one thigh. Spreading her legs with my hand, I saw there was also ample blood on the fabric beneath her.

I looked shamefacedly into her eyes. "I hurt you, didn't I?"

"Yes," she said.

"And you didn't even get there," I said.

I laid my hand on her mount. She flinched but then, realizing my intention, held herself still. With two fingers inserted, I twirled her clitoris, slowly at first but building momentum rapidly. Her legs clenched tightly on my hand and she began to surge toward orgasm. When she came, it was small and hard-clenched. After it was finished, she thrust my hand away and relaxed utterly, her arms thrown wide.

"I'm sorry," I said ruefully. "I wanted not to hurt you."

"I guess it just has to, the first time."

"Is that why you wanted to do it with a stranger?" I said. "Just to get it over with?" I tried to make the words easy, but they didn't come out that way.

She rolled over, sat up beside me. "Got a cigarette?"

I found the pack and the matches, lit one for both of us. We sat side by side on the edge of the sofa bed, naked, used up, passing the cigarette back and forth. She was remote again, even in this intimacy of sharing.

"Well, at least you've taken care of the cherry," I said. "If that was the problem."

"Yes," she said with a wry twist of her mouth. "I have, haven't I?"

She stubbed out the cigarette in an ashtray at the head of the bed, got up and found her purse. I watched as she opened it, to take out a flimsy pair of pants and a bra.

"You can take a shower if you want," I said. "Sorry, there's no tub."

She did not look at me. "Yes. I'd like a shower."

I got dressed while she was gone, trying not to listen to her movements just the other side of the bathroom door. If I paid attention, I would want to fuck again before she left. That would not be right, given her post-coitus attitude. She would be sore tomorrow morning, anyway. Maybe I ruined it for her completely I thought moodily. Maybe she never will like fucking, now that I've botched her first try at it.

She came out of the bathroom fully dressed. I stood up. "I'm sorry it didn't turn out so good," I said sincerely.

She came to me, leaned the weight of her body against me. It was a totally abandoned, completely trusting, movement.

"Thank you, Mr. Dorn," she said, whispering the words. "Oh, I do thank you."

"My name is Jerry," I said foolishly.

She had put her arm around my waist, her head against my chest, and she was holding me tightly. Then, before I could make a move, she was gone, the apartment door closing so definitively behind her flight that I knew I would not see her again.

I was unduly disturbed by the thought. For a long time, that night, I lay awake staring into darkness. I wanted to see her again. I wanted to know her, as I did not know her now. I could not accept tonight's adventure as an experience so extraordinary it could never be repeated. Yes, I tried to tell myself cynically that it was one to put in the book—not the book I was writing, but the book of my life. For once, at least, through a rare circumstance, I had fucked a really beautiful woman. Always and forever I would be the cock that had bloodily torn her hymen.

But, most of all, I wanted to fuck her again and again and again. It was a new experience to lust exclusively for the one woman capable of assuaging my appetites. I had never been in love, so I didn't recognize the symptoms.

Next day, on campus, I looked for her unceasingly. I did not see her. Not for two days; but then, on the third day, we passed each other on a walkway. She spoke a greeting, friendly and impersonal, and walked on.

I turned to watch her. So that's that, I told myself, and mentally shrugged my shoulders. But even as I did so, I knew I would not, could not, accept it.

I didn't know anything to do about it. I couldn't go to her room, call her on the telephone, ask her for a date. I was bereft of all devices; all I had in my favor was her memory of my plunging cock in her virgin flesh.

Early that evening, when a knock sounded on my door I thought it was the paperboy, come to collect. When I opened the door, Maria stood revealed. Dumbly, I stood aside.

She entered, closed the door behind her. "I didn't plan to come back, Jerry," she said. "I thought once would be enough. But it isn't enough."

She walked on into the living room, me following, and dropped her purse on the sofa bed. Turning, she came abruptly into my embrace, her strong arms clutching me. I tried to kiss her, but she did not want to be kissed. Instead, she slid down to clasp my hips, pressing her face against my crotch.

"I knew you'd do it right," she said. "You'd be gentle with me, you'd let me take all the time I needed. That's why I came to you, Jerry."

"It was pretty lousy, though," I said in a shaky voice. "You'll have to admit that it was a lousy lay."

She looked up into my face. "And you?" she said.

I could only tell the truth. "I haven't thought about anything else since the minute you left."

Her hand found my zipper, pulled it. I watched her face as she reached inside my fly, found what she was seeking, and brought it forth. She would take me in her mouth, now, and I didn't know whether I could stand it. But she only laid her cheek against my rigid tool, rolling it against her velvety skin.

I remained erect, with her kneeling before me, while she cherished the cock that had deflowered her. I knew, as well as if I had been inside her head, that she was remembering the act in successive detail. Including the pain. It would have been cheating to leave out the pain.

When she rose to her feet, she began undressing. "I was so sore I could hardly walk," she said. She made a small laugh. "Suppose it had been somebody who couldn't have cared less how much it hurt?"

She must have known, as I had known her thoughts, what I meant to do first to her naked body. She sat down on the bed, leaning back against the bolsters, and opened her knees for me. I knelt, and parted the lips of her pussy with a thumb on each side. The flesh was very young, very pink, so delicious looking that my mouth began to water. I could smell the musky odor, terribly exciting as her scent grew stronger with desire. I could see the rigid little clitoris peeping out of the intricate folds of its sheath. I put my mouth directly on it, taking it in completely. She sighed deeply, as though she had been holding the tension for much too long. As I plied my tongue, her hips began to wring, and she fetched an immediate orgasm so complete that it left her limp and helpless.

103

But I was not limp. Standing up, I took off my pants. She lay with shoulders slumped against the bolster, her legs braced wide on the floor. Her pussy was open and waiting. I walked my cock into it, going deep and hard. She gasped, and gasped again on my second thrust, and already, her legs locking on me, her hands tearing at my shoulders, she was coming again as I rode her hilt deep. Her head was thrown back and she almost screamed, for I was coming too, a hot, liquid flow so sudden that I was still trying to retard it.

Five minutes after her entrance, we had used every bit of the sexual tension that had built between us since the parting. Even so, I couldn't bear to abandon her flesh. Half-limp, leaning over her on braced elbows, I moved gently inside her while she lay quiescent, a dreamy look in her eyes, a half smile on her lips.

"Good, Jerry?" she whispered. "Was I good?"

"If it was any better, I'd die," I said. "How about you?"

She smiled the dreamy, absorbed smile.

Unable to sustain for long the posture I was in, I took her by the shoulders and, without disengaging, moved her lengthwise of the bed. I could then lie comfortably along the length of her body. A surge of tenderness moved inside me. My pussy, I thought. Nobody's been there yet but me. So it's mine.

Finally, realizing that a rest would be necessary before we could advance into the next phase, I rolled away, to lie on my back. She got up on one elbow to look down into my face. Her long black hair fell tickling against my chest.

She giggled. "I tore your shirt. Did you know that?"

"Maybe I'm the one who's bleeding this time."

Tenderly she examined my shoulders. "No. Just a scratch. Want a cigarette?"

"I've got some . . ."

She rolled across me, found her purse, sat down on the side of the bed. She put a cigarette into my mouth and lit it.

"Are you glad I came back?"

"Yes," I said. "You?"

She brooded. "Of course." She lifted her eyes. "But it's going to take a while, Jerry. You'll have to fuck me a lot."

I smiled. "That won't be hard to bear."

She grinned. "I thought . . . that first time . . . I thought you'd never get with it."

I had to frown then. "You'll have to admit, you sort of laid a load on me, Maria. Arriving out of the blue, saying what you said, then letting me know you were still cherry . . ."

She put a finger on my lips. "Hush. Hush now. We're past all that now. Aren't we?"

I kissed her finger, then opened my mouth and took it in with a sucking motion. "Yes. Long past it. Let's fuck."

Maria, hour by hour, day by day, was a continuing delight. Having her was an experience akin to watching a red, red rose unfold from bud to full-blown flower. Every hour we were naked together, she showed me a new increment of sensuousness and passion. She was eager, inquisitive—and totally absorbed. I came, I thought, to know her in all intimacy of detail. Unlike so many women of Latin blood, Maria was lithe and long-legged. Nineteen years old, she was coltish still in her bodily structure, awkward yet graceful. Gazing upon her naked, one realized that she would become in time an extraordinarily complete and lovely woman. As far as I was concerned, she was already beautiful beyond any woman I had ever known.

Her sexual energy could not be curbed. Quite simply, even childishly, she wanted to fuck from morning to night and then to morning again. I was forced to explain that a man's sexual system simply doesn't provide as many erections as a woman could desire and demand. But even during the necessary hiatuses, she continued to explore assiduously with her hands, her mouth, her tongue, keeping me in a constant state of titillation even at times I knew it would be futile to attempt the complete act.

On the days I did not have to go on campus, she came to me before daylight. She had her own key, so my first warning of her presence would be her hand creeping warmly into my crotch, cupping itself to my scrotum as she leaned to kiss me. Opening my eyes, my first vision of the day would be her lovely face, framed by the black cave of her long hair, brooding with a thoughtful passion. I would lie still while she fondled and kissed and stroked me into a morning readiness.

Not pausing to undress—with me knowing all the time, in that peculiarly intense sexual awareness of such matters, that she was naked under the single demure garment—she would straddle my hips and ease herself onto my cock. For a minute, two minutes, she would sit grinning at me, my cock buried upright in her cunt. I could feel her soften and warm and oil herself with her own juices. Only then did she begin fucking me, her hips plunging with the quick rotary motion she had learned herself, until I was gasping on the brink.

She had also learned measurement and control.

She didn't like to finish the first fuck of the day anywhere except on her back. So, clasping my shoulders, she would roll us, still locked together. When I came up into the saddle I was already into the full stride of fucking, with scarcely a stroke lost between us. Sometimes I would go on for minutes, sometimes only a couple of beats were required before she began to reach for orgasm. I could always tell when she was on the way, for invariably she clamped her teeth over her lower lip. Catching by signal the big wave of her being, I began to ride her surge, settling deeply into a long, luxurious stroke. More often than not, so mutually attuned were we, we would come simultaneously to the climax.

However, if I lagged behind, as soon as she was finished she would fuck me furiously from underneath, often fetching a second, less intense, orgasm of her own when I did come. But if I failed her, as inevitably happened at times, the disappointment damped her so completely that I would have to wait for a new effort at the very beginning of things.

She was remarkable in her virtuosity of the flesh. I had always understood that young girls green in experience find orgasm exceedingly difficult; that, indeed, years must often elapse before they succeed in achieving nirvana without manual stimulation. Apparently, Maria had awakened sexually in one single instant, for, beyond that first fuck, she experienced no such difficulties.

Nor was she, as one would have thought, orgasm-crazy. Often, she did not seem to need that kind of release, and did not strive for it. Instead, she would fuck slowly, thoughtfully, lasciviously, culminating with a small, voluptuous shivering of the flesh. At other times, she indicated a preference for the manipulation of my hand, clocking a tight, intense masturbatory orgasm before I got in her.

Liking such variety, she became a woman of many inventions. She developed signals, sometimes conscious but often, I believed, totally unconscious, to indicate a desired change of pace—from rapid plunge to a sensuous wallowing, from long stroke to short stroke, from straightforward fucking to a hip-grinding rotation. She liked me to kiss her breasts, to put my mouth on her cunt, to be licked with my tongue from crotch to belly to breast and back again.

More curiously, there would, without warning, be times when nothing satisfied her. Shifting fretfully under me, she would complain that I was too heavy, that she couldn't breathe. Taking the major position did nothing, at such times, to improve the flavor of the experience. She could not find an ample rhythm of fucking, but seemed to be constricted, her muscles locking, her breath laboring. After one of these occasions during which the salt of my flesh had lost all savor, she would become moodily distracted or unexpectedly touchy for an indeterminate period before she would suddenly rediscover her gusto for fucking and being fucked.

Her restraint in one matter also puzzled me. She would fondle my penis with her hand, she would often, with an excess of affection, lay her cheek warmly against it. She would even kiss the throbbing head with delicate tenderness. But never would she take my cock into her mouth. I could not reconcile such constraint with her otherwise open candidness of the flesh. Finally, one day, I bluntly asked her to suck me off.

She paused, startled, to gaze up at me. I saw a cloud of something very near to pain pass swiftly through the clear depths of her eyes. She sat up, making an awkward, youthful movement of it, turned her head, looked at my cock. I told myself, with a great, warm anticipation, that she just hadn't thought of it before. She would, in answer to my request, recognize the sensual possibilities and . . .

"I'm not . . . sure I'd like that," she said in a low voice.

"You like everything else," I said. I laughed. "At least, I haven't struck anything yet you haven't taken great pleasure in."

Stilly, she regarded my penis. Reaching forth a hand, she touched him with the tip of one finger. "I'm . . . afraid of it. That way, I mean."

I was more puzzled than ever. "Afraid?"

Her face was sober. "I've . . . I've felt that you've wanted me to . . . do that . . . at times. But . . ."

I grasped her arm, pulled her close. "If the thought disgusts you, forget it," I said. "I've got enough to keep me occupied, God knows."

She was huddled small against me. Putting her hand lightly on my chest, she moved it down the slope of my belly, encircled my cock at its jointure. Her eyes were closed tightly, as though, like an imaginative child, she was pretending to be blind.

"I always . . . thought a man's thing was . . . enormous," she said. "When I was a girl, I imagined you men walking around with this great thing between your legs that would just stuff me fuller than I could stand. I thought it was like a stallion on a mare, and wondered how it could be managed."

My male vanity was piqued. "Sorry to disappoint you," I said.

She twisted around to look into my face. "Don't take me wrong, Jerry. I'm not disappointed. It's just

109

. . . I can't explain my feelings about a man's thing. So don't make me try. Please."

She was still holding my cock. Her hand moved up, then downward, peeling him tightly. I could feel the sticky warmth of her palm.

"Forget it," I said. "Let's fuck."

She sat up. She leaned over my hips, gazing upon my cock. Her long hair teased at my thighs. In spite of myself, I surged up toward her mouth. It was so near, so tantalizingly near. She flinched, avoiding the taking; but she kept gazing with wide eyes. I could sense that a tangled complex of emotions was moving in her like dark tides.

At last, her body as rigid as if my hand were pressed at the back of her neck, forcing her to the distasteful task, she leaned downward until her closed lips rested against the glans. I could feel the warm stir of her agitated breathing.

"Maria," I said. "You don't have to do it."

Her mouth opened—I felt the stronger gust of her breathing—and her lips slid around the glans with an excruciating slowness. Her mouth held me head deep, without suction, for a pent moment. Then, with a savage abruptness, her lips shaped and hardened and she drove herself on him until the head was deep in her throat, gagging her. She withdrew, wiped her mouth with her hand, and went deeply upon him for the second time.

I wanted to tell her that she did not need to violate herself in this way. But I was enthralled by the sensation, and simultaneously involved in an effort at control, for I did not want to come in her mouth. But her deep-throated and desperate commitment had brought me close, so close—there are times when a

110

resistance only creates a terrible desire—and I did come.

She took it. She took all I could give her. She was not gagging now; I could feel her strong swallowing, once and then again, and suddenly her mouth was as hot and frantic as her cunt in the throes of spontaneous orgasm.

She sat up when it was over and looked at me with deeply brilliant eyes. Her mouth was a bruised, crushed, beautiful thing, no longer simply a mouth.

"You've got to fuck *me* now," she said. "You've got to, even if you can't."

I had no problems about fulfilling that demand. I laid her on her back and went into her, to find her cunt different from what it had ever been before. She was open as she had never been, hotter and more liquid, and I seemed to reach deeper than I had in all the fuckings up to now. She kept her eyes closed tightly, as though she were dreaming—or wishing that she was dreaming—all the long way to a slow, soft, spreading climax that shuddered gently through every cell of her body.

She rolled away with her back to me and lay silent for long minutes. Understanding that she needed this time to herself in order to absorb the experience, I quietly lit a cigarette and smoked it.

Finally, without facing me, she said, "You'll be leaving the college soon, won't you?"

"Just one more week," I said.

"I have to go with you now," she said.

Oddly, I understood. Her necessity arose not from the fucking, but from having swallowed my semen. Otherwise, she would have left me, when the time came for leaving, with only a bittersweet bank of memories to commemorate our occasions. Now, all that was changed. I could accept, emotionally, the profound alteration these last few minutes had wrought in her. But rationally it made no sense at all.

"Do you think that's wise?" I said.

Violently, she sat up on the side of the bed. "Is anything wise? Ever?"

I stared at her back. She had a lovely back, the skin deeply olive, the waist sloping into the female width of her hips. Below the small of her back, at the base of her sunken spine, was a tiny patch of fine black hair.

I put my hand on the patch. "We'll have to get married, then. Do you want to be married?"

She turned her head. "It doesn't matter. I just have to go where you go."

"All right," I said. "That's all right with me."

With the understanding that we meant to stay together always, our days and nights changed in texture and meaning. We could even begin to talk of love.

Now, on No-Name Key, I was far down the beach from the house. The sun was above the horizon, bringing with it the day. Stopping, I looked backward. Would I leave now, as previously decided? . . . or would I come downstairs naked tonight, prepped to reveal the story of my sexual life?

Was it possible to stay? I would have to tell Maria to her face all these feelings and meanings of the two years we had lived together in a marriage that had dwelled never in place, never in time, but only in being. I would have to talk with the same honesty Maria had found in relating how she had tasted so tentatively George's enormous cock in her mouth and in the gateway of her hairless pussy.

112

I had never put much faith in the Freudian ethic. I did not believe that Maria had been shaped utterly and forever by that ten-year-old experience. She had, after all, come to me as one Maria, had departed as another. Surely Casey had changed her also, and Tony Two. I found myself wondering, with an intense curiosity, what kind of woman she had been with them in comparison to how she had been with me.

Slowly, almost reluctantly, I began walking toward Maria's mansion. My thinking kept slow, reluctant pace. After all, how much had I understood—how much did I understand now—about why she had singled me out? She had simply come to me, asking to be fucked. And, in the end, she had departed . . .

Two years. We had loved each other, deeply and truly and passionately, for two years whole and complete. Drifting in time, drifting in place—for Maria had wanted neither time nor place—we had lived our life together in motels, in barrenly furnished apartments, we had owned only what would fit into the trunk of my car.

Of course, I had soon discovered that Maria, whose father was dead by the time I knew her, was possessed of wealth so great, seven or eight or ten millions, that I could not even visualize it. Those riches made no difference; I declared my resolve to use only the money I could earn with my writing, and Maria acquiesced without a murmur of argument.

Nowhere did we leave a trace of our passage. Whatever room we made love in, that room was altered only by the memory of having made love there. This mode of living seemed to suit Maria; when Maria was contented, so was I fulfilled.

There were many rooms, with many memories, for we fucked, God yes we fucked, we learned the other's

113

body and taste and temperament far better than we knew our own. The touch of her finger, the brush of her lips, the canted poising of her pussy as she shaped herself to receive me, spoke volumes of meaning and experience and memory. We fucked not singly but cumulatively, each occasion containing all previous occasions as well as something unique of its own. Yet there never came to us the blight of repetition and rote. Each time I mounted her, we entered into a new territory of ourselves, an infinitely variable experience of sensation and sensuality.

I knew that, on the rare occasions when she went down on me, she would hesitate before the act, brooding upon an unfathomable reaction within herself before she would gulp him deep into her throat, taking him violently into orgasm. I knew that when she kneeled over my face to fuck my tongue she would enjoy one quick shivery little half-orgasm before a long, slow, self-absorbed fucking; at the end, she would demand my cock deep inside her vagina for the climactic achievement.

Of course, though we were almost totally physical in our relations, there were the times between. During my working hours she would read, so totally absorbed she might as well not have been present, so that she was no distraction to the act of writing. When we talked, at meals or while driving, it was always on small topics, for she did not like to discuss books or ideas, or even herself. Whenever I attempted serious conversation, she would soon falter into irrelevancies, then become silent. I quickly learned to keep such thoughts for the writing instead.

It seemed to work, too, for I was writing better than I ever had. My novel was going well, and during the first year we were together I fulfilled a screenwriting assignment so satisfactorily I could reasonably count on another whenever the need should arise. There was, also, the annuity from my grandfather to fall back on. So I was richly happy; for the foreseeable future, we could continue to live in this nomad manner we had chosen. As I had never, before Maria, known love, so I discovered I had never known happiness. Now I had both, as well as success in my chosen profession.

Then—Maria went away.

It simply happened. One night on the road, we stopped for dinner at a nondescript restaurant with transport trucks parked before it. We had learned long since that, outside the larger cities where one could dine in style, such establishments could often be counted on for decent, simple food and excellent coffee.

While we ate, we could not avoid overhearing a trucker talking angrily into the wall telephone near the cash register. "Damn it, it can be fixed. I can fix it myself if you'll just bring me some tools." He listened for a moment. "Let me tell you. Let me tell you, now. I've got a load of watermelons on that truck and I can't wait all day tomorrow for you to find out what's wrong and do something about it." He listened again. "I'll buy your damned supper, and fix the thing myself while you eat. All right? Then get your ass over here."

He slammed down the telephone and sat down at the counter. "Son of a bitch," he said to the waitress. "Nobody wants to do their job any more."

"What a beautiful man," Maria said.

Surprised, I turned to survey the trucker. Maria

seldom made a comment about other people, especially a man. Wrapped up in our love, she seemed, indeed, to be unconscious of the existence of other males.

"Beautiful?" I said. "He's about the ugliest man I've ever seen, if you ask me."

True. He was big, with heavy shoulders and round meaty thighs, and he had walked with a clumsy, stumping motion of the legs. His face was craggy, knobby, with bushy eyebrows, and he must have been at least 40 years old.

"He's so angry," she said. "Maybe he's not beautiful except when he's so angry at the world."

While we ate, Maria kept watching him, until the chastised mechanic arrived and the driver went outside with him. When we walked to our car, we saw the two men with the cab of the transport truck elevated—it was an old, battered diesel job, no lettering on the sides. The driver's sulfurous commentary blistered our ears as we passed.

"A wildcat driver," I said in the car. "He's not running that old truck out of a trucking company terminal."

Half a mile down the road, we passed a nice-looking motel. "Let's stop, if they have a room," Maria suggested. "I'm tired."

In the room, Maria turned on the television, watched for a few minutes, turned it off.

"There might be something on another channel," I said.

She crossed to part the drapes and look outside. "Don't you need to get that screen treatment in to the agent?" she said. "You don't like to have the television on while you're working."

"I can do it in the morning," I said. "We don't have to check out until twelve."

Holding the edge of the drape in one hand, she turned to look at me. "I might want to fuck in the morning."

Spreading my arms wide, I smiled. "How about right now?"

She shook her head decisively. "No. Do your work. I'll take a walk so I won't bother you."

I was mildly surprised, for she was not overly addicted to walking. But, detecting a certain restlessness, I did not protest the unusual suggestion.

She went out, and I got down to work. I had got an idea today, while driving, about how to handle the ending, so I quickly became totally absorbed. I was surprised, when I had finished the last page, to realize that Maria had been away for three hours. Thinking she might be watching television in the lobby, I went to the front of the motel. The lobby was empty, except for the night clerk. Mildly alarmed by the lateness of the hour, I went outside. The parking lot was filled with overnight cars, but I did not see Maria. I looked down the deserted highway, knowing the truth. She had gone to the truck driver.

Returning to the room, I sat down on the bed. It may be just for the night, I told myself with an astonishing calmness, or it may be forever. Don't get me wrong; the realization that she had gone to another man was a dull ache deep in my gut. But somehow, somewhere, I knew, I had failed her. She had divined in the ugly truck-driving man, beautiful to behold in her sudden need, some quality of experience that I had not given her.

I waited for two days in that drab little roadside motel, hoping against hope. Only then did I pack the bags—hers as well as mine—and start off cross-country. For days I drove aimlessly, eight and nine hundred

117

miles at a stretch, stopping only to stumble into bed and sleep with exhausted dreamlessness, gathering strength for tomorrow's driving to absorb.

It was a bad time. It's a wonder I didn't kill myself, for my reflexes went all to hell, and my attention wandered so erratically that I would snap into alertness to find I had been traveling at a hundred miles an hour for a span of time I could not even measure. I shudder to think about it, for I am normally a cautious, steady driver.

I came out of it, one day, when I remembered the treatment I had mailed to my agent the day after Maria had left me. I was in a small town in Idaho named Mountain Home. I phoned the agent, to learn that he had been frantically seeking my whereabouts; the treatment had been accepted and he had stalled just about as long as he could, for I should have been at work now for several days.

I sold the car—I didn't want to see it ever again, or drive it another mile—took a bus to Boise, and flew to Los Angeles.

Two months later, Maria knocked on the door of my apartment.

"Well," I said, opening the door. "Hello."

"Hello, Jerry," she said.

She was wearing a dress I didn't recognize. She had not taken any of her clothes when she had left. Maybe the trucker bought it for her, I thought. I waited for her to come in. When she did not move to do so, I made a half-gesture of invitation. She entered and closed the door behind her.

"How did you find me?" I said.

"I called your agent. He told me."

Of course. So simple. When she had finally decided that she wanted to come back.

"You left with the trucker, didn't you?" I said. "The angry, beautiful man."

She looked at me for the first time. "Yes," she said. "But I'm back now, Jerry."

She was two feet away from me; I could have touched her in one stride. By appearance, she was unchanged. But she had changed; she had fucked another man. I had changed, too, because she had fucked another man.

"What went wrong?" I said. "Didn't he satisfy you like you thought he would?"

She sighed, sat down on the bed. It was a sofa-bed remarkably similar to the one on which I had first seen her naked.

"He was a mean bastard," she said.

I watched her face, her eyes, change with the memory.

"We were only three miles out of that town when he pulled into a rest stop," she said. "He parked away from the other trucks. The drivers must have been sleeping, anyway, because no one was in sight. He looked at me and said, 'All right, baby, put it on the line. Or take the long walk back to where you came from.'"

"So you put it on the line," I said.

Her eyes were candid. "That's why I went to him. But I told him I didn't want to do it in the truck, out there in the middle of nowhere. 'I don't care what you want,' he said. 'It's what I want that counts.' And he reached for me."

Sitting on the bed in my furnished apartment, she put her arms around herself and shivered. "It was like he didn't know any way to take a woman except by force. He ruined my dress. He nearly ruined me." She looked up into my face. "He made me bleed again. And he didn't care whether I liked it or not. He was a mean son of a bitch, and he hated women like he hated the whole world."

I was shaken by her calm, matter-of-fact recital. "So you left him. Why didn't you come back then? I waited in the motel for two days, believing there was a chance you would."

"I stayed with him."

"After being treated like that?"

She nodded. "He was a wildcat trucker, like you said. He'd buy fruit and haul it to the nearest large city, to sell in the market. Sometimes, he'd park his truck on the side of the road, set up signs, and sell it direct to the consumer instead. He could make more money that way, you see. But it took longer to get rid of a truckload." She paused. "He did more of it, with me along. He'd make me stand so the passersby could see me. A lot of men stopped to buy fruit."

"I guess it got better, then, after the first time." I was watching her face, wondering when I could bear to touch her.

She shook her head again. "Every time, it was like he wanted to kill me with his cock all over again. He fucked me in the truck. He fucked me in cheap little motels and even, once or twice, in those bunkrooms at truck stops that are so small you can hear the people breathing in the next cubicle. We always made a lot of noise fucking and so those other men would look at me, when we came out, knowing. It made him proud for his buddies to know, you see."

"Noise?" I said.

"He liked to hurt me," she said. "When he wanted to make me hurt, he'd squeeze my nipple, hard, between his thumb and his finger while he was getting his. Once the cops came, at a motel, because there was so much noise."

"But you liked it," I said. "I didn't treat you that way, so you liked it."

"I hated it," she said. "But I couldn't quit."

"I guess he threatened you, if you left him."

She shook her head, annoyed by my stupidity. "No. It wasn't like that, I told you." She stood up, wandered a semicircle in the room, stopped with her back turned. "Down under . . . all that anger . . . he was scared of himself. Don't you understand that?"

"No," I said. "I don't."

"Jerry, the only time he was gentle with me was when I would suck him off. He fought me doing it, but he wanted it, too. I'd have to catch him unawares to get my mouth on him. But then . . . Jerry, he'd clasp my head in his big, rough hands and lie back with his face out of my sight, talking so kindly, with such an enormous gratitude. For a long while afterward, he'd hold me close and smooth his hands all over my body, back and sides and legs, over and over again. His hands were so strong and so rough, with the palms all one big callus. But gentle, oh, so gentle. Afterward, he'd have to be twice as mean for a while."

"I can remember how anxious you always were to go down on me."

She came to me, laid her hand into the curve of my neck. "My sweet Jerry," she said. "I've missed you so much."

"Yeah," I said. I was holding my neck rigid, I discovered. "I can tell."

"He'd even hit me, Jerry," she said. "I've got bruises. Look."

She began to take off her clothes, as self-absorbed

121

as a child showing a sore place for the sake of sympathy. There were deep purple marks on the insides of her thighs, a hard knot on her left breast. Turning around, she displayed welts on her back.

"That's where he whipped me," she said. "With his leather belt."

"So he was a sadist, as well as a suppressed homosexual."

She shook her head. "He only whipped me once. He had left me in a motel outside of Salt Lake City while he went home for the weekend." She glanced toward me. "Did I tell you that he had a wife and six children? Six."

"No," I said. "I don't think you told me that."

"Yes. So he had to go home, and I was to wait on him, he said."

"You could have left then," I said. "He'd never have found you."

"I know. But I didn't. And when he came back . . ." She sat down again and folded her arms tightly around her naked body. "He just walked into the room, the belt in his hand, and started whipping like a wild man. He said he knew that, the minute he was out of sight, I had started fucking somebody else and by God I was going to pay for it."

"So that's when you gave it up," I said. "About time."

She shook her head, annoyed again with my obtuseness. "No. I stayed another week."

"What did it take to make you leave?" I said. "Or is this just a friendly visit?"

"It was just suddenly over," she said. "Just like that." She snapped her fingers. "I sucked him off, one more time, the thing he liked so much and yet couldn't stand because it took away all his great anger, leaving him only a man. Then I walked out of there and called your agent."

I gazed down at her, sitting naked on my bed. "So it's over," I said. "Until the next time."

She looked up at me. "Fuck me, Jerry?" she said. "Fuck me nicely."

I stared at her, this woman who had lived an experience with another man. A woman who could narrate the details in such quietly fatal words, without reserving either the bad or the good. Not only tell it, but tell it to me, Jerry Dorn, who loved her, who was the Adam of her flesh.

Even with all this, I knew. I had listened, hadn't I? So I would also take her tenderly into my arms, I would with love and gentleness heal all the aches and bruises she had brought home. Yes. Because I loved her, my spirit could forgive.

I took off my clothes and lay down beside her, embracing her gently, feeling her flinch and then relax as I began to kiss her, warming her lips and then her body, coaxing her until she broke through into cleansing tears.

"All the time I was with him, Jerry, I never got to finish," she said. "He didn't want me to get it, so he wouldn't ever wait."

"Hush," I said. "Hush now. I'll finish you a dozen times before the night is done."

As I said, the spirit was willing. But my flesh had jealousies I had not reckoned with. When I was hovering over her forked waiting, my cock, refusing to keep my promise, remained stubbornly limp. I put it inside her, stuffing it in limply with my hand, and began working frantically to raise a hard. But it was no use.

She looked up, a terrible grief pooled in her stricken

123

eyes. "I've ruined it, haven't I?" she said. "I've ruined it, Jerry."

"It'll be all right," I said. "Just take our time, that's all."

But there was not enough time, to the end of the universe.

In the days that followed, we tried. God, yes. Away from her, thinking how we had once been, I could come to a stand. She could raise me with her mouth, or by stroking with her hand. But my recreant flesh, rather than quickening at the moment of entrance, remembered without fail the alien cock her cunt had accommodated. And remembering, died.

For a week, seven days and seven nights, we labored to rebuild our world. Then sadly, hurtfully, the repeated failures too painful to endure, we parted.

So I lost Maria, finally and definitively. We parted not in anger, but with a great regret; with no tears, yet sharing a large feeling of friendship. It was only that my flesh blamed her flesh, not my soul her soul.

I had nearly reached the house by now, and the long, empty beach was behind me. If I went upstairs, packed my bag, and departed from No-Name Key, would I be failing her again? I had failed, the first time, in gentleness and in love. But . . . failure nonetheless. It had been my fate to induct a girl named Maria into the mysteries of sex. But there had been, within the girl I had so greatly cherished, a woman also named Maria who had possessed a wealth of feminine treasure I had not opened.

A year later, I had divorced Maria in order to marry again. On her, I had begot a son and a daughter. But the experience of Maria had left a rich stain on my soul that no woman, mother of my children though she might be, could eradicate. Helen, coming to sense my reserve, started to drift away. I did nothing to stop her. She had at last left me, after telling me, at the bitter end, that she did not believe I could love anyone. So little did she know.

After this second failure—so deeply a failure I did not even care—I had known better than to seek Maria in the warm holes of random females. There were a few casual affairs, true; but I fled them the moment my partner began to evidence signs of serious intent. These last few years, finding the search for physical relief too tedious for the meager rewards, I had become practically celibate.

I looked up at the house, thinking, Maybe I ought to go to Maria now, find out quickly whether the flesh remembers still—or whether my cock will stand and be joyful. Wake her out of sleep, as I had done so often in our days together, take her warm and soft and drowsy into the sensuous continent of ourselves we had once known.

But she had made it clear that she would not accept any one of us in such a solitary fucking. Only with the three and the one to make four, three penises and one vagina; only in the ultimate togetherness she had dreamed of in her vision of rescue from her past, her future. If I meant to try her, try myself, it could be only within the terms she had established. If I truly desire to fuck Maria, I told myself in flat terms that could not be denied, I must come downstairs naked tonight. I must take her bodily in the sight of the others.

I shall. I shall.

Or—I shall not.

There remained yet another factor to consider. If, in the moment, my readiness should wither away, would that small death occur from ancient memory; or simply because of the public nature of the act? I had never performed before the sight of men. If my cock should refuse the gate, I would never even know the reason why.

I shall. I shall.

Or—I shall not.

You ought to leave, a small voice told me despairingly. You had Maria once—at least the limited young Maria who had then existed. But you lost her. Suppose you found her again, this new, ripened Maria—only to lose her once more? It won't bear thinking on. Or risking.

Yet somehow, in the midst of the pauses and hesitations, I had already decided to venture all. Tonight, once the unknowing servants had departed from No-Name Key, I would descend into the midst of the others wearing only my cock, whether ready or unready.

I had come painfully to the simple truth. Maria needed me. But that was not all. I needed, also, to try, for once in my life, to become a part of something larger than my little self. It might be that such an accomplishment was not in me. But I could only join in the scout of the territory ahead.

I shall. I shall.

Coming up from the beaches of morning, I entered again into Maria's great house. And, this time, I meant to stay.

Chapter 5

We met at breakfast, decorously clothed; throughout the day we continued to act out before the servants the charade of a conventional house party, swimming in the pool, drinking bloody marys before lunch and taking a siesta during the enervating heat of early afternoon. We were all waiting for the night to fall, when the departing servants would leave us to pursue the secret life that belonged to Us—not individually, but collectively.

I was the key. In the immediate implementation of my decision, successful or unsuccessful, lay the fate of Us. I had acknowledged, during my before-dawn walk, both the responsibility and my reluctance to accept it. Always I had been solitary, individual, apart. But—did it matter how, under what circumstances, we fucked? After all, I found myself suddenly wondering, how much of our manner of sexual intercourse can be attributed to instinct, how much to mere social conditioning?

There was no doubt of it—there stirred within me a small animal of excitement, a constant realization that Maria, her body, was available. It was not a matter of imagination; the sensuous awareness moved in me independent of all ratiocination and daydreaming.

The idea of a woman is so important. She must live in your unconscious, as well as in the conscious ... or else she is only a warm hole, satisfactory for the immediate physical pressure, but nothing more. A man can masturbate in a woman as surely as with his hand.

Maria was the only woman who had penetrated to the unconscious layers of my being. That ancient adventure of breaking her hymen was clothed, in my memory, in the garments of legend, like a tale of ancient time—more real than the air I breathed, the food I ate, the thoughts I had thought today. In that legend, I was, for the once and only time, a Hero.

I slept soundly during the siesta, no longer bedeviled by the erotic dreams that had troubled last night's slumber. But when the sound of the departing motorboat woke me, I had my hand warmly in my crotch, cuddling a marvelous erection. I got out of bed and stood looking down at myself. I'll at least go ready and willing, I thought wryly. No one can doubt for a second what's on my mind.

In that moment, I endured the last fierce struggle between my conventional soul and the new collective self coming alive inside of me. I picked up my shorts and began pulling them on. But I paused, standing with one leg in, one leg out, my hard cock burgeoning between.

It was up to me. If I went downstairs clothed and inviolate, Maria's plan would be scotched, whether for good or for evil. Did I want to ... could I ... bring it to an ending? I thought of Maria's face when she should see me yet armored in clothing. I dropped the shorts. I picked up my cigarettes and my lighter. I walked naked out of my private room into the ambience of Us.

128

The long corridor was empty. I walked deliberately, with a bravery I had not expected to possess. I saw no one in the downstairs reception room. I paused before the French doors, gazing with a sudden apprehension into the pool area. Were they waiting in their nakedness to see whether my puritan soul would allow me to enter into the new life of Us? Or, worse yet, would I be the only one to expose himself foolishly, the others safely clothed?

I went on, not daring to give myself time to think it out. The pool area was empty. I hesitated, irresolute. Maybe it would be better to retreat to my room and wait until the others had gathered. But if I should retreat, I knew as surely as I have ever known anything, I would never again muster my courage to the sticking point.

My legs feeling awkward and clumsy, I crossed to the bar and sat down on a stool, the seat cold against my buttocks. I poured a double shot of bourbon over two ice cubes. I sat holding the glass in my hand, staring at it, before I tossed it back in one gulp. I fixed a second drink, adding water this time, and sipped at it in a more civilized manner.

Smoking a cigarette and drinking my drink, I sat naked and alone at the poolside bar. Consciously or unconsciously, my back was turned to the French doors, and I was unaware of Maria's presence until I felt her soft, warm hand on my bare shoulder.

"My sweet Jerry," she said, the words a whispering caress.

I spun around to face her. Her eyes were large with the threat of tears, her mouth trembled. "I couldn't tell, all day, whether you'd do it or not." Her voice was trembling, also.

I glanced toward the French doors to see if the

others were coming. "I wanted to leave," I said. "I meant to leave. But . . . "

She slid against me, putting her arms around my neck. "But you didn't."

I remained sitting. Maria, standing, pressed her naked belly against the outside of my thigh. Her upper body was warmly gracious as she leaned into me, her hands moved over my bare skin in a well-remembered flutter of touching. I slid down to take her into my arms, my erectile cock sliding against her thigh as though seeking the gateway to old delights. Her hands were doubled behind my head, bringing my mouth down to her mouth. Her lips were warm and soft and hard, avidly seeking.

She stopped the kissing. "Give it to me now," she said breathlessly. "Let me have it again, Jerry."

With a backward wriggle of her buttocks, she slid up on the edge of the stool opposite. Her knees opened, showing me the mound of rich black hair. I could see the waiting slit of pink flesh, and I was already moving toward the Mecca of its delights.

"Wait," she whispered. "Wait."

Though I did not know why, I waited. She sat ready before me, so still, and gazed upon my rampant cock. Her lower lip slowly sucked up, her teeth clamping it hard. Her eyes were brilliant. I needed her so badly, in this moment of suspension, I feared a sudden ejaculation, and I clenched the place inside me that would hold it until I had at least had a taste of her.

She looked into my eyes. "Jerry. He won't die now, will he?"

"There's only one way to tell," I said shakily. Tremors were chasing each other through my body

130

like wayward bolts of lightning. With a delicate touch of my hand, I elevated my instrument the requisite inch of adjustment and walked it into her, lodging the turgid head against her clitoris. I felt the harsh brush of pubic hair as the glans slipped through the thicket, to press apart the twinned lips and enter into the antechamber of her cunt. Her clitoris rested against the very eye of my cock; I was so sensitive I could feel its tiny pulsing.

I waited, a wave of panic washing suddenly through me, for my cock to quit on us. I looked desperately into her face; the memory of once-upon-a-time failure is so nearly impossible to erase. Her eyes closed as her knees clamped firmly against my sides. She was remembering, too—but the good times, not the bad—as well as feeling my cock now, as she teasingly fucked her clitoris against me. There was no faltering of the flesh; rather, the contrary.

After a time of this, she opened her eyes and smiled a slow, delicious smile. "Now," she said. "Let me have it all."

She shifted, in that subtle way of a woman opening herself, and with one long easy thrust I went deeply. The vista of her cunt seemed to open infinitely, even as it flowered with heat and moisture, and I leaned harder and harder, seeking the ultimate depths.

For a minute that might as well have been an eternity, Maria's pussy gripped me hilt-deep. We were not still; I was tasting her, remembering her, and she was tasting me, flesh in flesh. I was so sensitized that I gasped with the tenderly harsh hand of her gripping, there in that narrowed place where I had once bloodily torn away her hymen.

Maria raised her chin, leaning her head back in a long, luxurious reaction. "I guess a woman can't forget the first man," she said softly. "There's never another cock quite like it, no matter how beloved."

I began to fuck. She answered spontaneously, gripping her hands on my shoulders to brace against the rising beat. I began to hear her breath, pulsing in short, hard rasps tuned to the rhythm of our fucking. And, delightfully, there came a new thing—a softening and spreading of her pussy that allowed me, seemingly, to melt inches deeper—that had not been a part of the young Maria.

I placed my hands against the slopes of her breasts, thumbs resting on the nipples, and gave myself to the experience. I had just started to feel the first faraway urge toward ejaculation when the intrusive voice suddenly intervened.

"Now, fellows! It's not fair to start without the rest of us!"

I halted, thinking dismally, I can't keep on, I can't . . . and yet I've got to finish.

Maria turned her head. "Hello, Tony," she said. "You bastard."

She was laughing. I could not look at him, but stood staring over Maria's shoulder. Tony came close, I could feel him near, and I knew with a deep-struck horror that Maria was leaning to kiss him. As she did so, her cunt closed on my cock in a clenching reaction. My tool, uncaring of the source, quickened with the stimulation and sought to take up the task of completion. I held myself rigidly passive, refusing to accept the boon.

"Ummm, Tony, you always did kiss so good," Maria said. "Kiss me again."

Tony put one hand on my shoulder this time, pressing me against Maria even as I flinched away. As he gave her a long kiss, she slid her hips forward on the stool and began to fuck me.

I refused to participate. But I could not refuse awareness of the complex sensations flowing from her intricate movement. Involuntarily, I responded. When I did so, Maria took her mouth away from Tony, giving me her exclusive attention. Triumph thrust hotly through me; my rampant, ready rod had won her. I meant to keep her, too, take her all the way, even if Tony Two was watching.

"Don't let me break anything up, darlings," Tony chirped in his light-toned voice. "I'm just after a drink, myself." He clapped a hearty hand on my shoulder. "Keep it up, old man. I'm cheering you all the way."

I looked at him for the first time. The naked boy, so beautiful and sure inside his beautiful body, was grinning at me. My eyes dropped to his cock. He didn't even show a hard; it dangled, so large it was almost grotesque, between his legs. I became, suddenly, murderously angry.

"Why the hell don't you go away?" I snarled.

His smile mocked at me. "Sweetheart! That's not the rules of Maria's little game."

Unperturbed by my glare, he went behind the bar, lifted the lid of the ice bucket, and began to put cubes into a glass. While I stared malevolently, he measured Scotch, poured soda, and lifted the glass with delicate relish to his lips.

I was still inside Maria, but nearly as soft as though she had already looted my load of semen.

"Jerry," Maria said.

I wouldn't look at her. I would quit now, go up-stairs, finish myself with my hand, and put on my clothes. No-Name Key would see me no more.

"Jerry," Maria said urgently. "Pay attention to me, Jerry."

Tony Two laughed. "Maybe he wants to fuck me, love," he said to Maria. "Ever had a pretty boy, Jerry? It's nice."

"Shut up, Tony," Maria said. "Jerry . . . "

She began. Not hard, not demanding; very tenderly she slipped her pussy back and forth on my cock. The loving tactic brought me back in spite of myself. Still staring at Tony Two, I was, without being really aware of it, fucking with short, hard thrusts. It was, I realized suddenly, an act of revenge to take her while Tony was on the cold outside, looking in.

Maria's thighs locked against my sides. "Jerry!" she said. Her voice was sharp and trembling and I had to look at her. I was astonished to see the tears pooled wetly in her eyes. "That's not nice, Jerry," she said. "You don't feel like Jerry any more."

In a rush of love, I let go of the anger. Though I did not move, could not move under the clamped arrest of her thighs, I sensed with an uttermost sensitivity the subtle flow of her response to the change in me. Holding completely still, she rushed precipitately into orgasm. After the first shock of recognition, I began coming with her. We were, from one second to the next, totally immersed in each other's juices. Tony Two stood watching, his hand holding the glass suspended, his face harshly intent. As I began pumping semen, he stepped de-liberately away from the concealment of the bar to show me his cock hugely erect, as though he were

134

participating fully in the ecstatic mingling of our juices.

I leaned weakly against Maria. She was kissing me all over my face in a quick smother of caresses, laughing and crying at once.

"Wonderful, Jerry," she kept saying. "Wonderful, so wonderful. We've got it again, and I needed it so! Just wonderful!"

"Maria," Casey said, "come here."

I pulled away, feeling her slide down from the stool. We turned, Tony looking also, to see Casey standing naked inside the French doors.

"Goody, here comes cock number two," Tony said. "Maybe there'll be one left for me."

No one paid attention to Tony. Casey remained where he was, showing a good hard without the least sign of self-consciousness.

"Maria," he said again.

Maria remained by my side. "There's no competition here, Casey," she said quietly. "We're all together."

"All right," Casey said. "But come here."

With a lingering touch of her hand for me, she began to move toward the cowboy. When she reached him, she sank to her knees in a lithe movement, taking him with her mouth. He put his hands on his hips, his body braced forward, as her arms encircled his thighs. He stared at me, as I had stared at Tony Two, but the anger had already faded as he yielded to the sweet influence of her tongue.

Tony Two made a strangled sound. I looked, to see him putting down the glass and crossing, as though pulled by an invisible force, toward the man and the woman locked together by their passion.

135

He came close, very close, one hand reaching out to cradle Casey's scrotum. He was on his knees beside Maria. "Let me finish him, love," he said, his voice hot, wanting. "Let me taste him. And then . . ."

Casey gazed at the two, the man and the woman, kneeling before him in sexual supplication. There was an enigmatic smile on his face. He leaned, his hands fitting into Maria's armpits to lift her.

"There ain't but one way to go on with it," he said.

He carried Maria to a cushion-padded lounge chair and laid her down. He stood over her for a swift moment; then, so suddenly I couldn't believe it, he dropped on her like a jockey into the saddle, his rapid hips dipping his cock into her in a frenzied cross-country posting.

So quick, so hard, so fierce, it was too sudden for Maria to answer with a complete response. But she loved it, she loved it, she took him deliriously with quick, hard thrusts of her own as he drove the semen into her like liquid nails. In an instant it was done and he was out of her, walking with his slightly bowlegged roll toward the bar.

For the flash of a second, I thought he meant to attack me. When I recognized his intent, I moved aside, shoving the bottle of bourbon within his reach. He drank from it, two long, hard swallows, put the bottle down, and grinned crookedly at me.

"I've never had a woman another man's got ready —at least to my knowledge," he said. "So I guess you could call us brothers under the skin now."

The wry words were exactly right to sweep away the residual tensions. Suddenly it did not matter that we had shared her within minutes of each other, instead of over a span of time.

136

Tony spoke up plaintively. "What about poor old Tony Two? Is he going to get left out just because he's gay?"

Casey turned to him. His voice was amused. "Son, why in the world didn't they call you Tony Ten? That would fit the case a whole lot better than Tony Two."

Tony stood with arms akimbo. "Laugh all you want to. But everybody has fucked or been fucked except me. I want my share, that's all."

"I don't even know what you like to do," Casey said roughly.

Maria rose from her padded couch. "You're not being fair, you know," she said chidingly. She turned to Tony. "Come on, Tony. It's your turn now. With me."

Tony Two, with Maria's sudden attention, had retreated behind the bar. His expression was tentative, uncertain; he was suddenly bereft of all his brightness.

"I'm not . . . " he said. He cleared his throat. "I'm not . . . sure I can make it with a woman any more, Maria."

Maria, going around the corner of the bar, wrapped Tony Two warmly in her arms. "I'm still Maria," she said.

His face was miserable. "But what I really want . . ." He looked at her defiantly. "I want Casey to fuck *me*."

"Me?" Casey said, startled.

Tony Two looked at him. "God, yes. When I saw you climbing Maria, Casey, I nearly *died*." His voice faltered. "But you're a hotshot cowboy, aren't you, a man and a half. So you wouldn't think of it."

I was surprised by Casey's reaction. With a

trembling hand, he was pouring too much whiskey into his glass. "I'm afraid you're right," he said tightly. "That . . . sort of thing . . . is out of my line."

"Tony," Maria said. "I've had Jerry tonight. I've had Casey. Now I want you." With the words she had reached her hand to his great cock. He submitted to the affectionate gesture, was even responsive. But his eyes remained blank, hopeless.

"I can't, Maria," he said. "I simply can't."

Maria ceased her ministration, shifting her hand to rest warmly against his waist. It was touching to watch her gentle understanding.

"But you liked to fuck me, Tony. Then. So why not now?"

He would not look at her. "You were my chance to be straight, Maria. It didn't work, not for long. So I'm afraid to try again. Because I know . . . "

Maria glanced at me, at Casey. "Jerry was supposed to tell his story tonight," she said. "I think it ought to be Tony Two's turn instead. Agreed?"

He looked so broken, so vulnerable, that a great sweep of pity moved through me. I nodded. "I think that's a good idea."

She put the palm of her hand against his cheek. "Tony. Will you tell it? Exactly how it was with you?"

In a convulsive gesture, he put his arms around her shoulders, holding on. "Yes," he said brokenly. "Yes. I will."

Maria made her voice brisk. "All right. Everybody fix a drink now, and settle down to listen."

"But none of you are like me," Tony Two said, shrinking from the ordeal now that it was imminent. "So you won't understand."

"We'll try," Maria said. "Won't we try, fellows?"

"Remember, Tony, you belong with Us now," Casey

138

said gravely. "Tell me what you want to drink, so we can get started."

Tony Two glanced at him gratefully. Recovering a modicum of brightness, he said, "Scotch, of course. And, right off the bat, you've got to understand one thing. I'm not ashamed. Not the least bit. Because I am what I am."

TONY TWO'S TALE

I never had a chance to be anything but queer. Even when I was a little boy, too little, I knew that some men looked at me in a very special way. Of course, I didn't understand that it was because I was so pretty, prettier than most girls, and had this good body. I never did grow all out of proportion, like most boys. I didn't have any idea of my real nature, I really didn't. Why, I bragged about screwing girls, just like the other fellows, talked dirty and rough like they did. Of course, horsing around, wrestling and so on, I'd get these feelings, and wonder why I couldn't sense those feelings in my friends.

Dad was always a little worried about me—I know that, now. He had me enrolled in everything that came along, Little League baseball, and earning Boy Scout badges, all that. I was sent away to camp every summer. Dad figured it would make me tough and hard and mean, just like the other boys, and so become a man he could be proud of. And yet—Dad caused it to start, he was the one who set me up.

The summer I was 14, he had to go to a big business convention, and Mother wanted to go with him because it was in New York. So this friend of the family volunteered to drive up and get me. They hadn't told me anything about it, so I was surprised

139

when Mr. Harris showed up and gave the camp management a letter from Dad, advising the camp that he was to take custody and see me safely home. Mr. Harris and Dad were great friends; they were always having poker nights, and every fall they went deer hunting, up in Minnesota, for a couple of weeks.

I hadn't ever liked Mr. Harris particularly. Maybe because Dad was always holding him up as the kind of man I ought to want to be. Mr. Harris, you see, had been a pretty famous football player in college. I remember that, every time we were over at their house, Dad would ask him to tell me all about the cups and photographs and stuff on the walls of his private den. The photographs were old and faded and they looked like somebody had taken them a couple of hundred years ago, with those old-style helmets and everything. Football bored me, anyway.

Mr. Harris was a big man, broad in the shoulder and heavy in the leg. You could tell he had been a lot of muscle when he was young. He had gone to seed by my time, with a sagging waistline and jowls under his jaws. His wife was a quiet woman that I don't remember ever having much to say, and there were two little girls, both younger than me, who were so whiny and bitchy I couldn't stand them either.

"I guess me and you will have us a long trip together, Tony," Mr. Harris said jovially when we met. "We'll have plenty of time to talk about football. You won't mind that, will you? Aren't you going out for the team this fall?"

"I don't know," I said.

"Your Dad wants you to," he said seriously. "You ought to think about that, son."

140

Mr. Harris was very hearty and friendly while I was getting packed up, talking to the camp manager and helping me at the same time. I felt uneasy; it was going to be a long trip, because the camp was so far up in the mountains it would take two days' driving to get home.

It was pretty much of a drag. Mr. Harris kept up the jovial act for a large part of the day, telling in detail about old football games he'd been in, and helped win, and then he got on to how he'd try to persuade Dad to let me come hunting with them this fall. I'd like to shoot a deer, wouldn't I, and have somebody smear the first blood on my face?

He reached over to clap his big hand on my shoulder. "I intend to be the man to blood you, too," he said, laughing. "That's something a boy never forgets, if he lives to be a hundred."

About the middle of the morning, he bought me a milkshake and a hamburger, and for lunch we stopped at a nice motel restaurant. He had a couple of beers, and offered to let me have one, if I wanted it. I said I had better not.

The afternoon was different. Mr. Harris talked less and less, until finally we drove silently for a very long way. I was glad when he turned on the car radio to fill the gap between us.

I still felt uneasy, and I still didn't know why. I was tired, too—you don't ever get much sleep the last night of camp—so I went to sleep in the car. I was brought awake by Mr. Harris stopping the car in front of a motel.

"I guess this is as good a place as any to spend the night," he said. "Look all right to you?"

"Yes sir," I said. "It's fine."

He slid his eyes toward me. "I think I'll just register

us as father and son." He laughed a little laugh. "Don't want anybody to get any funny ideas, do we?"

"No sir," I said. "I reckon not."

When we walked into the motel room, carrying our overnight bags, there was a flutter of fear somewhere inside of me. Excitement, too—I'll admit the excitement. Both the fear and the excitement came from a strong feeling that Mr. Harris had been trying to act, all day, exactly as he always did, but hadn't quite been able to for some reason. I sat down on one of the beds and watched him getting a whiskey bottle out of his overnight bag.

"Want to run get some ice, like a good fellow?" he said.

I found the plastic container and hunted up the ice maker. When I came back he had his coat and tie off, lying sprawled on one of the beds. The television was on.

"Know how to mix a drink?"

"Yes sir," I said. "I think so."

I made the drink, brought it to him. He took a swallow, lit a cigarette, and lay back with a big sigh. "Ah, that's good," he said. "Nothing like getting in early at the motel after a long day of driving." He was studying me. "I'll bet you could use a real tub bath after so long up there at the camp."

"Yes sir," I said. "I guess I could."

"All right. I'll give you first crack. But don't take long. I'm pretty hot and sweaty myself."

I undressed in the bathroom. The tub felt good, after all those skimpy, cold showers at camp. I wished I could loll in the warm, soap-sudsy water for a long time. But, remembering Mr. Harris' remark, I got out pretty quick and began to towel myself off.

I was putting on my underpants when Mr. Harris

hollered, "Hey, Tony, come out here and let me have a look at you. I want to see what kind of football material you'll make."

I hesitated. But then I put on the underpants and walked out into the room. I couldn't keep myself from doing it, even though it scared me more than ever.

Mr. Harris was bare to the waist now, his big belly bulging out over his belt. His shoes were off and he had a fresh drink in his hand.

He grinned at me. "My God, boy, you're built as pretty as a girl. Come here and let me see if you've got any muscle."

I took a reluctant step toward him. When I didn't come any closer, he heaved himself up off the bed and came to put his big hand on my shoulder, turning me for an all-around look. He ran his hand down the slope of my back, all the way to my ass and over it.

"Yes sir, pretty as a roan colt," he said. He was massaging my biceps now. "Some good muscle there, all right. Start your training program, lift a few weights, run a lot . . . I'd say you've got what it takes for the backfield."

I moved a step away. "If you want the bathroom now, I'll get my clothes out," I said.

He was pouring another drink. "You're pretty shy for the locker room, though, coming out here with those shorts on." He leered at me suddenly. "I'll bet you're raising yourself a nice crop of hair down there."

So embarrassed I didn't know what to do, I just stood there. He went back to the bed, gulping at his drink.

"Come on. Shuck off those shorts and let me see what kind of equipment God's given you."

I didn't move. He was about half-drunk already and the fear was beginning to override the excitement.

He heaved himself up on an elbow. "Listen, fellow, I don't like all this prissy modesty. Why, in a locker room, the fellows will be walking around buck naked and you won't think a thing about it. You know why? Because everybody in that locker room is a man, or else he wouldn't be there. So you don't have to be afraid of that sort of thing. Understand what I mean?"

"But I . . . " I said.

"Ain't ashamed of it, are you?" He was grinning now. "What's the matter? Got a little old peanut you don't want to show? Is that it?"

My legs were beginning to shake. But I didn't know anything else to make him shut up about it. I knew, from having seen other boys at camp, that I didn't have to be ashamed of my cock. Very slowly, I pushed down my underpants.

He stared for a still minute. Then he whistled, long and low. "Man, you are going to have women all over you," he said. "Tony, you're hung like a horse."

I was worried I'd get a hard-on, right there in front of him. I guess I was too scared. But I felt a warm flush of pleasure at his admiration.

He laughed. "Yes sir. God's gift to women. That'll be you." His voice changed. "Been giving it plenty of exercise, I reckon? Running it through your fist?"

I shook my head, a hot flush moving all over my body.

He chuckled. "Boy, don't try to deny it. When I was your age, I beat my meat so much I'd be crazy as a bat if those old tales were true." He took another

144

swallow of his drink. He was still gazing at my cock, continuing to shake his head in wonderment. "What about up there at camp? You boys fool around with each other much?"

"No sir," I said, my voice tight in my throat. "A counselor sleeps in the tent."

"I don't believe it," he said flatly. "You can't keep boys from fooling around, I don't care how hard you try. You ought to see what goes on in a football training camp. And a pretty guy like you?" His eyes were shrewd. "I'd bet a dollar you've been bent over a footlocker a few times. Now, don't lie, boy. It's not anything to be ashamed of. Not when you're a man among men."

He finished his drink and stood up, stretching a long, luxurious stretch. "I guess it's time for my bath now," he remarked and began taking off his pants.

I watched him undress. He looked so gross out of his clothes. I couldn't help but stare at his cock. It was short and thick, and he had a little half-hard on.

He saw me looking, and laughed. "I've always said it ain't how much, but how," he said. "Course, I've had to say that. What I wouldn't give for a cock the size of yours."

Deliberately, he walked over and, before I could move, took me in his hand. I flinched, but he gripped hard enough to hurt and I had to ease off. In spite of myself, I was growing in his grip.

"Quick on the trigger, too," he said. "What it must be to be young."

He left me then. My clothes were still in the bathroom, so I pulled up my underpants and sat down on the other bed. The television was still going. I watched it without being able to follow the old movie that was on. After a while, Mr. Harris called

*for me to bring him another drink. When I took it
into the bathroom, he was in soapy water up to his
waist. I handed him the glass, trying not to look at
his cock floating with its head on top of the water.
Noticing my underpants, he laughed at me.*

*"Boy, I'm going to get you out of that bashfulness
if it's the last thing I do," he said. "That's a promise."*

*I returned to the bedroom and waited. Yes. Wait-
ing, even though I didn't know what I was waiting
for. After a while he came out, naked as a jaybird,
and fixed another drink. He sat down across from
me.*

*"Now listen to me, son," he said seriously. "Your
body's nothing to be ashamed of. If you'll notice,
I don't mind walking around naked in front of you.
So why should you mind being naked in front of me?"*

"Well, sir," I said. "I just don't feel right . . ."

*He slapped my knee. "That's just what I mean. You
don't feel right. Are you afraid you'll look at a fellow's
cock and want to suck it? Is that it?"*

*"No, sir," I said, mumbling the words. "I don't
think so."*

*He rose, swaggering naked around the room. His
cock, normal now, flogged about, and I couldn't
keep my eyes off of it.*

*"A real man doesn't have to be afraid of anything
like that," he said. "He's sure of himself, you see. It's
these half-queers that show all this bashfulness. Take
my word for it. They're like a woman, they think you
might want to do something if you see them naked.
Understand what I mean?"*

"Yes sir," I said. "I reckon so."

*"Now I'm going to have another drink, and a nap
before dinner. You can watch television if you want,
it won't bother me."*

146

He went to sleep very quickly without finishing the next drink. I watched the old movie, then a half-hour film on fishing, then the news. All the time, I kept looking at him, lying there naked on the bed. I had never seen a grown man naked, though I had seen boys, and I was fascinated by the difference. He had so much hair, and there was a brown, wrinkled look to his cock. There was a solid, masterful presence in his flesh.

He must have been dreaming something fierce, because he kept groaning and shifting around, and he got a pretty good hard-on. Finally, he went to sleep so soundly I had to wake him up when I began to be afraid the dining room would close. He got up sour and grumpy, washed his mouth out with water and then a swallow of whiskey, and we got dressed.

His disposition improved while we ate, he was being jovial again, and I began to think it was all over. Especially when, again in the room, he got into bed, under the covers this time, and said, "We'd better plan on an early start tomorrow. Good night."

I don't know how late it was when I woke up in pitch blackness with Mr. Harris on the bed beside me, his hand inside my pajamas. He was working my cock very slowly, and I remember the roughness of his palm—he played a lot of golf—so that it hurt and felt good at the same time. Somehow, he knew the moment I was awake, though I had decided almost immediately to pretend I was still asleep.

His voice startled me. "Feel good?"

I didn't answer. I tried to turn carelessly away, as though doing it in my sleep. But I didn't fool him. His hand gripped my cock, hurting, and he reached his other hand over my hip to hold me flat on my back.

147

"You're awake and liking it," he said, a growl in his voice. "So lie still, damn it."

I kept still. He moved his hand to cup my balls. I couldn't help opening my legs, because his other hand was stroking at me, finding the hard little nipples on my chest and gliding the roughness of his palm over them, then stroking down into the softness below my rib cage.

"You're a pretty fellow," he whispered. "You know that, don't you? Oh, how you know it, you little prick-tease." Leaning heavily over me, he put his mouth on mine. Trembling, I jerked away from the warm kiss.

"Mr. Harris!" I said.

There was no stopping him, though. He heaved on top, pressing me into the mattress, and I could feel his cock between my thighs like a stick of fire. He was holding my head clamped with both hands, kissing me, and a passionate desire began to move inside me. But I didn't know, yet, what it was I wanted him to do.

"I'm going to show you," he whispered. "Be quiet. I'm going to show you, now."

Before I could understand, he rolled away and his strong hands were turning me onto my belly. When he got on top again, he seemed so much heavier, crushing me with his oppressive weight. Afraid, shaking with the fear, I began to cry. I knew he meant to do something terrible. I wanted him to do it. At the same time, I was terrified by my ignorance.

His breath was warm against my ear. "Be still, now, or I'll hurt you. And don't make any noise. I'll hurt you for that, too."

I knew there was no way, now, to stop what was going to happen. In that final yielding, I thought a

*very strange thought. I believed this was why Dad
had sent Mr. Harris instead of coming himself. He
knew what would happen, he had wanted it to happen, he had chosen Mr. Harris to play the part, as he
had chosen Mr. Harris to hunt with, and play poker
and golf with, and talk about football and baseball
in their proper season.*

*His big hands were braced and strong, spreading
my buttocks. He grunted when he hunched up to
press the hard head of his cock against my anus. Feeling sorry for myself in my helplessness, I whim-
pered, thinking about my mother. How would she
feel if she knew? She would understand this terrible
thing, because didn't Dad do it to her, those times
they made those sounds of bed-creaking and hard
breathing and groaning in their room at night? And
didn't she like it, with the awful liking that was growing in my fear, like a flower in a field of weeds?*

"Just relax, and it won't hurt."

*Mr. Harris spoke in his normal voice, instead of
whispering as before, and somehow his tone made it
seem so much more natural and inevitable. The darkness helped, too; it was not the Mr. Harris I had
known and disliked, it was only a Mr. Harris cock,
a Mr. Harris weight, a Mr. Harris passion for me. I
made an effort to obey, as the head of his cock pressed
harder and harder against the tight bind of my
sphincter. But when he broke through the magic
ring, I had to cry out. His hand was over my mouth,
anticipating my scream and smothering it.*

*I was panting, and my body had broken out in a
cold sweat. I hadn't believed anything could hurt like
my asshole was hurting with his thick cock. He was
ruthless now, banging hard against my buttocks, ripping deeper with each shove, and every time I tried*

to scream through his blunt fingers, and struggled forward to escape him.

When he stopped, his cock was all the way in me. It felt enormous, and I could feel his balls hanging against my thighs, a warm, heavy weight, and his body crushing on top of mine seemed to weigh a ton.

He was breathing hard, with a grunting sound, and I wondered why he wanted to do it if it hurt him, too. I began to hope that he would get out of me now and it would be over with.

"Let me get a pillow under you," he said in his everyday voice. "A pillow will make it better."

With one hand he lifted my middle, holding me snugged into the curve of his body, and shoved a pillow under my stomach. Moving his hand downward, he found my cock and gripped it gently . . . not stroking, simply holding it.

"Now it's going to get good," he said.

There in the darkness, he began to fuck. He went at it very quietly, even gently, and though it did hurt, some, it wasn't nearly as bad as before. I lay still, breathing deeply, my eyes widely open on darkness.

It took several minutes for the next thing to happen. Somewhere inside me, a long-held tension relaxed and my ass began to soften and warm and make him welcome. A tremendous wave of sensuousness moved through me, like a tide coming in.

"Ahhh," he said gustily. "That's it, boy. That's it!" He began to fuck more swiftly, with an increasing thrust, and my ass was rising back rhythmically against the sweet cock, cherishing gratefully each separate inch instead of trying to run away.

I can't describe how it was. I was spreading under him, opening, becoming warmer and softer, and

150

there was no longer any pain, only the enormous tidal waves moving slowly, and slowly, and then with passion; so that, coming full circle, I wanted him to punish me roughly, hurt me again—but I had conquered him, he couldn't make it hurt no matter how hard he tried, I could take everything he had. The greatest tidal wave of all began to gather, sweeping all the way out to my fingertips and down to my toes. I was tingling and alive all over, and his beautiful cock was throbbing in a new phase, flooding my anus with his come, gallons and gallons of it, and I was moaning with the sheer joy of what had been wrought inside my lovely body.

He lay still on me, finished, and I waited, not wanting him to go away. It was like being in the warm spring sun after a long winter, the day you take off your winter underwear, you know, and go barefoot. I had the same warmth of spirit for Mr. Harris, a deep gratitude for an act of nature. I was, like spring makes you feel, awakened into a new life.

He withdrew finally, rolling away his weight. "You came, too," he said. "Did you know that you came, too?"

I didn't try to answer. I only turned, putting out a hand to touch him. When my hand found his side, I moved close against his male warmth.

"Mr. Harris," I said. My voice was trembling with love.

He did not respond, but lay stiff and still. "By God, boy, you really like it, don't you?" he said.

He got up, leaving me abruptly, and went into the bathroom. I lay waiting for him to come back. There was soreness in my ass, but also in my tender flesh the memory of how it had felt during the good part. I yearned for him to return and begin again.

151

When he came out of the bathroom, though, he got into his own bed. Apparently, he went to sleep immediately. I lay in the darkness for a while, remembering over and over again what had happened. I couldn't understand how it could hurt so terribly when it was so good, so right. It did feel right, you understand. All sorts of vague notions and half-understood feelings had coalesced tonight, so that for the first time in my life I knew my flesh, its reasons and purposes. I slipped from thinking into the most easeful sleeping I had ever enjoyed.

I woke up all over and all at once, completely aware not only of the day but of the night before. Mr. Harris, sitting fully clothed on the side of his bed, was smoking a cigarette and staring at me. Lying there very quietly, no longer afraid, I looked at him from under the corner of the sheet. I felt shy and loving. He was such a beautiful man, and remembering it, too.

When he saw that my eyes were open, he looked away. "So you're finally awake," he said gruffly. "Do you have any idea what time it is?"

"Did I oversleep?" I said. "I'm sorry, Mr. Harris." I stretched, feeling luxurious; only then did I realize how sore I was.

"Ten-thirty," he said. "We ought to have been on the road for two hours."

I grasped the sheet to throw it back. "I'll hurry," I said contritely.

"Wait a minute," Mr. Harris said.

He was regarding me with a curious expression—as though he were frightened now. Instead of me.

I hope you aren't planning on telling your dad about this trip of ours," he said. "I'll tell you now, he won't believe a word of it."

152

He stopped, as though waiting for my response. I didn't have anything to say. The thought of mentioning the adventure hadn't occurred to me. After all, it was my idea that Dad had planned it this way.

Mr. Harris went on, his voice low and even. "All I have to do is deny it, because your dad knows about you. He told me, once, he was afraid you might be queer. I didn't believe it—not till last night." He stared into my face. "But you liked it, boy. You loved it. Isn't it the truth?"

I didn't try to avoid his eyes. "It hurt, there at first. But then . . ."

He nodded. "I felt you give it all, fellow. Like a woman gives it. So it won't do you the least bit of good to tell your folks I grabbed your cherry. Understand what I mean?"

I was watching his face. "I didn't mean to tell them."

His eyes wavered uncertainly. He stood up. "Come on, let's get some breakfast and hit the road."

At breakfast, I had a ravenous appetite. Mr. Harris didn't eat much, but drank a lot of coffee and smoked half a pack of cigarettes. Back at the room, he hustled our suitcases into the car in a great hurry, complaining about the late start. Once on the road, he concentrated on driving fast. I had hoped we could talk, discuss fondly how marvelous it had been, but he didn't seem to have much conversation of any type. After a while, I turned on the radio, found a good rock station, and gave myself to the music, mixing up the beat of the sound with the beat of his body against my buttocks last night, and feeling warm and sure of myself. He didn't object to the music, either, like most grown people would have. Maybe he didn't dare.

When we stopped for a late lunch, I was hungry

again. On our way once more, I began to think about being at home tonight, sleeping in my own bed. At the same time, watching Mr. Harris out of the corner of my eye, I was wondering, as I had all day in a warm consciousness of love, how it was that a person could change so much overnight. He wasn't Dad's friend any more, he was my wonderful man, sagging gut, rough hands, and all.

The middle of the afternoon, we stopped to gas up the car. I went to the bathroom. Mr. Harris waited until I came back, went himself. When he got into the car, he did not drive away immediately, but sat with both hands on the steering wheel, looking straight ahead.

"Listen, fellow," he said. "There's no law says we've got to get home today. Understand what I mean?"

I sat very still. "Dad and Mother are at home," I said carefully. "They'll be expecting us."

He turned his head, looking deeply into my eyes, and I felt a throb of excitement. He wasn't through with me yet, like I had thought this morning. Nor I with him.

"Cars break down all the time, don't they?" he said urgently. "Nobody could argue with that, could they?"

"I don't think so," I said.

He grinned, open and friendly for the first time today. "The car just broke down. I think it's the fan belt."

I pointed to a drive-up telephone at the corner of the gas-station lot. Mr. Harris drove the car into position, took the receiver down, and put in a dime. He went through the ritual of a collect call, then said in his heartiest voice, "Hey, John? This is Bob. Now, don't get yourself into an uproar, there's nothing seriously wrong."

He listened for a moment, then said, "Just this one thing, John. I blew a fan belt, back down the road about a mile. Had to be towed in here to . . ." He named a small town we had passed miles back.

He listened again. "The thing is, the fellow here at the gas station doesn't have the right belt in stock, and he can't get it until in the morning. That's why I called, to let you know."

He listened again. "Not to worry, John. There's a motel right down the road, I can see the sign from here, and we'll be on early in the morning. O.K.? Just wanted to let you know so you wouldn't worry." He listened. "These things happen . . . Nah, it's no trouble, it won't matter whether I'm in the office tomorrow or the next day. Wait a minute. You'll call Ethel for me? Fine. Take care, now."

When he hung up the phone and looked at me, I could read in his mouth and eyes the hungry anticipation of our stolen night.

"See how easy it was?" he said, and put his hand cupped around my thigh. We laughed together, each in a full understanding of the other.

Though it was still early in the afternoon, we stopped at the very next motel. I stayed in the car while Mr. Harris registered us, trembling again but with excitement this time, no longer ignorant of myself, of what would happen soon now, so soon.

Once in the motel room, I hurried to get ice without waiting to be asked and mixed Mr. Harris' bourbon and water. Sitting on the bed, having watched all my movements with hungry eyes, he took the drink from my hand.

"You can have one, too, if you want. But make it sparingly."

I poured a splash of bourbon into a glass, added a

lot of water. It tasted strong and harsh in my mouth, but it warmed the fire in my flesh.

"All right," Mr. Harris said. "Take off your clothes."

I began to undress, taking my time about it, very much aware of his eyes. It was a good feeling to know, here in the subdued light of the afternoon room, that he wanted me so badly. When I was naked, I had a real hard-on, and he was breathing in light rasps through half-opened lips, his eyes glued to my cock.

"Good God, boy, what a dong you do have," he said as though discovering it for the first time. He grinned, his tongue moving over his lips. "A damned pity women ain't going to get the use of it."

I took his glass, letting our fingers touch, and fixed him another drink. I placed it ready to his hand and sat down on the bed to watch him get naked. With the grossness of his flesh, the hairiness of his chest and legs, he looked more like a bear than a man. I wondered how I could have seen him as ugly. He was not ugly, only hard and masculine. Even the drooping roll of his belly didn't bother me.

He stood before me naked, cock up and eager, and took a hard swallow of whiskey. I sipped from my glass in imitation of him. My head began to whirl; from the bourbon, perhaps from the anticipation of being fucked again.

"Come here boy," Mr. Harris said. "I want you to suck it."

It jarred me. "What?" I said.

He was impatient. "You know what I mean. Come on!"

I sat still. "But I thought . . ."

He grinned. "We'll get around to what you like. Right now, it's what I like."

He walked toward me, sitting there on the bed, and put his cock against my face. I didn't understand. I only stared at his thick, blunt cock, the head half-way out of the uncircumcised sheath. Then, because he bruised my lips with it, I knew he wanted me to take it into my mouth.

My stomach moved queasily. Once, last summer, I had watched a sixteen-year-old camper make a smaller boy do the same thing. The little fellow, frightened and submissive at first, had vomited at the end, on and on into the dry retches.

I looked up. Mr. Harris' face was tense, hard, waiting. I love him, I told myself, and leaned to shape my lips around his tool. As I did so, he began a fucking motion. I held my mouth right for it, gagging slightly but not letting it show. The taste was so strange.

It was only a minute or two before he drew away. "Like it?" he said.

I looked up at him. "If you do. But I'd rather . . ."

His voice was quick, harsh. "I know what you'd rather. But you don't want to be hasty, fellow. The longer you make it last, the better it gets. Here, let me show you how to do it."

Pushing me on my back, my legs rising, he went down in one hard swift gulp. He slid his hands under my hips, lifting me to his mouth, and he was all over me, giving me such a flurry of sensation I couldn't sort it all out. He gulped me deep, slid me out between hard-edged lips, he licked his tongue around the head, first one way and then the other, he had me so wild I quivered with each new surprise.

I wanted to come, and tried to get away, but he wouldn't let me. He stayed with me until the last possible instant, standing up to grin down at me as my cock shot high a wad of stuff, the liquid remainder boiling down the stem to wet my scant growth of hair.

"Now that's the way to go about it," he said. He lay down on his back beside me. "Try it again, now an expert has taught you how."

Half drunk, I suppose, as well as in love and sexually excited, I was ready for anything. My great and only desire was to please him. So I went down with thought and instinct and imagination, remembering what he had taught me. I meant to take him all the way to come, too, and stay with him through it; but he stopped me before he was near.

"Let's don't waste it," he said, taking me under the armpits and lifting me to lie along the length of his body. "A woman can go down on you. But she can't do for you what I'm going to do now."

I threw my leg over him in an ecstasy of delight with the promise and began to kiss him. The taste of his cock mingled with the taste of his lips, and I was frantic with desire. He kept me company; his hands were sliding up and down my rib cage and feeling between my legs; when he turned me on my belly a great stab of joy shot through me, for I knew we were equally ready.

It hurt—not as much as last night, but some—as he entered into me, harder and more eager than before, more careless of my flesh. Knowing all that lay beyond, I didn't care, I only settled myself under him and by the time he was well inside I was already experiencing the distant beat of the tidal waves rolling in on my horizon.

I didn't come externally this time, it was all inside, but it was complete, so sweetly smothering I couldn't stand it. I had gone ahead of him, so I began to thrust back against him as he thrust upon me and I could sense every beat and throb of his gathering impulse. I was in a continuous trembling orgasm

158

until I felt him begin, and then I tightened into the total response that brought my semen spurting at the moment his did.

He rolled away immediately, panting hard, gulping for air. I crawled close against him, holding him with one arm across his great barrel.

"Was it good?" I asked tremulously, full of love and longing.

He gulped hard, swallowed, breathed again. "Boy, I've fucked everything you can imagine—from women to queers to ten-year-old whores in Hong Kong. But I ain't never fucked anything that likes it the way you do."

Those words made me proud. "It's not me," I said fondly. "It's you."

He turned to face me, staring deeply into my eyes. His eyes closing, he kissed me tenderly, holding my chin with his hand.

"You are something, Tony Two. You are something."

Sadness moved in me, a great sensation of loss. "But this is the last time. When we get home . . . "

He sighed happily. "We'll find ways, boy. There's always ways. Of course, we'll have to be careful. I'm a man with a reputation to think about."

"Yes," I said. "I understand what you mean." I laid my hand into his crotch. It was sticky, warm. I thought about taking him into my mouth again, but I felt too languorous to follow the idea.

"Fuck me again?" I said.

He laughed a small laugh. "Give an old man a chance to recuperate, fellow. I'm not as quick on the return serve as I used to be."

An idea moved in my head. "Then I'll fuck you."

I was already getting him turned on his belly. I

didn't have the least idea what it would feel like; I simply wanted to make him as happy as he had made me. Suddenly, I was aware of him sitting erect. In the next instant, a fist slammed into my face. It knocked me sprawling to the floor between the beds. I was shattered, afraid again all of a sudden. I stared up into his glaring eyes, the whole side of my face aching.

"What did I do wrong?" I said, beginning to cry.

He leaned close, his face snarling. "You don't think I'm queer too, do you?" he said harshly. "You don't think you can shove your cock up my ass?"

I got to my knees. "But I thought . . . "

He spurned me with one foot, knocking me backward. He rose, straddling over me. He looked like a mountain, looming up there.

"There's one thing you've got to understand, first and last. I'm a man, by God. I fuck people. I don't let people fuck me."

I was crying, my hands huddled over my face. "But it feels good, Mr. Harris. I only wanted to make you feel good."

"That's because you're a homosexual, boy. A homesexual needs a man's cock, just like a woman." Calmer now, his tone was becoming explanatory. "It'd ruin me for the rest of my life if I let anybody do to me what I just did to you. Understand what I mean?"

"But you sucked me," I said. "That's . . . "

"That's just fun along the way, fellow. What counts is what you finish with. You want to finish with my cock up your ass, right?"

"Yes," I said humbly.

"All right. That's the way you like it, that's the

way I like it. And that's the way it's going to be. Now come here."

His hands were coaxing me up off the floor. Humbly, submissively, I arose, and let him lay me down on the bed again. Yet there was a certain victory in the very submissiveness, so that when his cock was up my ass again I was somehow the winner. I lay humbly and quietly and peacefully and made him fuck for a very long time before I let myself respond.

It was different this time, tender and loving, for he wanted to show how sorry he was for hitting me. Also, it took him a long time to get an orgasm, so that I was having my secret little inside sensations for a long time before we got to the bottom line. When we were through, I knew that, though he might be on top, he might be doing all the striding and thrusting, I owned him, he didn't own me. I didn't need to fuck him, not the way he needed to fuck me. I only needed to submit my ass to his ministrations.

We slept, then went to eat dinner. When we returned, we began upon a wild night. Like a bridal couple, we explored each other's bodies, each other's needs, each other's responses. We turned on the television, so the noises couldn't be heard, and I began to work on his cock with my mouth, bringing him ready again. Here I learned another kind of victory; I could get a rise out of him even when he wasn't nearly ready to rise. He fucked me twice before we finally went to sleep and again, a nice tender warm farewell to our honeymoon, as soon as we woke up the next morning.

When we arrived at home, about eleven o'clock, I knew my place in life. I was a homosexual, seeking a male cock to satisfy my needs; and knowing my attractiveness, knowing my beauty, knowing my power, I felt strong and sure of myself.

For two weeks, we didn't have a chance to exchange even a secret word. He was in the house a couple of times, but Dad was always there and Mr. Harris carefully didn't pay me any more attention than was usual. I began to suspect that, returning to the normality of hometown life, he had decided it was foolhardy to continue our affair. I was pretty hurt, I can tell you. For the first time, I knew the pangs of a disappointed love.

Then Mr. Harris came to the house one day just after school had let out. Of course, he knew Dad wouldn't be at home, that time of day. We were even luckier; Mother had gone shopping, and I was alone in the house.

I let him in and then just stood there, looking. He glanced at me with darting, greedy eyes. "Where's your mother, son?" he said in his usual hearty voice.

"She's gone downtown, Mr. Harris."

Before the words were out, his arms were around me. I held him close, raising my mouth for his kiss.

"All I've done is think about you, boy," he said, whispering the words harshly. "But I've got to be careful. Understand what I mean?"

"You don't have to be afraid now. Come on. Hurry."

Dragging him by the hand, I started upstairs. In my room, I closed the door and started to unbuckle my belt.

"Just take 'em down," he said in that harsh, needful voice.

I got into position across my narrow bed. With trembling hands he pulled down my underpants.

I heard his breath suck in at the naked sight of my buttocks. Standing half-crouched, he pegged himself, hard and certain, and began fucking with a quick, jerky movement, his hands gripping on my shoulders.

Just as it started to come into being between us, I heard the front door open and close. He heard it, too. He stood with bent knees, his cock thrust deep, and I could feel the trembling of his body.

"Tony Two," Mother called. "Are you home?"

I thought I would faint. Mr. Harris was as badly frightened as I was. But he began to fuck again, recklessly desperate to get the orgasm. I tried to help, knowing he couldn't quit if she came into the room. Even as we heard her footsteps on the stairs, he managed a skimpy come, jerked himself out, and began fumbling at his zipper. I jumped up, pulling up my pants, and she was at the door, saying, "Tony Two! Are you in there?"

"Yes, Mother," I said shakily.

Mr. Harris, turning wildly, grabbed my canoe paddle off the wall behind my bed. He was inspecting it with frenzied care when Mother opened the door.

"Why, hello there," he said jovially before she could open her mouth. "Tony was showing me his camp paddle." He held it out, admiring it. "Now, ain't that something?"

The camp I went to, when you passed a swimming test, got your first-aid certificate, or learned how to make a leather pincushion, they'd put it down on the paddle and you were supposed to bring it home and cherish it the rest of your life. Well, maybe I would; it had certainly saved us, because Mr. Harris was up Shit Creek in more ways than one. But he had the paddle.

163

Mother, in the doorway, looked at us rather curiously, I thought. *I guess we did look a little flustered, and strangely sweaty. Or maybe I only imagined it.*

"I came over to see old John," Mr. Harris said, *eyeing her archly. "Since he's not home, it'll give me a chance to talk to you."*

Mother unconsciously preened herself under the sexual glow of his regard. He was always flirting with her.

"You know John's still at the office, this time of day," she said in her best flirting voice.

"Well, to tell you the truth, I tried to call John about the poker game tonight, but I couldn't get any answer on his office phone. So I thought I just might catch him here."

"Can I give you a drink? He shouldn't be much longer. He said he'd be home early today."

"Delighted. You run right down and get it all ready. I'll put Tony Two's paddle back where it belongs and come right along."

Mother glanced at me. "Have you done your homework?"

"I was just fixing to get started," I mumbled.

Mother left. We listened to her all the way down the stairs. Mr. Harris let out an agonizing breath. "We can't risk that again, that's for sure," he whispered.

"Then how . . . " I said yearningly.

He thought for a minute. "Can you get downtown on Saturdays?"

"Yes," I said, whispering also. *"I think so. Most of the time."*

"I'll . . . be in the office Saturday afternoon. I can always make the excuse of work. Know where it is?"

164

"The Brill Building," I said.

He slid his arm around my shoulders, holding me hard for a quick second. "Then . . . you'll be there?"

"Yes," I said breathlessly. "Yes."

He went on downstairs, and I sat down to my homework. Then, remembering how he had been so arch and suggestive with Mother, I suddenly began to imagine him making love to her on the couch in the den where the bar was. Seeing him so vividly, doing to Mother what he had done to me, I was eaten alive by a flaming jealousy. I couldn't stand it, so I went downstairs, only to find them talking amiably over their drinks. But I stayed with them until Dad came home.

Mr. Harris and I went on together for a good while. But it wasn't ever what it had been those first two nights. In his office on Saturday afternoon, it was always one quick hump and then hustle me out of there. Indeed, instead of becoming more confident as time went on, he seemed more and more certain that his luck was running out and if he kept pushing it he'd be caught making love to a 14-year-old boy. He made a hundred promises about how we'd get away together sometime, each more frantic and sincere than the last.

But it never seemed to come off, and one Saturday afternoon, while I was waiting for the time to go up to his office, a man on the street gave me the eye. I had already learned to recognize my kind of people, you understand. Until today, I had ignored the secret signals; but now, on an impulse, I turned into a drugstore, pausing in the doorway for an instant to allow the attractive stranger an opportunity to see me.

I went to the magazine rack and began leafing

through the first random magazine I saw—a *Popular Mechanics*. In a couple of minutes, feeling him beside me, I knew he had taken the signal. His hand, slender and wan, reached out to pick up a magazine. I didn't look at him, he didn't look at me. But I don't need to tell you that I didn't go to Mr. Harris that afternoon.

In his beautiful apartment, for the first time I performed the part of the man as well as the part of the woman; and I learned that men could fuck face to face, instead of only in the position of animals. Brent was younger than Mr. Harris, thin and handsome, elegant in his dress, fastidious in his taste. He lived alone in an apartment which he had decorated with loving care. Brent much preferred being fucked to fucking, but since he was congenial about everything, we went on together for a decent length of time.

For weeks, I successfully managed to avoid Mr. Harris. Finally, one day, he cornered me in the den when Dad went down into the cellar to bring up more beer.

"Tony," Mr. Harris said, laying his hand pressingly on my arm. "Tony, I've missed you."

Muttering an evasive reply, I turned away; but not before I saw the tears in his eyes.

"Saturday?" he said hopelessly. "Saturday?"

I faced him squarely, remembering, not the good times, but how he had raped my waiting innocence. "I'm sorry, Mr. Harris," I said blandly. "My Saturdays are all taken up, these days."

He put a hand to his face, looked at the wetness on his fingertips. He opened his mouth to cry out against my unjustness. But already Dad's footsteps *were clumping up from below. Mr. Harris turned his back, going to the window to look out into the emptiness of the lawn. That was the end of Mr. Harris, and the beginning of the life I lived until I met Maria.*

By then, of course, I was confirmed in the gay life. I had had a dozen serious affairs, and no counting of the casual encounters. I had discovered that the love life of a homosexual is a constant repetition of the same hopeful theme, like a piece of music played over and over until the rhythm becomes engrained in the bone. And you learn to recognize the ending notes, too.

First the first meeting, the jockeying of gesture and innuendo until each other's needs and desires are revealed; then, for a while—a very brief while —the glow of fulfilled love, along with all the hopes of stability and permanence that every homosexual, I suppose, dreams of but rarely achieves. The moment a relationship is solidly established, it seems, each partner hastens to betrayal before he can himself be betrayed. Afterward come the bickerings, the jealousies, the frantic reunions and redeclarations of fidelity, leading to the destructive tearing at each other, when all the unforgivable words are spoken . . . until finally the bitter parting, leading to the next frantically sought encounter, to start the music again from the top.

There are, of course, the floaters, the prowlers, totally cynical about the processes of love among men, who seem to enjoy the constant change of partners. That was not me; I wanted love, constant and fulfilling. With each new lover, I assured myself that this time it would be different, and believed

167

it until the closing notes were sounding inexorably in my heart.

I had, of course, long since left home. The day after graduation from high school I had headed for Florida, seeking the sun and the good life. I was working as a lifeguard for a Miami Beach hotel when I met Maria. She wasn't staying at the hotel but had a small apartment nearby; she had made some sort of arrangement with the management to use their pool and beach. You can do that sort of thing with the kind of money Maria had. She probably owned the hotel, for all I knew.

I must say, I was reasonably happy. I took my regular turn on the stand, down on the beach or at the pool, but the rest of my time was my own. I was living with a very nice fellow, an older man named Roger who had promptly established our relationship on a very solid basis—money. Every Monday morning, just like the tooth fairy if you'll pardon the expression, I'd find one hundred dollars in bills under my pillow. He wasn't jealous-natured, either. If I disappeared for a day or two he never asked where I had been. There simply wasn't as much money the following Monday. I was satisfied with the arrangement. After all, there was a certain stability—and whatever permanance I might desire.

A lifeguard at a resort hotel is pestered by women, of course. I was still a virgin in that department and as far as I was concerned I meant to stay that way. I'd go out with one or another vacationing female, and even hustled a few come-on gifts of jewelry or clothes. I'm afraid I was a disappointment, though, for I treated them with the respect due a lady, which wasn't exactly what they were looking for.

Maria, I recognized from the beginning, was different. Within a week after first appearing on the scene, she always spoke to me in a direct, friendly manner. Then we got in the habit of having a drink in the bar after I was off duty. We seemed to be able to talk— never anything serious or profound, simply chitchat about people we knew, places we'd been, experiences we'd had.

Maria was my first friend. With people of my own sort, there was always the matter of sex. Escorting women, I had to act straight, even though I had no intention of going all the way, and that always made for a certain tension. Maria didn't seem to be involved with sex at all. She lived simply and quietly and completely alone. Only after several weeks of established association did she invite me to her apartment. It was a plain place, quite impersonal except for her books; the living room was crammed with books and records. Her only extravagance was an expensive hi-fi system on which she listened to every kind of music you can imagine, from rock-and-roll to Gregorian chants.

We had known each other for three or four months —which, in the transience of Miami Beach, practically constitutes a lifetime relationship—when Maria asked me to escort her to a concert. We had a great time and from then on, whenever she needed a male escort, she would ask me. Whenever I could make it, I did. I had never had such an undemanding, yet fulfilling, relationship with anyone, man or woman.

About that time, Roger went away. It happened in the same manner we had come together, with everything up front. One night he simply told me that, since he was leaving for Majorca for an indefinite stay, I ought to look around for another place to live. I was disturbed, at first, and asked if anything was the matter.

Smiling, he patted me on the bare shoulder. "We've been very good together, dear," he said. "I always believe in quitting while I'm ahead."

That was that. The real surprise came when I mentioned to Maria that I was looking for a place to live.

"Why don't you move in with me?" she suggested.

I gazed at her, sexual suspicion suddenly alive. Had it all been a quiet plan, and now the time had come to give it the old college try?

She must have read my mind. She smiled and said, "Tony, I know you don't care for women. But we're friends, aren't we? . . . and I do have that spare bedroom." She put her hand on my hand. "You'd actually be doing me a favor. It's not only that a woman living alone has her difficulties—I get pretty lonely sometimes, too."

I thought about it. In certain ways, it could make things difficult. It would be impossible, for instance, to bring someone home. On the other hand, how often, really, did I want to come to my own place? I hadn't been able to bring people to Roger's apartment, either. Also, I had become accustomed to living beyond my means; the prospect of an efficiency apartment commensurate with my working income was not pleasant to think about.

First, however, I had to find out how much she knew about me.

"How did you know?" I said.

She laughed. "Tony Two, any man, by now, would have had to make a pass, just to keep his male franchise." She became serious. "It's one of the things I like about you, Tony. We're good company for each

170

other because sex doesn't get in the way. I won't interfere, I promise."

A small suspicion remained in the back of my mind. "Well, we could try it for a week or two," I said cautiously. "While I look for a nice place I can afford."

The first night or two with Maria, I was pretty nervous. I lay awake for an hour after going to bed, expecting her to approach me in darkness. But pretty soon I had relaxed into our close companionship that demanded only that we be good friends.

The next phase began quite as innocently. One night I came in rather late, to find Maria reading and listening to music. Going into the kitchen, I prepared to scramble some eggs for a late supper. Once I had the eggs ready for the skillet, I glanced up, to see her standing in the kitchen doorway.

"Hungry?" I said. "I can break in a couple more eggs. No trouble at all."

"No," she said. She was still gazing at me. "Tony, why are you always so sad when you come home late?"

"Sad?" I said. "You're not insinuating that Tony Two is a down-in-the-mouth guy, are you?"

"Yes," she said. "Tony, don't you like your life?"

I picked up the bowl and poured the mixture of eggs and milk into the skillet. "If I didn't, I'd surely change it, wouldn't I?"

So intent on parrying her concern, I wasn't aware of her nearness until she touched me with her hand.

"Tony. What is it like?"

I dropped the spatula, grabbed it before it hit the floor. "What's what like?"

She drew away. "I know it's none of my business. But we are friends, aren't we?"

I was busy turning the bubbling mass of eggs. "Yes,"

171

I said. "Of course." In the back of my mind I was thinking that I should have known that sooner or later she'd make her move.

"I am hungry, after all," she said, sitting down at the table.

"Take these, then, before they get cold." I put the eggs on a plate and set it in front of her. I began breaking more eggs into the mixing bowl. She ate while I scrambled the fresh batch and sat down opposite her. Finished, she lit a cigarette.

"I'm just curious to know what it's like to . . ." she said, and then her voice hesitated.

I glanced at her. "What it's like to be a queer?" I said. "It's like any other human thing, good and bad all mixed up together."

She flushed. "I've never known anyone . . ."

I was staring resentfully. "What about your sex life?" I said. "I haven't seen enough of it to know what it is you go for."

She was avoiding my eyes. "Me? I don't have one." She tried to laugh, failed. "I was married once. Since then I . . ."

"Do you want me to take you to a butch bar?" I said. "Is that it?"

Her eyes came back to my face. "You're being cruel now. Deliberately cruel."

"You're pretty mean yourself," I responded. "I haven't interfered with your private life, have I?"

"Tony," she said then, "have you ever had a woman?"

"No," I said. "What's more, I don't want one, if that's what you're thinking." I stood up, wondering how long, starting in the morning, it would take to find a place of my own.

She looked up. "Tony, I can't stand it when you

172

come home night after night looking so used-up. Do you have to work so hard at being so bright and gay? Is it worth it?"

I looked away. "It isn't a matter of whether it's worth it or not. It's just the only game I drew chips in, that's all."

She stared at her hands lying palm up on the table. "Maybe it isn't your game, and that's why it's so hard on you. Have you considered that?"

My voice felt rough in my throat. "Maria, if you want to get laid, look somewhere else. I'm just your apartment mate. Understand what I mean?"

I stalked out of the kitchen and into my room. I shut the door, hard. I waited. I couldn't hear anything. Slowly I undressed, put on my pajamas, and got into bed. But I was still waiting, there in the darkness. I knew it was not finished by my abrupt departure from her presence. It had only begun.

I was all mixed up. Where in me had dwelled the cruel savagery I had used on her? . . . this lovely woman who was equally lovely inside, and so was a true friend. Of course, the fact of beauty, the fact of woman, didn't matter with me. Or did it? For the first time in my life, I suddenly found myself trying to imagine how it would be to make love to a woman.

I couldn't do it. There wasn't enough knowledge on which to build an act of the imagination. My entire impression of the deed consisted of a man sticking his foolhardy cock into a wet, hairy, warm hole that, equipped with all the mysterious mechanisms for grabbing the seed and making it into a baby, did strange writhing things to it. I had come out of exactly such a hole—could I desire passionately to entrust a cherished part of my cherished body to its

173

untender mercies? It was so vividly real, the very idea made me slightly sick to my stomach.

Switching gears to escape, I began remembering instead what I had experienced before coming home tonight. I had gone to a bar after work, where I had allowed a charming fellow, a tall blond Viking type, to pick me up. Strangers, we had wasted two or three hours in a sexual sparring match before finding out who liked what. In his garage apartment, a cheapy place with walls made of sheetrock, I fucked him and then he fucked me. My sole residual sensation of the encounter was the extraordinarily hungry look on his face as he stroked my muscles, and then the astonishment, and actual fear, when he saw the size of the cock I proposed to shove up his ass. But he loved it —he told me afterward that it was like his first time all over again.

But he knew, and I knew, that we would not see each other beyond tonight. That's the trouble, I thought sadly, lying in the darkness waiting for Maria. No matter how hard you try, you don't ever get a man. We all seek a marvelous masculinity; but the moment you have a person you know that he's no more a man than you are. If he was, he'd be with a woman, wouldn't he? . . . not with you.

Maria had wanted to know about the sadness. Well, there it was.

Even Mr. Harris. He had advertised his maleness with so much rough talk, the hunting, all the carefully masculine things. He had taken me like a real man takes a boy, rough and half-raping. I had felt myself truly fucked, and I had liked it. But the last time we had talked, Mr. Harris, with tears in his eyes, had shown himself to be only one more like me.

174

I look for the older ones, I told myself in the darkness, because the first one was older. I had always played the Greek myth of the mature man and the beautiful boy. It didn't work well any more, because I was not the boy I had been. I had acted out the role too many times with too many half-men. I had consented to accept their pretensions in fair exchange for my own.

But suppose—just suppose—a woman had started me instead of a man; a woman like Maria, mature, kindly in her heart, with an instinctive understanding. Yes. I felt it. There was in her an understanding that could take me by the hand and lead me out of these blind alleyways.

A light, firm tap sounded on the door.

"Come," I said.

Maria entered. "Tony," she said. "I was being very unfair to you. I'm sorry."

I spoke into the darkness. "You were only telling the truth. The truth always hurts, I guess."

I knew she was closer to me than on first entering. "I want to understand. I want to help—if I can help. And I could, if I could only understand." There was a pause. Then she said, "Tony, take me to a gay bar tomorrow night?"

I sat up in the bed. "Maria. You don't want to see what goes on in a place like that. You wouldn't find it . . . very pretty."

"You are my friend. I want to understand what life is like for my friend."

"Have you ever seen one man kiss another man?" I said harshly.

A paused silence, while the image I had given her swam through her mind.

175

"You see?" I said. "We pretend it's natural and normal and oh so much fun. But you don't want to see it, Maria. I don't want to show it to you."

Another silence. Then, very quietly, "All right, Tony. I guess you're right."

A sliver of light, from where she had opened the door, sliced across the room. Before it could disappear, I said, "Maria. Come get into bed."

She was a brave woman. I heard the rustle of her garments as they fell to the floor. In the next instant, she slid naked against me and put her arms around me. I began to cry.

I hadn't cried for so long I really didn't know how. But, because she held me, rocking patiently back and forth, I learned it all over again, letting out all the anguish in my soul while she crooned her comfort to replace it. Some long time after I was emptied of tears, I went to sleep with her still holding me.

When I woke the next morning, she was gone. I was grateful for her absence. I dressed slowly, fearful she was still in the apartment and I would have to face her in the daylight. I couldn't do it, I knew; she had come naked into my bed and the only part of her I had used was a shoulder to cry on like a little baby. I came as quietly as possible into the living room, poised to flee the apartment. I would find someone to send for my things.

She stuck her head out of the kitchen. "You've got 20 minutes to climb up on your stand down there at the beach and look gorgeous for all the panting ladies. Breakfast?"

There was no escape from her cheerful matter-of-factness. "It'll have to be fast," I said.

"Coffee and doughnuts, then. How does that strike you?"

I ate coffee and doughnuts and hurried to work. All during the long shift, I kept staring at the far reaches of the ocean, thinking about Maria. And about myself. I came straight home, only to find the apartment empty. Taking one of her books, I tried to read. I was too restless. Her books were too heavy for me at the best of times, all about psychology and territories and greylag geese and their aggressions and rituals. It didn't make any sense to me. When I heard her key in the lock at last, I was surprised at my anticipation.

She came in smiling, swinging an elegantly striped box from one hand. "A new dress," she said. "Terribly expensive. But terribly beautiful."

"Model it for me." On the infrequent occasions she bought new things, she liked to get my approval. Our tastes nearly always agreed.

"Not now. I want to do some talking first."

Something tightened inside of me. "Yes? What about?"

She sat down facing me, placing the dress box on the floor beside her chair. Her face was serious.

"Tony, I think we ought to get married."

I sat up straight. "Married?"

She nodded. "Are you game?"

I couldn't get around the astonishment. "Why would you want to marry me?"

"Because I think it's right—for both of us. I've got money, so you won't have to do anything—anything at all—that you don't want to do. Work or play. Do you understand?"

I looked away from her. "Fine for me. What about you?"

She waited until my eyes came back to her face. "I need a friend. I need a lover, if I could find the right

177

one. But more than anything else in the world, I need a friend."

I was staring now. "You know that I'm queer."

She moved her hand. "If you don't want to make love to me, you won't have to. But . . ." She paused, and for the first time I noticed how deep were her eyes. "But maybe, just maybe, you might learn to like the idea."

"You were in my bed last night. Nothing came close to happening, except me bawling like a baby. What kind of man is that for you?"

"You had a lot to get out of your system, Tony. It was exactly when you were able to cry that I knew we ought to try it. Marriage, I mean. Now—all you have to do is agree that we have good possibilities together."

"There ought to be something solider than possibilities," I said. "I can't see anything in it for you, any way you look at it."

She leaned forward tensely. "Can you be someone I can love?"

I rose, began to walk the room. The big jump off an undreamed-of cliff had its attractions, all right. Perhaps, with Maria in my bed, I could—I would—want her. Suddenly, with a terrible, deep yearning, I found myself wanting to want her. For the first time in my life, I had a chance to wipe out of my flesh and my soul all those half-men, Mr. Harris and Roger and the others like them, who had possessed my body.

I faced Maria. She was already standing, ready for the decision.

"You know what you may be letting yourself in for."

"I know," she said. "But do you know?"

I took a deep breath. "All right. I'll marry you."

178

We waited the three full days required by Florida law, continuing to live in the apartment as friends without once touching each other. But God, how we talked. Or—I talked. It was like a dam bursting. First, I told her all about Mr. Harris. Then, one by one, I went through the significant others, how I had loved them and hated them, had loved and hated myself. Maria only listened. But how she did listen, with love and affection and an increasing understanding, even when I only wept and could not find the words to tell how it had been with me.

The strangest thing of all, though, was the secret of the dress she had brought home that day. She had bought it to get married in . . . as though everything had been settled before the first word was spoken. It was a species of magic. I sought also a further magic, psyching inside myself a faith that the ritual of ceremony would make a man of me. I came to believe it. I truly did; and on our wedding night I went in to her.

There had been a candlelight supper, with wine and good talk. Just the two of us, for our witnesses had been strangers. After a long lingering at table, I went warm with wine to my room, where I undressed and put on my very nicest pajamas, all red and gold. Then, without knocking, I walked into her bedroom. But my legs were trembling.

She was standing, still clothed, before the full-length mirror. I wondered what she saw, in this moment. She looked at me over her shoulder, a swift alteration changing her face. She reached one hand behind her, struggling to lay hold of the zipper. I went to help, heard the faint burr of the metal teeth separating. I let the wedding dress fall about her feet. With practiced ease, she unhooked the wired

179

bra, letting me see her breasts. A chilling wind gusted through me. She was a woman. She wasn't built right. Not for my lust.

With a swift, stooping movement, she was out of her pants and stood naked, the gauzy fabric like a cobweb in her hand. With the objectivity of the uninterested, I had always counted her beautiful. All those woman-curves going the wrong way, the gross patch of thick black hair that showed nothing to take delight in: ugly. She was ugly.

Fleeing from my cruel eye, she lay down on the bed. "Take off your pajamas," she said. "Let me see you. Please."

I would not show her a useful cock, so I was ashamed to make myself naked. It would hurt her to know that the sight of her nakedness had destroyed whatever warmth of desire had been in me.

"Turn out the light," I said shakily.

Obediently she reached one arm, plunged the room into darkness. I took off the pajamas, feeling air strike cold against my flesh, and stumbled toward the bed. I walked into her groping hand; it touched my thigh, moved up, then inward to find my balls; at the last, with a feverish grasp, encircling my cock. She gasped, realizing its size, even though limp. I remembered suddenly how Mr. Harris had said that I would be God's gift to women, if only I weren't queer.

I remained still while her palm stroked warmly, concentrating fiercely on the fact that here in the darkness was a loving hand. Because I could no longer see the woman, I began to rise.

"Touch me," she whispered. "You'll have to touch me, too."

Sitting down on the side of the bed, I put my hand on her belly. It was softly curved where, to be provocative, it should have been washboarded with muscle. Taking a silent breath, I slid my hand over her hairy mount. Her hips moved up. I didn't dare adventure further; I had an acute awareness of the woman-hole beneath, demanding of me, devouring of me, with the dire threat of never letting go once I had fallen in.

"You can get in me now," she said "If you want to."

I didn't move. I wanted to—to try, at least. But I didn't know how to begin.

Her hand stroked steadily, building a worthy tool. "You have a beautiful cock," she said, whispering. "A cock like I've never felt before. I want it inside me, I want to feel it, I've never had one that big."

I could not respond, though I wanted to. Or—I wanted to want to. But I could only sit cold and far away, even as her hand was keeping my erection. At last she stopped talking, she took away her hand, she shifted over on the bed.

"All right, Tony. Just lie down. I'll do the rest."

I placed myself beside her. I was staring up into the darkness, when a blacker darkness loomed over me. It was Maria. In the next instant, her cunt gobbled at my cock in a stutter of hip movement, swallowing it up even as her weight oppressed me, and I could feel the scalding, acid juices eating at my tender flesh. I struggled, in a sudden frenzy, to escape my fate. She wouldn't let me go, she was stooped ravenously over my body, her hips were beginning to pound and her cunt was sucking my cock off at the roots. I remembered how I had tried to scream when Mr. Harris had violated me; only he had kept his hand hard on my mouth. Maria wasn't smothering my cries, so I could scream now, couldn't I?

181

Slowly, realizing my helplessness, I quit fighting her. She stopped then, breathing hard. "All right," she said. "Let yourself feel me now. Like I'm feeling your great big beautiful cock deeper than any man has ever gone. It's a good feeling, Tony. Don't deny that it's good."

I could sense her warmth, her love, her need. But she was too heavy, her flesh too loose and womanly, insisting on its femaleness with the eating warmth of her cunt. It was a hole too juicy, too greedy, Maria was a terrible female holding me captive to her juices.

"I can't . . . I can't breathe," I said.

Without answering my complaint, she eased her weight, leaning forward on her elbows. It brought her closer, too close, but she was being gentle now and I thought of how fond we were, how each liked the other as a companion, we were married, for God's sake. Soon there would be good talk as we lay side by side, finished with this terrible new experience. We would be together as in my barren life I had never been with anyone.

Despite all I could do in the way of conjuring magic, my erection ebbed away inch by inch, even as she ground her hips with artful energy, working to keep me on line. When I slipped out of her entirely, she let it all go into utter failure, coming down off me to lie huddled against my side. She was shaking all over; when I touched her cheek with my regretful fingertips, I found the wetness of tears.

"Not your fault, love," I said "I'm just not built that way. I tried to warn you."

"It is my fault," she said. "I just can't make you know how much I do love you."

"We can love each other without fucking, can't we?"

She moved beside me, coming closer. "But a man

and a woman . . . can't be together without it. So much of sex, really, is in the mind. If you could only get it fixed firmly . . . " She was turning. Her voice came as though from far away. "Take me, Tony, like you'd take a man."

A sudden thrill shot through me. Putting forth a hand, I discovered that she was on her stomach, ready. I found her buttock. It moved softly under the thrust of my palm. But it was something I knew, wasn't it?

"I'm awfully big, Maria," I whispered.

"It'll just hurt the first time, won't it?" she said. "You told me that, remember?"

I drew away. "You're a virgin there? I've never taken a cherry. I don't intend to start with you."

"If you can love me like that, then love me like that. We've got to make something tonight."

I had already realized, with shame and glee, that the proximity of her ass had laid an enormous erection on my cock. The aroused need pulled me suddenly on top, my knees inside her knees, and her buttocks were rising. I liked the feel as I clasped her into the curve of my body. I would be Mr. Harris, raping a willing victim. I fitted my cock into my hand, aiming it—but, at the last second, something, perhaps another Tony Two entirely, suffered in advance her outrage of scream and sweat. With an intense love, I aimed my terrible erection for the other place.

She gasped with a delighted surprise as I slid up tight into her cunt. She began a joyful paean to my flesh in a marvelously intricate writhing of her whole lower body and, because her buttocks were snug against my thighs, I could take her and keep on taking her, reaping one spontaneous orgasm after

183

another out of the rich harvest of her ready flesh.

I did not come. She was too loose, too wet, it was not close enough to home. But when she reached a stopping place she turned under me, bringing her frontside up, the juicy cunt swallowing anew my erect cock. There was a second of fading on my part; but she reached around my hip and found my anus with her finger.

"Fuck me now," she said. "Fuck me, goddamn it."

With the words, her finger drove against the sphincter, sweetly piercing, and I began to come. I came mightily, again and again and then again, until I had collapsed, finished and empty, in her stroking arms.

The remaining hours of our wedding night were quiet ones. We had broken too many barriers, had spent too much emotion, to dare ourselves further. We lay side by side, our bodies casually touching, smoking cigarettes in the darkness and talking like the good companions we were.

Only once did she approach the questions that had been raised.

"Why didn't you take me . . . there where I said?"

"I didn't want to hurt you."

"Why didn't you want to hurt me?"

"Because I love you."

"Oh, Tony," she said, and turned to snuggle tightly against my body. For the first time, I laid my mouth on her soft mouth and kissed her soulfully.

So we began to learn how to live together sexually. My major struggle was against the deep fear of her vagina. Getting into her was like plunging into a great, hungry mouth. I could manage it only from the rear, her buttocks snug and warm in my lap

184

while I held tightly to the envisioned possibility of
her anus. At that, only her finger masturbating my
anus could bring the sperm boiling out of me into
the greedy maw of her cunt.

So many taboos, circumscribing severely our hard-
held territory of love. I would not, could not, touch
her clitoris with my tongue. When I tried to force
myself, I would have to hurry into the bathroom to
rid myself of the overpowering scent of her pussy.
On the other hand, I never once consented to violate
her ass, though she often urged me to avail myself
of its desirability. Maria owned to her own repres-
sions; she could not go down on me, either. When
she thought of doing so, she confessed, the image of
the men who had preceded her in the act came
too vividly to mind.

All these barriers . . . yet we had love, we had
companionship, in us dwelled an undying hope that
we could win through to a complete trust of the flesh.
We had one thing, at least, going for us; for the first
time in my life, I desired to be a real man, instead
of only desiring to make love to one. That, alone,
was worth the travail.

Too soon, however, another danger loomed on our
horizon—a peril that I could not seem to make Maria
see. She began to be obsessed with the need for a
deeper understanding of my nature. She approached
the topic in a hundred different ways.

"I can't imagine how it must feel when a man
fucks you that way," she might say.

"I guess it can't be explained, not really," I re-
plied, hoping to turn her aside.

"Do you have orgasms?"

"Yes," I said uncomfortably.

185

"Like the orgasms you have with me?"

"Not exactly. In fact, it's completely different. I don't want to talk about it, love."

But she would persist. "Different? In what way?"

"It seems to last longer, spreads deeper and wider. It . . . Please, Maria."

"Then it's a woman's orgasm, is that it? Like when I come with you in me?"

"I don't know how a woman feels. So I can't say."

She would brood, then, while I waited, hoping that the subject was finished. And so it would be, for a time, until she came back to it, as she did over and over again. Until one night she said:

"Tony. Fuck me like that. I've got to know."

I shook my head. "That's been decided since the very beginning. No."

This time, though, she wouldn't let go, persisting in her devious pleading until she had opened a rift of tension and distrust in our love. I could not tell her that I was deathly afraid of liking it too much, causing me, in spite of the best will in the world, to lose my precarious hold on the ability and desire to fuck her normally. I knew, as surely as tomorrow, that such desertion would bring us, sooner than later, to a parting of the ways. Maria, though a woman who had dared to marry a homosexual, needed, and would eventually demand, a cock in the fore-ordained place at reasonable intervals.

She would not give it up. "It won't be the same," I told her time and again. "A woman can't feel like a man, no matter how hard she tries."

"But you don't have the right to deny me. We need all the ways of coming closer together. And this one . . . I can learn something of what you feel, and so . . .

186

I had just fucked her in our fashion and was lying back enjoying a cigarette, feeling smugly that it had come off particularly well. The smugness began to turn into irritation.

"Will you please shut up about it?" I said. "If you can't, I'll go to my old room."

She got out of bed. I thought she was angry. But she only went into the bathroom and returned, holding a jar of Vaseline in her hand.

"I bought this today. If you use it, it won't hurt at all, I'm sure."

"Maria. Please!"

She was staring down. "You've already got a hard-on, just thinking about it. You want it worse than I do."

I could not deny it. "All right," I said. "If I do it, will you suck me off?"

She did not hesitate. "Anything. If it's got to be a swap-out, I'll do anything you want."

Somehow, that harsh statement liberated me into violence. With abrupt hands, I pulled her down on the bed and flipped her onto her belly. Straddling her, I smeared Vaseline on the head of my cock, dabbed a handful against her anus, and leaned against her. I was being Mr. Harris all over again, she was the young me, and when I ripped into her, hearing her cry out, I laughed and plunged ever more ruthlessly. And God forgive me, I raped her, I didn't care for the pain, I gloried in her sweating and squirming, and after I had come, deep in her ass, I regarded with pride the ring of blood around the base of my cock.

She was utterly collapsed, her face hidden. I stared at her shoulder blades. "Now you know," I said bitterly. "Now you know, don't you?"

187

She did not move. She was defeated, beaten, completely conquered. The Maria that I had loved had been whipped out of her by my violence. Strangely enough, I felt more a man, in that moment before she spoke the words that destroyed me, than I had ever felt.

She moved, and I let her get out from under me. She sat on the side of the bed, her face in her hands.

"It's so damned unnatural, Tony," she said softly. "It scares me to the bone. I couldn't have believed it was that perverse to all human nature."

I remembered, against my will, that she was older than I was. The men had always been older. Her words, showing me that unwanted wisdom, tore up something inside me that has never been repaired.

Getting up off the bed, I put on my street clothes. I left her flattened and used amid the sweated, blooded sheets. I took my time, knowing she would not chase after me. On my way out, I stole the money in her purse. It was nearly five hundred dollars.

That same night, I bought five willing half-men for fifty dollars a head. In a fancy motel room, they fucked me one after the other, five times worth, until I was ruined and collapsed and finished forever. There toward the end, it became painful. That was what I wanted; I wished it never again to be passionately fulfilling to be fucked in the ass. But, of course, it nearly always is.

I did not return to Maria. The thought never crossed my mind. I went on my merry way alone through the world I knew so well, that I hated so awfully.

Chapter 6

It was very late when Tony Two had finished telling his story. No one, it seemed, was ready to call it a night; there was a pervasive feeling that somehow the tale remained unfinished. Tony Two had started telling it in sadness and self-pity, progressing successively through a self-bravery, a defiant brightness, a dry, serious quietness. At the end, when he had moved to sit before Maria, leaning against her knees, he had come to a complicated amalgam of boyish bashfulness and adult bitterness, with trace elements of irony and self-knowledge. I, for one, could not begin to sort it out properly.

Maria, at least, arrived immediately at the kernel of his meaning. Her hands cupped over his bare shoulders, her eyes bright with unshed tears, she said, "I failed you so badly, Tony. So badly."

He twisted around to look into her face. "Failed me?" he said. "I had all the equipment necessary to become a man, including the desire. And God knows I had the opportunity if anybody ever did. The spirit wasn't there, that's all. So how can you count it your fault?"

"I became so fascinated with perversity. I forgot completely that I had contracted to make you know the sufficiency of straight sex, when it's combined with

189

love. I made you take me your way instead of leading you into mine."

Tony looked at me, at Casey. "A real man likes everything there is to like about a woman . . . the smell of her pussy, the taste of it, the way it swallows him whole when he goes into her. He yearns for it, he doesn't fight it like I did." Sadly, he shook his head. "I was caught too young. So I didn't have a chance, did I, really? At least, I can always make that excuse. But if it hadn't been my right road, I wouldn't have stayed on it, would I?"

Maria moved her hands soothingly on his broad, muscled shoulders. "That's not important. Not any longer. It's how you feel about it now. We've all got a better chance, here together on No-Name Key, than we've ever had. So tell us how you feel about it tonight."

His eyes were troubled. "Just like the other time—I want to *want* to make love to you. Not simply to a female . . . to *you*." He took a deep breath. "I kept thinking about it last night. Even my dreams were about you coming naked into my bed, like you did that time before we got married." His eyes had gone away from us, gazing into the lighted pool. I watched rippling reflections of its gentle movement washing over his face. "But at the same time, I've been hot as hell for Casey to fuck me."

I glanced toward Casey. His face was a study in contrasts. He was so wholesome looking, so out-of-doors American, with his rugged features, his weather-beaten skin, the wiry horseman's body.

"But of course I won't get him, will I?" Tony Two said quietly. "All I can do is watch him climb Maria, get my kicks that way."

Casey continued to gaze at Tony in such a way

190

it moved a revulsion inside me. If Tony Two, as he had once taken Maria by the sheer power of his perversion, should take Us in his quirky direction . . . but surely this was not what Maria intended.

"Why do you need to change, Tony?" Casey said. "Hell, everything is possible for everybody; we all know that. I'll fuck anything with a hole in it . . . anything for mutual pleasure. The only difference between you and me is the matter of personal experience."

I would have to disagree. Quickly, before it was too late. With all the compassion, the understanding, that I now felt for Tony Two, the possibility did not exist that I could make love to his beautiful body. He might feel himself female, receptive, passive . . . but I was aware of the great instrument nature had given him.

"I suppose what you say is true, speaking physically," I said. "But love, sex, is so much a matter of the mind and of the soul that the body alone cannot rule."

"That's where we've all failed, isn't it?" Maria was looking at me, and I was warmed by her immediate understanding. But then she went beyond me. "Where we are still failing. Because there remains the truth that only Tony Two, of the three men on this island, has laid his story on the line."

I did not flinch. "I was ready. You know I was ready, Maria."

"Why does Tony have to change, that's what I'd like to know," Casey said in his persistent voice. "We aren't trying to make new people here, are we? Only digging out the real people hidden inside all our lying dodges."

Tony looked at him. "Because there's no real satisfaction in it," he said. "It's like I told you. When I get a man, there must be something too much like me in him."

Their gazes were locked. "Are you telling me that if I shoved it up your ass, I'd turn queer?" Casey said. "Don't believe it, Tony boy. I might go some roundabout roads. But I know where it's at, at all times."

"We're forgetting something," Maria said. "Making love—truly making love—is not an exercise in self-satisfaction. You seek to fulfill the person you have come to love. I couldn't get it across to Tony, somehow, that when he fucked me it was for my pleasure, not for his. And vice versa."

Tony Two's eyes became bright and seeing. It was himself that he saw. "I've never thought about it that way. I . . ." He paused, his face showing the disturbance of a newly acquired thought. "I guess maybe that's what's wrong with homosexuality. There's so much self-love to it, so much narci . . . narci . . ."

"Narcissism," I said.

He looked at me. "Yes," he said. "Looking into your lover, you want to see yourself—as though he were nothing more than a mirror. Yes. I've sought out mirrors all my life. I have been made into a mirror for others. Yes."

"You haven't made me understand yet why you want to quit," Casey said stubbornly.

Tony turned to him. "Because every day you keep getting older, if you want to know," he said angrily. "The kind of love we've got is for the young. The ugliest sight I can imagine is an old queen." He subsided, his mouth trembling. "I'm nearly thirty," he said in a low voice. "I've been around too many blocks too many times. When I walk into a gay bar, I can see all their cold eyes, like adding machines counting up the years."

"Good God!" Casey said softly. "Good God Almighty!"

Tony's head was bowed. "I don't know why I can say it tonight, say it all." He was breathing hard. "Even when I was young, I kept thinking, every time, how to make it last. But how can it last? . . . you look into the other person and see only yourself. While he seeks himself in you. And every year that passes you see yourself that much older. A fellow can't keep on bearing it, because he knows, more surely every day, that time will defeat him in the end."

"It's hate, then, not love." It was I who spoke into the poignant silence. "Self-hate. That's what you keep seeing in the mirror of your lust."

Tony glared. "And what do you look for in your lust for the body of a woman, wise man? Tell me that."

I stood up. "I'm not seeking my like," I said. "She is, at least, my natural opposite."

"Wait a minute," Maria said. "Let me think."

We fell silent. Maria sat on the edge of the lounge chair, her knees pressed against Tony Two's back, her hands on his shoulders. Her eyes, watching the turned-away curve of his cheek, were deep and perplexed, yet brilliant with something I couldn't recognize. Or didn't want to.

"Let's go back to first things." Her voice was so near to a whisper that we had to strain to hear. "Talking only confuses what we're trying to talk about, wraps it up in so many words that mean so many different things to each one of us."

She sat silent again for what seemed an interminable period. Beginning to feel restless, I got up and went to the bar for a fresh drink. There was the taste of stale tobacco in my mouth from all the cigarettes I had smoked. Outside, I thought, the beach stretches clean and empty, and in the early morning the sanderlings will run to and fro. No-Name Key will keep ever in its old way, while we . . .

I was afraid to know where Maria would take Us now. Not for Us—for myself. How deeply could Jerry Dorn meld himself into the three and the one? It was no longer whether I wanted to merge my individuality, only how far I could make myself go.

Maria, rising, took the long padded cushion from the lounge chair and placed it on the tiled floor. I turned to watch. Fussily, like an overly neat housewife, she shifted it about until she was satisfied.

"Tony," she said, "lie down."

Tony, without a word, obeyed. I walked over to join Casey and Maria. Stretched naked on his back, he was beautiful: the wide shoulders, the muscles sloping smoothly down into his waist, the muscular round of his thighs. I had to admit, in my secret soul, an envious regard for the great cock that, even as I gazed, lifted its head alertly.

Maria, her head down, her face shadowed by the long hair, was kneeling beside him. "You're going to fuck me now," she said with a soft urgency. "Not because you need me. Because I need you. Will you let me have your lovely prick, Tony? Please?"

He turned his head away. "If I can," he said. "I will, if I can."

She put out her hand, fingers curling to embrace his cock. "It's Us, Tony. Male and female. Us."

Uncertainty crept into his face. "I can't feel it, Maria. I . . ."

Maria lifted her head. "Casey. Put your hand on him. You too, Jerry."

Casey, understanding more quickly than I, dropped to his knees and cupped his hand into Tony's scrotum.

"Jerry?" Maria said, glancing up.

"I . . ." I said. My voice strangled in my throat, stopping the denial.

Her reply was quick, harsh, impatient. "Then go away. Just go away!"

I had thought it would take courage to deny my role in Us. Instead, I discovered, I was not brave enough to abandon them to limitation. A moral coward, I kneeled into the group. Maria, taking my hand, grasped my reluctant fingers around the stem of Tony's prick.

It was strange to touch another man. I could feel it beginning to throb into an erectness. The harshness of his body hair scraped against the heel of my fist, harsh and soft. Sharing so intimately the erection that was coming into his flesh, I was getting a hard-on. When Maria bent her head, it was as though her mouth was on me, too. Tensely, I looked at Casey. He was ready also, the instrument up and ready between his crouched thighs.

Maria raised her head. "Tony," she said, the words, her voice, hypnotically repetitive. "It's Us now, remember. All the male, all the female, loving you. Needing you. Wanting you. It's Us that'll do the fucking." It had become a seductive, rhythmic crooning. "When your cock goes into my cunt, it'll be Jerry and Casey and me and you. So get up and do it now, for all of us. Do it."

I think a dead man would have risen to the call. Tony came to his feet in one swift movement. We were kneeling before him, obeisant to the kingly cock enthroned between his rippling thighs. Maria, in a long flow of body movement, took his vacated place, rolling onto her back, her legs, her arms, lifting.

"Put it where it belongs, Tony," she cried out. "Put it there NOW!"

He started down into her as though diving head-deep into her flesh. Just at the final commitment, he wavered between desire and revulsion. It was, we knew, the old fear of the birth hole. Simultaneously, Casey and I put the flat of our hands to his naked buttocks and pushed. I heard the sigh gusting out of Maria as his cock penetrated her vagina.

Tony, sunk to the depths, lay without movement, breathing hard. Casey, straddling his buttocks, began to make fucking motions, as though demonstrating a skill to a laggard child. Tony Two began to move with him and somehow it was both of them fucking Maria through the singleton agency of Tony's great tool.

Maria, taking them both into the upward-reaching grip of her legs, began to rock with the combined thrust. Not to be left out, I took my cock in one hand and laid the other on Casey's back, where I could feel his strong surge of muscle. It brought me into the fucking of Maria; somehow I had in my cock the sensations of her rippling cunt. I even knew when she began to come.

Casey drew away, allowing Tony to continue alone, and stood with me over the fucking animal at our feet; all animal now, yet human too, so human, for Tony, caught by her come, was ejaculating in one pounding surge after another, his buttocks rippling and tightening as he drove the semen deep into her receiving flesh.

Finished.

Immediately, Maria came out from under Tony, leaving him flat on the mat, and cried out, "Take him now, Casey. You've been wanting to. So go ahead and take him," and Casey was crouched over Tony, cock in hand, a grimace of desire and determination showing on his face. Tony received Casey with a voluptuous slow-motion presentation of his ass. I didn't see any more, for Maria was ready for me now, saying, "Come on, let's don't just stand here watching. Let's fuck."

She was down on her back and I was kneeling between her opened thighs, gazing avidly upon the pussy that would now be mine. Impatiently she encircled my waist with her legs, drawing me strongly into her, and I could feel the wetness of Tony's come, soaking her so warm and ready that she was immediately into orgasm. I did not allow her to take me along for the first, or even for the second. But when I hear the hungry moaning of her third, mingled with the equal sound of Tony and Casey getting theirs, I let it all go in one complete and utter surrender of my banked puissance.

Casey was the first to get to his feet. "I always said I'd fuck anything with a hole in it," he said shakily. "I reckon I proved it tonight." He began to laugh.

Maria, turning on her side, laid her hand on the nape of Tony's neck. "See, Tony?" she said. "You see now?"

He was lying with his face hidden in the curve of his arm. He shifted closer to Maria and reached down to lay his hand on her mount. Maria, smiling, looked up at me.

"That's Us, Jerry," she said. "We're kind of wonderful, aren't we?"

"Wonderful isn't the word for it," I told her.

She sat up, holding out both hands. Casey and I pulled her to her feet. "I guess everybody could use a drink," she said. "Or, better, a cup of coffee?"

I wanted coffee. So did the others, so we trooped into the kitchen, where Maria made it while we busied ourselves preparing a tray. When we were ensconced comfortably beside the pool again, cups in our hands, we were truly together for the first time.

When Maria asked for my story, I did not hesitate to begin.

"I'm afraid it's not as spectacular as Tony's," I said in preamble. "In fact, sex didn't really mean much to me, even though I was nearly 30, until Maria came along. I had an episode when I was ten—though it was mostly the girl's idea, with me just going along for the ride. I took a break then, to think it over I guess, until I was 16. The back seat of a car that time, with a classmate I had grown up with, so you know what that was like—a wriggle and a squirm, then going off into a condom and thinking it was the greatest invention since Chinese firecrackers. That was followed by three college adventures, one after the other, none of which amounted to anything. About as conventional as anyone could possibly imagine." I smiled, taking a deep breath. "That was the vast experience and deep sexual wisdom I brought to you, Maria."

I began to tell them about me and Maria, in a depth

of detail that held nothing back. When I had finished, Maria said thoughtfully. "So that was it."

She seemed to shake herself, settling into a new mode. "Remember how Tony talked about mirrors? I was making a mirror out of you, Jerry, in which to look for George all over again. When you kept getting in the way, I used the truck driver for the same purpose—as well as against you, in a double kind of using." She shuddered. "My judgment was way off by that time. He was about as far from George as it's possible to be. Or maybe not." She frowned. "Maybe George was the other side of him, the hidden part he didn't like to show."

"Maria," I said. "Come here."

She came to me. I pulled her down into my lap, holding her close, feeling her warmth.

"Maria, I simply didn't know," I said slowly. "Do you understand what I'm telling you?"

She put her hand to my face. "I think so."

"Not just that I didn't know you. I didn't know myself, either. But even if I had—there wasn't enough of me, Maria. Not nearly enough."

"Maybe no man is enough for any woman," Casey said. "Have you thought about that?"

Maria looked at him. "That's not how love is supposed to be, Casey. One woman is supposed to love one man, forever and always. That man is supposed to love that woman. That's the way it's always been told to us, anyway."

Casey shook his head. "This is something I've thought about. A man is a pretty straightforward mechanism, when you get right down to it. His sex is a simple pipe of flesh that, under particular circumstances, will pump a portion of fluid. Once that happens, a man is over and done with—for an hour, a day, a week, all depending on the man. But a woman . . ." He shrugged. "Living up there on the ranch by myself most of the time, I've devoted a lot of thought to women in general. The truth about a woman is, she doesn't have to do, but *be*. So sex isn't a straightforward act for her, but a linked series of states of being. And never twice are those states the same."

I had pegged Casey as a simple-natured cowboy, a concatenation of muscle capable of exploding occasionally into a violence of feeling and action. But he sat among us now, speaking slowly and thoughtfully—and coming closer to the grain of the meaning of Us than anyone had yet succeeded in doing. We are all so much more complex than we will allow the world to see, I thought. Grasping the thought, I spoke it aloud.

Casey's reply was dry, deprecatory. "Complex? Let a fellow spend enough time by himself, no telling what ideas will come into his head. Your trouble, Jerry, you've spent a lot of time in solitary—but not alone, like I have, because your head is always populated by the people you're writing about." He chuckled. "Empty your skull, man, before you start to think. It'll help to spend some long winters in Nevada, too."

How eagerly he had taken Tony Two, I thought. There had been in him no sense of shame, no loss of manhood. As intensely curious about him as I had become, I couldn't help saying, "Maybe it's time you told Us your story."

"Yes," Maria said eagerly. "We've all talked now, except Casey."

Casey yawned, stretched, stood up. "Too late to

start tonight. I don't know about you fellows, but I'm dead sleepy." He looked toward the Gulf. "In case you haven't noticed, daylight's coming."

We were startled by the announcement; yet, on the other hand, it seemed that the evening had started so long ago, far away on the other side of so much history of Us, that it was like remembering back into the depths of a childhood.

Maria, sighing as though reluctant to let go of the night, stood up. She went to Tony Two, kissed him. I was next, then Casey.

"Goodnight, fellows. It's been . . . marvelous tonight, hasn't it?"

"Especially for me," Tony Two said, a throb in his voice.

We went together up the stairs, and kissed again before parting. I don't know about the others, but I was asleep in five minutes.

When I came awake, I was disoriented in time and space. Stumbling to the window, I realized anew the place-fact of No-Name Key. As for time, a sunset was in glorious progress. I was astonished. I couldn't remember when I had last slept a full day.

The servants would have come and gone, so I didn't bother about clothes before going into the corridor. I tapped on Casey's door, but got no answer. When I swung it open, to verify his absence, he sat up in bed. "What time is it?"

"Sundown," I said. "Have you been asleep all day, too?"

He ran one hand through his rumpled hair. "Must have." He yawned. "God, I'm hungry."

"I'm going down," I said.

"What about Tony Two? Is he up and around?"

"I'll check."

I repeated the process of knocking on Tony's door, then opening it. Tony Two was sitting in a chair beside the window. Here on the east side, he was getting only the reflection, in filmy clouds, of the sunset.

"There you are," Tony said.

"Been up long?"

"About an hour. I went downstairs, but no one was about."

"Casey is just getting up. Let's go down."

Tony rose with his quick, athletic grace. "What about Maria?"

"I haven't seen her. If she's still in bed, we'll let her sleep as long as she wants. All right?"

We went downstairs together. In the dining room, I inspected the steam table. It was laid ready for dinner. Casey joined us, lifting a lid or two.

"I'm interested in eggs," he said. "How about you fellows?"

The moment eggs were mentioned, my stomach craved them. Casey grinned. "I'm a pretty good ranch cook," he said. "Come on."

We followed Casey into the kitchen. Opening the refrigerator, he found a carton of eggs and, after further search, a package of bacon.

"Jerry, how are you on coffee?" he said. "Tony, you can look after the toast. Think a dozen of these eggs, scrambled, will fill the hollow places?"

Following Casey's directions, we busied ourselves. Soon the kitchen was redolent with the crisp smells of frying bacon, perking coffee, toasting bread. Casey, dishing the scrambled eggs onto a platter, said, "What about Maria? Shouldn't we wake her up for breakfast?" Hearing a sound, we turned simultaneously. Maria stood in the doorway, utterly shocking in her appearance. She was wearing a dress.

Such a short time ago, we had been less startled when she had come among us unclothed. I think she realized the irony of our reaction; she was grinning shamelessly at our nakedness.

"My God," Tony Two said apprehensively. "Are the servants still here?"

We were all gazing in rapt fascination. She was so lovely in the white frock; the fabric flowed softly over her dark-toned skin, bringing out the brilliance of her eyes, the temptation of her warm red mouth.

Maria laughed. "Sorry, fellows, but it's that time of month again. How are you at bridge, by the way?"

"I suddenly feel very naked," I said. "Can you hold breakfast, Casey, while I run upstairs and slip into something a bit more comfortable?"

"Please don't get dressed," Maria pleaded. "I love the sight of naked men. You can let a girl windowshop for the future, can't you?"

We laughed with her. But, by a vote of three-to-one, we overruled her. If she was to be dressed, we would be dressed also. While she carried the tray to the poolside, we trooped upstairs and returned decently clothed for our communal breakfast.

Incredible as it might seem after last night's shared sexuality, we segued successfully into a new, decorous phase of Us. We played cards and drank bloody marys—in honor of Maria's condition, Tony Two solemnly declared—and went to bed early to catch up on the sleep we still felt we had lost somewhere in the middle of yesterday. As a consequence, we were up early, next day, and for the first time went swimming in the Gulf.

The day after, we three men went tarpon-fishing —though Tony, devoting himself to renewing his suntan, refused an active part. The old Cajun took the boat into the mouth of a mangrove bay that led deep into the Everglades, ocean merging almost imperceptibly with swamp, a green bank of life that began with mangrove and turned gradually to cypress and a proliferation of lesser growth I did not recognize. We trolled for three hours before Casey took the first strike. He fought the fish with the determination of a bulldogger. John Kershaw handled the boat skillfully, keeping it in neutral most of the time, letting the big fish pull it all over the inlet, but shifting into reverse when Casey's reserve of line was reduced to the backing.

The big fish, mailed in its large silvery scales, lay at last alongside. "He's beautiful, Casey," I said. "A great fish. It took you exactly an hour and ten minutes to land him."

John Kershaw reached with the gaff, but Casey, lifting a hand, stayed him. "He fought hard, all right. So let's don't kill him."

The old Cajun, without a word, laid aside the gaff and knelt to remove the fist-sized lure from the tarpon's jaw. As he worked patiently, trying not to tear the mouth, Casey was kneeling beside him, paddling water with his hands through the fish's gills. They both stood up, leaving the fish free. For several minutes he remained alongside, his tail waving feebly, before he moved away.

Casey, after the tarpon had disappeared in a final swirl, turned to me almost apologetically. "You don't have to kill them, you know, unless you want a trophy. It's not as though they're any good to eat."

In this moment, I liked Casey better than I ever had. He had shown, beneath the violence of his nature, a substratum of feeling and respect for other lives, even that of a fish. Of course, the feeling could not be spoken; it would only have embarrassed both of us. But it was deeply felt, and simply understood, as we went deeper into the tangle of mangrove islands to fish for snook with light spinning rods.

For five days we lived in a hiatus of time and being It was as though this period of calm had been ordained by nature—as, indeed, it had been ordained by the female nature of Maria's body. All the agitations of simultaneous desire and repression, of anguish and self-consciousness, had ebbed away. It had become completely natural to be clothed or unclothed, depending on our activities, whether playing bridge or skinny-dipping in the surf.

With the temporary abandonment of communal sex, we had also, by tacit consent, abandoned the discussions. When we talked, it was of matters light and easy, such conversation somehow bringing us closer in friendship and understanding. By moving away from the insistent pressure of sex, we discovered that we could enjoy each other's company in game and skill and good talk.

The first phase of Us had come to an end. We realized it, in our individual selves, yet we remained serene, confident. There was no frantic sense of loss; understanding that further adventures of the body and of the mind waited in the near future, we were content to abide the good time.

The fifth night of the hiatus, I remember, I said quietly to Maria, "Are you happy? Is this what you wanted?"

Her face glowed with her reply. Her answer in words was not needed. "I've never been happier, Jerry. Never. I am . . . *right* . . . for the first time in my life. I am cherished."

I had to think about the word she had used.

205

Cherished. A word, a meaning, that had been dropped out of the language of love so long ago it now existed only in the ceremony of marriage, not in the manual of endearments.

"What about you, Jerry? Maria said. "You and Casey and Tony Two?"

My answer was not ready, in so many words. Tony Two filled the gap.

"It's so wonderful to be here, I can't think of going away."

Going away. I had, perhaps, been deliberately avoiding the thought of departure. Yet it would come. It would have to come.

"Jerry?" Maria's voice was softly insistent.

We were stitting so close, enjoying a nightcap before retiring, that I could have touched them all with one full-length sweep of my arm. "If you had told me that I would share a woman I loved with two other men, I wouldn't have believed it," I said slowly. "Except—it isn't a sharing, is it? It's realer, deeper."

"Thank you, Jerry," Maria said. Coming to me, she laid a sweet kiss on my mouth. "You were the farthest away, there at the beginning. But now, I don't know why, you're the closest to the core of Us."

I looked at the others. They were smiling, watching Maria with me. And it was true; I was no longer alone, I had both friends and lovers. Achieved only, I realized, by the communality of our sexual opportunities.

Maria, going to Casey, put a solicitous hand to his shoulder. "What about you, Casey?"

He looked up, a tight smile showing. "The only time I've been able to like other men was riding winter line with a buddy, or going on a week's hunting trip up in the mountains. Times when no women were around. Have you quit being a woman, Maria?"

She smiled, laying a finger tenderly on his lips. She seemed to understand precisely what he had told her. "Of course," she said. "I'm just a fellow now, like everybody else on No-Name Key. Except I can feel like a woman any time I want to." Her hand tightened on his shoulder. "Tomorrow night . . . I intend to be the woman of the world." Her brilliant eyes swept to include me and Tony Two. "Tomorrow night we can fuck again. And I'm ready."

She walked away, going to the tall French doors without looking back. We watched her disappear, then looked at each other. The same thought lived in our minds.

Chapter 7

We began the first night of the new phase in this way:

Maria said, "Before anything else, Casey must tell Us his story."

We looked at Casey. Casey was looking at Maria. "Are you sure you want to hear it?"

Her eyes were locked into his. "Yes," she said. Her voice was steady.

His eyes did not veer away. "Then the first thing I have to tell you is this; you're not the best fuck I've ever had."

CASEY'S TALE

I didn't have a woman until I was 20 years old. Not that I was so laggard, though I was raised on a box-canyon ranch—the same place I'm working now—40 miles from town. I didn't need a woman.

The year I turned 14, my daddy gave me, all my own, a palomino filly to break and ride. The prettiest little thing you ever saw, but wild as a buck. She had been sired in the brush by a big old palomino stallion that kept a band of mares up there above us in the mountains. Because they used a spring a few miles from the house, we'd catch sight of the band once in a while. My daddy never bothered them until he rode out one day with the hired hand to help him and caught that little filly for me.

When I saw her, for the first time in her life she was wearing a seagrass halter and she looked like she'd kill a fellow, given half a chance. I went wild right there on the spot; there had been horses around all my life, but I hadn't ever owned my own mount.

"There's just one thing," Daddy told me, grinning at my excitement. "You'll have to break her yourself. Nobody else will lay a hand on her."

Easier said than done. Though I spent every minute I could spare from the ranch work, and going to school, it was a week before she would let me touch her. The first lesson that filly taught me was patience. I would ease over the corral fence, talking to her, while she watched me out of the corner of her eye. Every time I nearly had the lead rope, trailing on the ground, she would sidle away. When I finally got my hands on it, she would circle me warily, keeping the rope at full stretch.

Standing in the center of the corral, turning with her circling, I'd tell her a hundred times over how beautiful she was in the sight of my eyes. She was buckskin all over, a rich chocolate brown fading to a lighter tone on her muzzle. Her head had fine, boxy lines, her barrel was tight and smooth, her legs were as slender as a thoroughbred's, what you call deer-footed. Her spirit was as lightly alive as a thoroughbred's, too, with a fire behind it you had to respect. I didn't have a name for her yet, because it had to be the right name. I didn't aim to name her until I had been on her back.

The first week, the old stallion hung close to the home ranch. We would hear him in the night, making *his trumpeting call. I was afraid he might break into the corral, so every night, though walls spooked her, I put her in a stall. It was only after he had given up that she let me touch her. It was like a miracle. For an hour I had been holding the lead rope while she circled with dainty disdain. All the time, little by little, I had been taking in rope. I had often done the same thing before, but this time she didn't seem to notice that I was closer and closer—until, suddenly realizing that I was right by her side, she stopped dead still. Trembling all over, I put out my hand. I felt the shock of my touch go through her, like a rattlesnake had struck. She blew her breath, stomped her front feet—but she didn't move away. Instead, she bent her neck and blew warm breath against my hand, smelling me. If I hadn't been 14 years old, I'd have had to cry.*

You can break down a yearling by riding them before their bones set. I put in the time gentling her, until she would follow me around like a pet dog. Every night I fed her grain, brushing and curry-combing her while she ate. She grew fast, and wasn't she sleek and pretty!

One day, I got out an old saddle and showed it to her. It spooked her, right enough, but after I carried it around in my hand for a while she got used to it. One day I swung it up on her back. She ran right out from under it, and it was a week before I could get close to her again.

You see, I didn't want to break her, the way we usually broke our riding stock, by just climbing on and riding her out. When the time came, I wanted to step grandly up on her, with no trouble at all. First loosely on her back, then the surcingle fastened more and more tightly, I talked her into accepting the saddle.

210

Then I filled a towsack with dirt and began coaxing her to carry the dead weight as I walked her about the corral.

I waited all winter and most of the spring before I tried getting into the saddle myself. By that time, I was pretty confident. The confidence was misplaced. That palomino filly, after a trembling minute of outrage, went out of her cotton-picking mind. She reared until I thought she was going to fall over backward; she came down sunfishing, and on the second turn I came out of the saddle like I had been shot. She wasn't through yet, either, not by a handful of beans; while I lay in the corral dust, stunned and shaken, she charged me. I put my hands over my head and rolled for the fence in a flurry of dust and hoofs. I was lucky to get out of there alive.

We had come to the stopping place in no uncertain terms. Gentle, obedient, loving, as long as I had my feet on the ground; but the second she felt my weight, she had only one idea—to throw me off, and kill me. I tried to be as stubborn about it as she was. But Daddy began to talk about how I'd better think about selling her for rodeo stock. It was his theory that I'd made her too much of a pet, spoiling her to the point of uselessness. I wouldn't hear of selling her, and swore I'd ride her if it killed me.

It derned nigh did. She must have thrown me a hundred times. Finally I fell wrong, coming out of the saddle, and broke my arm, and Daddy forbade me to get on her again.

It was a humiliating situation. Wherever I went, that filly would follow me, as affectionate as a ten-dollar whore. She'd nuzzle at my shoulder to get my attention, or punch me in the back with her nose. She'd do anything I wanted, even to silly horse-opera tricks

211

like lifting a hoof to shake hands, or kneeling and bowing her head—anything but let me ride her. So one day I was cooling my feet down at the spring—had gone to fetch a bucket of water—and she was cropping tender leaves nearby. I watched her, hate in my heart for her obstinate ways, and suddenly I was thinking, By God, if I can't ride you, I'll fuck you instead.

My breath locked in my throat. I was 15 years old, and you're just about as horny at 15 as you're ever going to get. The only woman I knew was the schoolteacher—Mama had left Daddy before I was five—and my class was all boys except for Sadie Weatherall, who had squint eyes and buck teeth and a personality to match. So all I had found to do about it was knock down my horniness with my fist once in a while. Until now.

Weak in the leg and hot in the groin, I took my feet out of the water and went to her. Petting her with one shaky hand, I eased her back against a rock of an appropriate size. She had got to where she could read my mind about wanting to ride her, but since that wasn't what I was thinking about she didn't spook the least little bit when I climbed up behind her and unbuttoned my fly.

Standing there cock in hand, I moved her tail aside and looked at her pussy, thinking about shoving it in there. I was about to come just with the thought. I put a finger in her to see how she would take it. When she only squatted slightly, I aimed and shoved.

Either one of you ever fucked a mare? I'll tell you, it is something else. A mare's cunt has got twice as much heat as a woman's. I tell you, when that sweet, fiery feel lapped my cock, I went crazy.

I reckon maybe the animal was pretty dern surprised at this new trick I was teaching her. But of course I wasn't any more than tickling her, because she was built for a stallion's tool, a foot long and as big around as your arm. For the first minute or two, she hunched her back and took it. Then she began to piss, the warm, stinging flood drenching the front of my britches. I was still fucking. I couldn't have stopped if she had been passing fire, and when I came it was like my backbone had melted. It was my first piece of ass.

I had a problem. It wouldn't do to go home with my britches soaked with mare's piss. Daddy, or the hired hand, would notice for sure and I never would hear the last of owning a mare I could fuck, but couldn't ride. I took off my pants, rinsed them out in the spring, and laid them on a rock to dry. Sitting in my shirt tail, gazing at myself, I marveled at how much pleasure could come from such a thing. The filly came up behind me and began muzzling my neck. I stroked her nose, thinking foolishly that she must have liked it too. Maybe she wanted some more. I began to raise a second hard and before you could say Jack Robinson I was backing her against the rock one more time.

She understood what I was up to this time, so it was harder to make her stand. But I reckon she thought anything was all right as long as it didn't involve carrying me on her back, because after some coaxing she let me fuck her again, standing patiently, her back hunched, as she took my pitiful member like she would one day take a stallion's grand offering. Reveling in the scalding heat of her pussy, I kept it going for a long time, stroking lightly, pausing at times to stand tight against her hips, soaking my cock hilt deep. I could feel the goodness all the way to my

213

toenails. Finally, of course, I couldn't hold it any longer and so I quickened my stroke, pounding like I was the palomino stallion myself, melting my cock in the great heat of her. When I drew out, I was so weak I could hardly get down from the rock. She had turned her head, watching me with her great liquid eyes, and I went to lean on her neck, devoured by my love for my beautiful palomino mare.

I want to tell you something else. When my pants were dry enough, I put them on. Then, not stopping to think about what I was doing, I caught her by the mane and vaulted up on her back. I sat there, feeling her quivering under me, and waited for her to explode. But she didn't. She only stood trembling for a long minute, in which I couldn't breathe, and then she curved her neck to look at me.

I've tried to imagine what was going through her head. Maybe she was figuring it all out, I don't know. She had kindly feelings toward me. She knew I had those same kindly feelings for her. I was a stupid human being, who wanted to do silly things like fucking her with my puny cock when she wasn't even in heat, and riding on her back. She must have made up her mind, in that minute, that she might as well go along with my strange ways. Without any urging, she struck out for home, singlefooting along under my weight as though she'd been carrying me for years.

For the next five years, I rode Sweetheart, and fucked Sweetheart, and loved her like a man ought to love a good woman. In all that time, I didn't cast the first eye toward a girl. Oh, I'd go to the social doings, barbecues and dances and such, I'd even drink a little whiskey, and maybe choose up a fight or two. On the way home, I knew, I could put my cock where it belonged, enjoy the loving a young

214

man needs, and not have to worry about the complications a woman's pussy can bring into your life.

When she was in heat I fucked her a lot, because I could stand behind her and watch her pussy wink, red and ready, and when I got inside her cunt would be working, stroking me like she wanted to stroke the stallion's great tool. Of course, every time Sweetheart came due, Daddy wanted to breed her. He couldn't understand why I didn't want a colt out of her. But the servicing of a mare had always seemed a cruel and hurting passion, the stallion bugling and pawing and biting the mare's neck while his great instrument ripped at her. I didn't want to subject Sweetheart to that sort of thing. Maybe I was jealous; maybe I figured that, once she had felt the real stallion cock, she wouldn't tolerate my puny fucking any more. I told myself it was because I didn't want her to get sway-bellied and ugly from toting a foal every year.

I suppose I would have lived my life a contented bachelor, never knowing what it was to fuck a woman, if Daddy hadn't lost the ranch. I was 20 when the bank foreclosed and I found out that Sweetheart hadn't ever really belonged to me. It made a streak of bitter lean when I saw her hauled off in a truck with the rest of the livestock. Daddy told me he'd found a job as night man at the local jail and had rented a house in town, but I said I reckoned I'd just go on my own way. He didn't ask why I felt so, and I didn't tell him. He went to his soft job—he died in less than a year, though as far as I knew there hadn't never been anything wrong with him—and I went to work on a dude ranch.

Dude ranching is something else. In a lot of ways, it's harder work than running cattle or horses . . . or

*herding sheep, even, though I've never sunk that
low. A dude is as ornery as a ten-year-old brush steer,
as unpredictable as a horse, and about twice as stupid
as a sheep. In addition, if they're female, more likely
than not they expect to get fucked.*

*The place I worked ran heavy to single women—
single, I mean, in the sense of waiting out their
residencies so they could divorce the current husband.
Some were old hands who had been the route two or
three times and looked forward to their stay amongst
the horny young cowboys. Others, sometimes young,
sometimes middle-aged, were pretty bewildered by
what was happening to them. But, one and all, they
seemed mainly intent on proving to themselves that a
man could still want to stick a cock in their hole and
move it around some.*

*A new hand got to be pretty cynical about the
whole process in pretty short order. The situation
certainly wasn't designed to increase your respect
for womankind. Listening to bunkhouse tales, I
learned more about the entanglements of sex than a
20-year-old boy ought, by rights, to know. Not just
tales, either—there was the elegant lady who walked
into the bunkhouse one night and offered twenty-five
dollars cold cash for each and every hard the assembled
hands could raise. When daylight came, she was still
standing to her word, and had laid out more money
than you would have believed. Last season, so I was
told, there had been a prim little schoolteacher type
you couldn't have touched if you'd been equipped
with the cock of a stallion, but she'd suck a fellow off
at the drop of anybody's ten-gallon hat. I heard all
about the weirdies, too, like the old lady, about 60,
who'd hire a fellow to flail at her with a rawhide
while she carried on in a way you wouldn't believe*

with a cock made out of ivory she'd bought somewhere in the Far East. Not to mention the movie
star—the most beautiful woman ever to stay at our
ranch, to hear the old hands tell it—who swore she
was still a virgin, and got her kicks being fucked in
the ass instead. So one time three guys ganged up on
her, in her cabin one night, and raped her the way a
woman ought to be used, and she had to be taken
away in a straitjacket. Even discounting a certain
amount for natural exaggeration, you had to believe
that people take a wider range than you'd ever have
thought possible while living on the home ranch.

We had nicknames for those dudes outstanding
enough to merit such honor. My first year, as I
remember, there was Miss Passion Pit, The Horny
Humdinger, and The Spanish Monster, amongst
others. It fell to my lot that the first woman I rode
was Two-Ton Gertie.

Actually, the name was something of a slander. A
big woman, all right, but young—no more than 30—
and shapely to boot. Just naturally built big, that's
all. She weighed maybe close to 200 pounds, but it
was muscle more than fat.

I sort of liked old Two-Ton Gertie. At least, she
knew about horses. We had to give her the biggest
horse on the ranch, to carry her weight; but she had
a sort of grace in the saddle. Those dude-ranch horses
can be pretty ornery, because they get accustomed
to being ridden by people who're scared of them.
It don't do to let a horse know he can bluff you. Two-
Ton Gertie could handle a fractious animal as well
as any cowboy; for that matter, she could handle the
cowboys as well.

First I knew she was interested in me, I was leaning on the corral fence watching a fellow named

217

Shorty sweating out a new dude's first ride, keeping the horse from spooking with one hand and holding the dude in the saddle by main force with the other, when I felt something feeling around my ass. I jumped and whirled, to see Two-Ton Gertie grinning at me.

"You've got the prettiest butt I've ever seen, cowboy," she said. "I just had to cop a feel. I hope you don't mind."

I was pretty red in the face—no woman had ever laid hands on my ass before. Anywhere else, either.

She started laughing at my reaction. "Ain't nothing to be ashamed of. I'd give half my ex-husband's fortune to look that good in tight breeches." She sighed. "Never in a million years. Will you saddle that elephant they let me ride?"

I caught out her mount and saddled him. She stopped on her way out of the corral gate. "I'd like some company today. Will you ride with me?"

We had our orders about keeping the dudes happy, so I saddled up, told Shorty where I was going, and we started off up a bridle path. My heart was in my throat, wondering what Two-Ton Gertie had in mind. Her attention was strictly on riding, though, and she went at it so hard and fast I had to hustle to keep up. Only when the horses were lathered and we were returning at a walk did she even speak.

"What's your name?"

"Casey," I told her.

"Casey, you ought to pay me a visit after dinner tonight. Who knows, I might have a little present for you."

There it was, then. I understood the gift she had in mind. Two-Ton Gertie was known to be straight-mouthed about her likes and dislikes, her needs and her desires. A lot of the women didn't wait to be asked; under such circumstances, an accommodating cowboy could count on a nice tip, so I had been told. As it happened, I hadn't been asked yet, flat out like that. Although I had worked at being friendly and courteous at all times, as instructed by the management, I really didn't have much idea how to go about letting a lady know I wanted to fuck her. I knew it was more complicated than backing her up to a rock and having at it.

So it wasn't exactly the size of my possible tip I had on my mind as I eased quietly out of the bunkhouse that night and walked to Two-Ton Gertie's cabin. I knocked. She told me to come in. I came in. She was sitting in a rocking chair before the hearth fire—it gets chilly in the mountains after dark—a drink in her hand.

"Want a drink?"

I figured I could use one, so she poured a shot in a glass and picked up a water pitcher. I wanted it straight, so I told her so and gulped it back in one hard swallow.

She was watching me. "I've always wanted to take my whiskey straight, like a man," she remarked. "As a matter of fact, I've always wished I was a man. A woman my size, she doesn't have much chance to be a woman, but nobody cares how heavy a man is. How are you at doing it dog fashion?"

"What?" I said. I heard her; I just didn't believe she had said it.

"Dog fashion," she said impatiently. "That's my style. Taking an ordinary-sized man in my arms, I feel like I'm holding a child. I've never once had a man even near to my own size. Ain't that a sad thing to say?"

Taking up the whiskey bottle, I poured a second

shot. She watched me critically. "Drink too much, you won't be able to get it up," she said. "Whiskey and sex won't mix. Don't you know that?" She was watching me very closely. "Haven't you ever had a woman, boy?"

"Oh sure," I said. "Lots."

Snorting a disbelieving sort of laugh, she got up out of the rocking chair. She had been wrapped in a flannel robe; when it swung open, I saw that she was naked under it.

I had never seen a woman's body. I was getting an eyeful now, all right. Her breasts were huge, not standing out but sagging with their own weight. She was thick around the middle, flaring widely at the hips, and her legs were like two white columns. Still, there was a womanly shape to her—not like a guitar, but more a bass fiddle. The snatch of hair between her legs was as heavy and matted as a throw rug and I could smell her body odor in the warm cabin, funky and sweaty, like she hadn't bathed after the ride.

She chuckled. "Like the sight of a woman, don't you? Even a woman as big as I am. Just look at you. Got it on already."

Moving close, she put her hand on me as frankly as she had felt my ass. I pulled away, beginning to tremble like a spooked horse; then I held still as her hand shaped itself on the outside of my pants. She rubbed slowly, watching my face, very close now, and the woman-odor kept getting stronger.

"Dog fashion?" she said.

"Any way," I said, the two words blocking in my throat like I'd swallowed a cactus burr.

She left me, climbed up on the bed. "Come on then," she said. "Ride me, cowboy."

I shucked off my pants and drawers. My legs were

220

cold, though the room was warm. I stopped beside the bed, looking at the big woman.

Crouched on hands and knees like that, her butt was like a mare's hindquarters. Her pussy was pooched out between her thighs, showing red and ready. Like you do a skittish horse, I touched her solidly with the flat of my hand. Then I slid it inward to find the wetness of her cunt.

"My ex-husband said that fucking dog fashion made him feel like he was fucking an animal." she said. "So don't fool around, I'm hot as a two-dollar pistol."

She did look like a mare. My mare, I thought, and felt it quickening in me. If I had to fuck a woman, this was how to do it, my hands on her haunches, her thighs against my thighs. Would she hump her back, as Sweetheart had always done? I was behind her now, laying my cock against her pussy. Closing my eyes, I slid inside. Her cunt was big, bigger and wetter than the mare's, but she didn't have the mare's heat.

Two-Ton Gertie was still talking. "My grounds for divorce are mental cruelty. That's supposed to mean when your husband makes you go down on him against your will. In my mind, it means he wouldn't fuck me the way I like to be fucked best of all. But I won't tell the Judge. That's right. You're there now. You're fucking now. Yes. Keep on. Just keep on. Yes. Yes. There. There now. There."

I had meant to fuck her as I had fucked my mare when I wanted to make it last, with slow, easy strokes, all the way out and all the way in. But, because she wouldn't stop talking, I lost control and began pounding at her with quick, hard drives. I wasn't exactly used to conversation at such times.

"Yes, that's the way. Ride 'em, cowboy. My husband was really a very nice man. But he felt so small in my arms. When a man feels small in your arms, he's small inside of you, too. God, I'd love to find a 350-pound giant, he'd just smother me, wouldn't he? I'd feel so tiny! Yes. Hard now. Hard. Hard, damn it, swing that beautiful ass cowboy, goddamn yes, fuck yes, fuck yes, fuck yes. Goddamn!"

I had my hands braced on her hips and my eyes were still closed, to keep me with my palomino mare. Two-Ton Gertie wasn't as good, she couldn't be, but she was all right because she was beginning to move inside, like Sweetheart did in heat, winking on my cock, milking away with a hot little hand, stripping me down. And talking, talking, always talking.

"Of course, he'd have to have a small ass. I can't stand the sight of a man with a heavy butt. That's what I liked about you, Casey, I just had to touch that pretty little ass today, like a baby reaching for candy. It scared you, didn't it? But you're all right now, you're in the socket, oh yes, oh yes, you fuck like a rabbit, don't you Casey, ride it out now, ride it out, it's coming now, I can feel it coming."

I don't know how she did it. Without moving her body at all on the outside, she was fucking me as hard as I was fucking her. Only at the very end did her great haunches begin to roil, like an earthquake taking place, as I shot it all in one big wad, slamming hard and then holding it while she milked me dry.

She heaved an enormously heartfelt sigh and rolled slowly on her side, looking at me as I braced myself on my knees, trembling all over.

"Goddamn, you're a fucking son of a bitch, aren't you?" she said.

I didn't know what to answer to that kind of statement. "Thank you, ma'am," I said, mumbling. I waited there in my shirt tail, not knowing what to do next. It hadn't come even close to what I had thought it would be like. I hadn't even known that a woman talked like that while being fucked.

"There's a 20-dollar bill over there in my purse on the dresser," she said. "I do believe it's got your name on it."

I got off the bed and found my pants. I began to put them on, so upset I had forgotten about my drawers.

"What's the matter with you?" Two-Ton Gertie said.

I couldn't face her. "Sorry, ma'am. I don't take money." The hot breath of anger gusted through me, so that I turned to stare into her face. "And goddamn you for offering it."

"My God, boy, I wouldn't have had the nerve to ask you down here if I hadn't thought you could use a piece of change as well as a piece of ass. You don't want to put me in the position of asking for favors, do you?"

My face was getting red. "I just don't want your money."

She must have believed me, because, sitting up on the side of the bed, she held out her heavy arms. "Casey, I didn't think they grew them like you any more . . . at least, not on dude ranches. Come here to Mama."

I went to her. She wrapped her arms around my naked hips and laid her face against my belly. In spite of myself my cock lifted its head as she held me close and smothering, her hands patting gently my naked ass.

Drawing away, she said, "Take off the rest of your clothes. I'm going to show you what fucking can be like."

223

She watched while I unbuttoned my shirt and dropped it on the floor. She sat regarding my erect rod, a strange expression on her face. She reached out to cup it in her palm, her fingers resting ticklish under my balls.

"The truth is, I'm your first woman," she said, gazing up into my face. "Isn't that so?"

"Yes ma'am," I said.

Sighing, she lay back on the bed, pulling her knees up. "Then climb on," she said. She chuckled. "It's yours, all two hundred pounds and a yard wide."

Her body swallowed me, seemed like, as her legs lifted around me. Her pussy was a great big field of warm flesh into which I melted like sinking into warm pudding. Except, this pussy-pudding was alive. I just wallowed, drowning in her. Both her hands were on my butt, pushing me deeper and deeper, and I was tossed helplessly in the roil of her body.

It was great and marvelous and so smothering I couldn't stand it for long. By main force, I got out of the grip of her legs and straddled her. Her arms were still holding me head deep in her great breasts, but I was on top now and in command. She wasn't talking this time, either, as I began to ride her mountain of flesh. I could not only feel her wetness, I could hear it, smackings and gurglings of her juices, for she was already coming, way ahead of me, and I raised up to watch her face, controlling her with the command of my hips like you control a trained cutting horse. I took her all the way through the course once, and then again, only this second time around I was fucking out my come into her bucking flesh.

When we were done, she wouldn't let me go, but opened her legs, letting me slide down deep, and began kissing me. Her mouth was so active and alive, *it was like fucking again, except that she was all tongue and mouth instead of all cunt and soon she had rolled out from under me, kissing down the length of my body to my cock, swallowing it in a little frenzy that made me come again, a small one this time but good, so good. I had my four fingers buried in her by then, and made her come at the same time I did.*

Two-Ton Gertie wore me to a frazzle that night. I was only 20, so it took a while. But with all her inventions and ideas she got me inspired and interested again and again. And then, fucking in all the different ways a woman can find to fuck a man, she'd use me up one more time. When I was finished for good and all, she let me go to sleep, and didn't roust me out until daylight was due to come.

"You sure you can't use that 20 dollars?" she said, laughing, as I got dressed. "God knows you've earned it."

I was still stubborn about it. "No," I said, without trying to discuss all the reasons.

She was sleepy herself now, even her voice sounded sleepy. "If I could pay you, I'd know I'd get you back again. This way . . ."

I buckled my belt and sat down to put on my boots. "I'll come back," I said. "Any time. That is, if you . . . want me to." I looked up. "I'm a small man, Gertie, and you said . . ."

She laughed. "If you can't get a big man, cowboy, a good little man will do. Take my word for it, you will do."

I came back, too, many and many a time, even though the other hands made fun of me for fucking old Two-Ton. Naturally, they figured I was coining money hand over fist—cock over pussy might be a better way to put it. I let them think what they wanted.

225

The fact was, I liked my big woman. She satisfied me.

More than that—though I never took a penny from her, Two-Ton Gertie helped me get the home ranch back from the bank.

It came about in this way. Two-Ton Gertie was not only a good rider, a good-hearted woman, and hell-on-wheels in bed; next to fucking, she liked to gamble. She spent all her spare time in the casinos; sometimes she'd win a bundle, some nights she'd drop a bundle, but she always went back for more.

I had learned, soon after going to work on the dude ranch, that I had a hot hand with the dice. I had tried the casinos, of course, out of curiosity, but I had better sense than to gamble in them as a regular thing. The house odds will get you sooner or later, I don't care how good you are.

One night after our usual long session in bed she asked me to go to the casino with her. I had avoided being with her in public, because of course I knew everybody who saw us together would believe I was a bought-and-paid-for stud. But this time, after some persuading, I went along and helped her lose a nice little roll that just about equaled my year's salary.

She swore I had brought her bad luck, because she nearly always won. I laughed at her and told her anybody was a fool to buck those casino odds. It developed into a strong little argument, until I finally told her that if she had any sense she'd look up one of the private games—there were plenty to choose from—where she would have a decent chance to win. She wanted to go right that minute, of course, and finally I called a place I knew and asked if I could bring a friend, even if she was a dude, to watch the action.

The crap game was in the back of a garage. I

226

wouldn't let Gertie get in the game, but only watch, as I had promised. I was hot that night, and walked out with 200 dollars on top of the 20 I had gone in with.

Gertie was pretty thoughtful on the way home. I was thinking of one last romp before taking off for the bunkhouse, but she had other things on her mind.

"You're a high roller, aren't you, Casey?" she said.

"I'm pretty fair with the dice, I reckon," I said. "But no good with cards. So I don't claim to qualify."

She was regarding me very intently. "You've got ice in your veins when you're in a game," she said. "I was watching you." She stopped, thinking for another long minute. "All you need is a bankroll to back you up." Her eyes became shrewd. "That is; unless you lose your nerve when the pot gets over, say, a hundred dollars. Do you lose your nerve?"

"I don't know," I said uncomfortably. "I've never gambled with that class of money."

"There are high-stakes games in this town, aren't there? Just like that two-bit one you were in tonight?"

"Sure," I said. "But you'd better not walk in with less than a thousand dollars. They'll nickel-and-dime you right out."

She took a deep breath. "I'll bankroll you," she said.

I drew back. "I've told you. I don't want your money."

"I'm not giving you money. I'm bankrolling you . . . for half the winnings. Is it a deal?"

It scared me. I had watched a few of those big games, but I had never played in them. I could feel sweat in the palms of my hands.

"I don't know whether I'd hold up in that competition or not."

"There's only one way to find out," Gertie said steadily. "Now come on, cowboy, climb into the saddle one more time so the lady can sleep good tonight."

We started out cautiously, but it didn't take long to learn that I could win as easily with a thousand dollars on the line as with ten. I stuck strictly to private crap games, and Gertie held the roll in between. We had set up as partners with 2,000 dollars as our capital; the stake fluctuated considerably, but she never did have to put in a new dime. As I entered bigger and bigger games, I got better—or luckier— so that by the time she had her divorce papers my half share was enough to make big plans on.

After one last wild weekend, Two-Ton Gertie went her way and I went mine. As we parted, there were tears in her eyes. "Casey," she said, "You're one hell of a guy. No matter where I am, what I'm doing or who I'm married to—you've got access to my ass any time you want it bad enough to come after it."

A hell of a woman, old Two-Ton. The day after she was gone, I went home to make a hefty down payment on a new mortgage, and so I owned the home place again.

But my little palomino mare was gone forever. Nevertheless, I was as contented as any man has a right to be, I guess. My work was cut out for me, restocking the ranch and getting it on a paying basis. Those first years, I couldn't begin to afford to hire help, so I learned to live alone, a lesson that has stood me in pretty good stead. Running cattle involved the hardest work, but required the least investment, so I started like that, though it was my ambition to raise horses. I was too far away from the fleshpots to think about wrangling dudes; besides, I was just as happy not to have the place cluttered up. The third year, I lucked into a reliable man, so I took a season at my old job, with a chance to fatten my bankroll by hard work and some judicious gambling—and even enjoy

228

a taste of nooky once or twice. I never took a dime from any woman, and when I returned to the home ranch I didn't find myself missing any of them, either.

The year I met Maria, my situation was pretty solid. I was no longer a hired hand, during my season with the dudes, but an independent contractor. I'd bring down a string of ponies and, working in cahoots with the ranch management, I'd guide pack trips into the high country.

It was a good life, take it all in all. You don't mind associating so much with the kind of folks who can enjoy and appreciate a long, tough pack trip. We'd stay in the mountains up to ten days at a time, living in tents and sleeping in bedrolls. I not only enjoyed the life, I was making profit hand over fist.

The first two or three days of the trip, I didn't notice Maria out of the ordinary. She was quiet and withdrawn and didn't cause trouble. Then, too, I had long since got in the habit of pitching my personal tent some distance from the camp whenever I could. The fourth night out, we were camped near a waterfall. My tent was completely out of sight, behind a bunch of rocks. I had just put on a coffeepot for my going-to-bed cup when I heard somebody walking around out there in the darkness.

"Who's that?" I called, standing up.

"Me," a woman said, and came on into the firelight.

It was Maria. I can remember yet, in full detail, how she looked. Instead of the flashy cowboy regalia all the dudes got into the minute they arrived, she was dressed more like a gaucho—a plain black silk shirt and wide-legged gaucho pants, the leather as soft as a glove, that struck her just below the knee, and a pair of scuffed riding boots. Her hat was flat and black, with a band made of silver conchos . . . she

229

had it pushed back on her shoulders now, held by the chin strap, which showed black against her throat. With her dark complexion, her black hair, it was just the thing. As I looked at her, I was thinking I wouldn't mind fucking her in the least, if that was why she had come to my private tent. But, of course, I had to play it easy until she showed her mind.

"This is rattlesnake country," I said. "I wouldn't recommend walking around in the dark."

"Your coffee's ready," she said. "Can I have a cup?"

I could smell it, just on the edge of boiling, so I hurried to take it off the fire. I was so busy I didn't have time to stop her from going into my tent. She came out immediately, carrying a large mug in each hand. She held them while I poured.

"Umm, that's good," she said, sipping at the coffee. "Your appetite is so great up here in the mountains, isn't it? Everything is twice as good." She found a flat rock and settled herself comfortably.

Yeah, I thought to myself. Including sex. There's something about being in the saddle all day makes a woman want to fuck all night. Why the hell didn't she latch on to Red or Shorty, instead of me? It was a sour thought, because I was tired from the long day and looking forward to getting up before daylight tomorrow. Still, a foretaste of possible pleasure began to warm itself in my groin. She was a beautiful woman.

"That comes from riding all day," I said.

I remembered her now—a good rider, and not given to complaints. Some people have an absolute genius for finding things to disagree with on a pack trip.

"The mountain air, too," she said. "So thin and pure, and with the pine smell." She laughed quietly. "If I ate at home like I've been eating on this trip I'd weigh 200 pounds."

Willing to ride with it, I found a rock and sat down. "If you think this is good, you ought to know my home ranch."

Which surprised me. I made it a practice not to talk about myself no more than could be helped. As far as the dudes were concerned, I was a cowboy for hire—though not at stud, like most of the boys. I fucked who I pleased, when I pleased, and kept my life my own.

She was watching my face. "Then you don't do this sort of thing all the time?"

"Only when I need the money," I said. "I've got the prettiest little spread you ever saw, back in a box canyon with plenty of grass and water."

"Why haven't we seen it, then? I'd rather stay there than at a big, plush place like . . ."

"It's a working ranch."

I said it short and curt, thinking she was being too inquisitive.

"Oh," she said. She sat finishing her coffee then, without trying to interrupt the silence. When she had drained the last drop, though, instead of going on back where she belonged she filled the cup and sat down again. That's a dude for you—think they own everything you've got. There was coffee at the main fire for anybody who wanted it.

Since I didn't know exactly how to tell her to go away, I waited.

She was watching the fire. "I think I'll be sorry when it's time to go back east," she said. "I've never been out here before. I like it. Better than I thought I would."

231

"Are you here for a divorce?" I asked.

She turned her head. "Why else?"

"You're so much younger and prettier than most of our clientele," I said. "I guess you must be getting a good settlement out of it."

She didn't seem to notice the insult. "No," she said. "My husband was younger than I. I had the money. But he left me. For another man. Or men."

She gave me the news of her life like reading it out of the morning paper. I sat watching, not knowing what to say.

"You really made yourself a mistake, didn't you?" I said finally.

She was looking at the fire. "I knew he was queer when I married him," she said quietly. "I thought . . ." She stopped. I could read the pain in her face. "But it didn't work out. It didn't work out at all."

I was trying to think how it must be for a woman, taking on a fellow like that. Knowing what he'd done with other men, yet willing to take his cock into her body, willing to love him, willing . . .

I couldn't figure how we'd got to talking like this, first about my home ranch, then about her marriage. I had to find a way to bring it to an end, I decided suddenly. It wasn't smart to get yourself too involved with any dude.

I stood up. "Do you want to fuck?" I said. "Is that why you came up here?"

I wondered whether she'd act flustered, or coy, or embarrassed. Most women choose one of those three responses when you put it on the line like that.

She only looked curiously at me. "I guess you get a lot of that, don't you?"

"That's why I carry a double bedroll," I told her.

She rose. I couldn't read her expression. "I suppose I could use a real man," she said. "Do you get paid?"

The anger I always feel when a woman mentions money made my voice sharp. "I generally do it for nothing," I said. "That way, I can quit whenever I take the notion."

She was still watching my face. "Most of the cowboys get paid, don't they?" she said. As though she were truly interested.

I laughed. "Oh, they'll accept presents . . . you know. Some of those fellows got twenty or thirty sets of cufflinks and a dozen watches stashed away against a rainy day."

"How's your supply of jewelry?"

I felt the anger again. "I don't wear cufflinks," I said. "And I can tell time by the stars."

Those words, for a reason I couldn't understand, made a change in her. She'd only been talking. But now, suddenly, she wanted to be fucked. By me. I could, I knew as well as you can know anything, take her down on the ground and shove it home, all in one move. But I didn't.

"What's your name?" she said in a soft voice.

"Casey," I said. "You know my name. How about it?"

She placed her coffee mug carefully on the rock where she had been sitting. "No," she said. "I don't think so."

So I had turned her on, then had turned her off. More disappointed than I wanted to admit, I watched her walking away into the darkness. "Make some noise," I called after her. "Remember, this is rattle-snake country."

So that was that; I put out the fire and went to

233

bed. But I couldn't get to sleep for the longest. I wasn't exactly thinking about her; I was just kind of restless.

Next morning, after flapjacks and coffee, I was too busy getting the group strung out on the day's ride to pay any attention to her. When I gave the campsite a last safety inspection and cantered my mount past the strung-out riders and the pack horses, I was surprised to find her waiting for me on the point.

Kicking her horse in the ribs, she moved him in close. "Good morning, Casey," she said. "Sleep well?"

"Fine," I lied. "How about you?"

"Like a baby," she said contentedly. "I didn't even dream."

I expected to have to put up with her chatter all day long; but I didn't know my Maria yet. She rode silently, loose and easy in the saddle, with an obvious pleasure in the day. Though we exchanged no more than a dozen words, I found that I was enjoying myself too.

After the lunch break, the situation changed. A hardeyed blonde who'd given me a speculative glance once or twice decided Maria needed some competition, so she moved up on my other side. I passed the afternoon riding between the two women, if the trail permitted. The blonde kept talking away all bright and blowsy, with an occasional not-so-subtle remark thrown at Maria. I expected a bad tension to start spoiling the trip. Maria didn't let it happen. She gave the blonde the same quiet, friendly mood she had shared with me through the morning.

That night, I was only on my third cigarette when I heard someone coming in the darkness. My breath caught in my throat. It would be her, Maria, and this time . . .

*It was the blonde. She came pouting into the fire-
light. "Why do you come off up here all by yourself?" she said. She giggled. "You do make a girl go
to a lot of trouble, cowboy."*

*"Maybe that's why," I said, standing up out of
politeness.*

*She came so close, her full breasts brushed my
arm. She was wearing a dress, white and fluffy, instead
of the cowboy pants she had had on earlier.*

*"We didn't have a minute to ourselves all day, did
we?" she said, as though we shared a conspiracy
against the woman who had ridden with us. "So I
just made up my mind I'd come and . . ."*

*Suddenly her hand had found my crotch, and her
parted thighs were rubbing the outside of my leg.
"Oh, Casey," she said, moaning. Her hand was busy
with the zipper. "Oh, Casey."*

"Come on," I said. "Inside the tent."

*She drew back. "You won't think I'm like this all
the time?" she said. "I'm not, Casey, I just . . . You
don't think that, do you? Casey?"*

"I wouldn't think any such a thing, ma'am," I said.

*Her hand was inside my fly, hunting home base.
"I never could stand these aggressive women," she
said. Her breath panted behind the words as she
clasped my naked cock. "A woman ought to wait on
the man, don't you think? But I . . . Casey, I got so
hot, thinking about you."*

*Thinking about her rival getting nicely fucked, I
thought; but I only said, "Inside the tent."*

*She calmed down. She took her hand out of my
pants. Walking into the tent, she glanced at the bedroll spread on the ground—the tent was lighted by a
lantern on the center pole—then turned, holding
out her arms.*

235

"You may kiss me now," she said graciously.

I obliged her. It was a hungry mouth; after a minute I drew away. I was wishing that it was Maria who had come to me. But she won't, I thought. For just that one minute she wanted to, very badly. But then, when I didn't do anything, she turned it off.

The blonde's fingers were busy unbuttoning my shirt. I wanted to do the job myself, but she pushed my hands out of her way, saying, "Let me."

She undressed me down to the skin, taking her time about it, pausing to feel my biceps, to lay her palm on my chest muscles. I stood like a stud horse being judged in a show ring.

"You don't look it in your clothes but, Jesus, you're strong," she said. She pressed her face against my skin and breathed deeply. "You even smell like a man."

"More like a horse," I said, trying to laugh.

She was serious. "You don't use all those deodorants and stuff that men put on, do you?" she said. "I hate that smell on a man. I just hate it." She stepped back, her eyes all over me like a pair of hands. "Lie down. I'm ready to fuck."

I disliked the tone of command. But, having a ready hard and nothing better planned for its relief, I obeyed. She stood over me, still dressed, gazing with full eyes. The old boy was red and dripping by now.

"Yes," she said. "Oh God, yes."

She straddled one leg over me and squatted. Before she was all the way down, I realized that she was naked under the concealing fluffiness of the white dress. The idea of what she was fixing to do made me so randy I thought I'd blow off right there. But then I felt the harsh touch of cunt hair, an instant before she settled herself comfortably, my cock buried deeply. I

236

arched like a bow, after a deeper reach. She said, "Be still now." She began to fuck, sitting heavy on my loins, her hips moving in an intricate pattern of back-and-forth as though she were in a rocking chair.

Her eyes were wide open, glaring. "Don't come now," she said. Her voice was harsh, tense. "Don't you dare lose it, you son of a bitch, you bastard, you goddamn man with your great big cock just waiting for some sweet lady to come along and fuck it for you. You're all alike, and if you lose it before I tell you I'll kill you."

She shut up then, her attention concentrated on what she was doing to me. Her face set in anger, she leaned forward to give herself more leeway. Her cunt seemed angry, too, slipping and sliding so fiercely on my tool, beating it down like it was a snake ready to bite.

When she began to get it, I knew I couldn't hold back. She knew it, too; she began telling me she hadn't turned me loose yet, she'd kill me if I came now, and she was farther forward, her hands strangling at my throat. At that moment, hearing a sound, I turned my head and saw Maria in the entrance, holding the flap with one hand, staring wide-eyed. The blonde looked, too, her hips writhing in the throes of a one-up orgasm.

"Get out of here, you bitch," she said harshly. "There won't be anything left for you. Do you hear?"

Maria took a backward step, dropping the flap between us and her. I was as cruel as the blonde had been; mentally, I was suffering an agony of shame, but physically I lusted with the blonde's lust as she started in again, saying sweetly, "I'll get you one now, dear. You'll like that, won't you?"

In my time, I had been fucked lying on my back;

but never like this. The woman was an absolute genius, and this time it was all for me, a great, generous, gracious reward for my total obedience. When I began to come—and it's always slower, at least with me, the way we were doing it—she went into an absolute frenzy of fucking, but so controlled that she kept me hanging by my fingernails for longer than I could have believed. But as the long fall began she refused to let me roll on top so I could fuck her like a man.

Afterward, she stayed in position. I could read in her eyes, her face, that she was living it all over again in complete detail, as self-centered as during the active fucking. Her eyes changed, became hard and hateful, as she relived Maria's intrusion. Then she smiled a slow smile of triumph, rose, and began tidying her dress with fussy little plucking gestures.

"Get dressed," she said. "You'll have to walk me back to camp."

That tone of assured command again, as though she had taken charge of my life. But, thinking about her stumbling over a rattlesnake—she'd do it, too, a dude like her would find the only rattlesnake in a square mile of mountain to get bit by—I got up and dressed. When I was ready, the blonde stood obviously waiting for me to do the polite thing. When I lifted the tent flap, she started through as regally as entering a ballroom. Then she froze.

With her immovable body blocking the entrance, I couldn't see. I pushed past her, to see Maria sitting beside the campfire, quietly smoking a cigarette and staring into the flames.

The blonde took up a stately march. She didn't glance at Maria, though Maria had turned her head to watch, a faint smile on her face. Head high and all

238

flags flying, the blonde stalked out of the firelight into the darkness.

I paused beside the fire. "I'd better walk her back to camp," I told Maria. "She'll get snakebit sure as hell if I don't."

Actually, I was pleased to have the duty; just at the moment I didn't know exactly how to face Maria. So I hurried, both to catch up and to get away from Maria. The blonde, when I came alongside, abandoned her stately defense and took my arm, clinging to it as though she were a helpless little thing. It was a triumph, all right, when she walked me into camp like that.

I returned to my tent more slowly. She'll be gone, I kept assuring myself. But she was still there. She had put on the coffeepot, and had two mugs ready and waiting. I stood staring at the edge of light. She looked up.

"Was it worth a watch?"

"I told you," I said. "I tell time by the stars."

I didn't know what to expect. What I did get was a burst of laughter, her hands gripping on her thighs, her head thrown back. So free and easy, I had to laugh with her, though mine was more on the sheepish side.

"The coffee's ready," she said.

We drank two cups apiece before Maria left for the main camp. She wouldn't hear of me accompanying her.

That was how we became good friends. But it was a strange friendship. Every day she rode beside me. Every night she came to my tent to sit with me before the fire, drinking coffee. We didn't talk much, or laugh much—and I didn't dare bring up the question of sex, after what had happened.

The blonde, of course, tried to be a problem. She insisted on riding point with me every day, and kept it up grimly past all sense. She even came, one night, to my tent; hearing her approach, Maria and I withdrew into the shadow of a boulder, clutching each other in smothered laughter. After she had left, I discovered a jewelry box on my bedroll. It was a pair of cufflinks as large as small saucers, ornate and ugly. She must have bought them, in preparation, before we had left the ranch. Maria began to laugh, but when I declared that I had a use for this fine gift she stopped abruptly—until I explained that I meant to give them to Shorty, with the understanding he would lay ardent siege to my blonde commandant. I did, and he did, so the blonde was no more trouble. I learned from Shorty, later, that she fucked him down to a nub, always in the same overbearing manner. The last time, when she was ready to leave the ranch, she didn't fuck him at all. She squatted, but only to piss all over him before he could get out from under. Shorty certainly earned his cufflinks.

All too soon, the pack trip was over. On the last night, Maria and I sat together over campfire and coffee, as was our habit. I had a sadness I hadn't felt since the day I had lost my sweet palomino.

"If you're taking another group out soon, I'd like to come along," Maria said out of a long silence.

"It's time to get ready for winter," I said regretfully. "I've got to get back to the ranch."

She was silent again, staring into the fire. "It's been good, Casey," she said. "It has been good, hasn't it?"

I said something, then, that I hadn't planned on. The words came out of a part of me I hadn't even known existed. "Maria. Come home with me."

She lifted her head, looked into my face. I held my

breath. Had I made a mistake? Had I been wrong all along?

"Thank you, Casey," she said. "Of course I will come."

Maria loved the ranch. She rode with me as I went about the chores of preparing for winter. Taking over the kitchen, she proved herself a good, though inexperienced, cook. I had never eaten a woman's cooking, so it tasted good to me.

At first Harley, the hired hand, was there, but he soon left to winter in the Big Bend country of Texas. During the lengthening nights, as arctic air moved down to close us off more and more from the world, we sat before the fireplace, as we had once sat before campfires, talking little, laughing little, simply living together like brother and sister.

I had no idea how long she meant to stay. With the first snow, I warned her that we could get snowed in, maybe for a week at a time, so if she meant to leave . . . She only laughed, saying she'd order a couple of pairs of thermal-knit underwear from Sears. I did not mention her departure again. Nor did she.

The real winter cold came down like a white-gloved fist, soon after, and we were locked into the box canyon until the sun should open up the road to town. Knowing it wouldn't last long at a time, I had always enjoyed being snowbound. With Maria to keep me company, it was even better.

On the third night of driving snow, a second sentence of surprising intent spoke itself through my mouth. We were sitting close to the fireplace, one on each side, for the cold air was creeping steadily stronger through the ranch house. A chill wind howled faintly around the eaves. I was contented, happy, easy in my soul; the home stock was safe

241

in stalls, the range cattle and horses were bedded up, I knew, in deep canyon cuts. Harley, during my absence this summer, had cut and stacked plenty of hay. Tomorrow, if the snow quit tonight, Maria and I would ride old known trails, snow breast-deep on the horses, to make the rounds.

All easy. All comfortable. And the woman here with me.

"Maria," I said, not knowing I was going to say it. "Why don't we get married?"

She remained still for so long I began to think, foolishly, that she had not heard.

"Casey," she said at last. "I don't think I've ever told you. I have a great deal of money. Millions."

I had to think about her answer. It was something I hadn't counted on. Many a dude-ranch cowboy has struck it rich by sticking his cock in the right pussy at the right time. So of course she thinks I found out how rich she was before I paid her any attention, I thought. Immediately, I knew that I was wrong. She hadn't believed any such a thing; she only wanted to make sure I was aware of the bad news.

"That wouldn't make any difference," I said. "Not as long as we live here."

She thought about that for a while. Then she said, "It wouldn't, would it?" Her voice began to be glad.

I didn't want to leave the slightest chance for a misunderstanding, so I laid it out carefully. "That's what I'd expect," I told her. "Just me and you, running the ranch, making our living."

She laughed. "Not even take an occasional season amid the dudes? Aren't you afraid you'll miss all those fine cufflinks?"

I laughed with her. "Not if I had you." My breath locked in my throat. "Because I love you, Maria."

I thought, at first, my declaration had wounded her instead of making her heart whole. Her eyes went dark, her mouth suddenly trembled. She said, "I love you too, Casey. But I haven't been very good with love."

I ignored the last part, because I didn't know how to deal with it. "Then you ought to marry me."

She was very still. "I've already been married, Casey. Twice. I didn't plan on trying again."

I hadn't heard about the other marriage. But I said, "That doesn't make any difference. And they say third time's a charm."

"The money—it won't make any difference either?"

"Not if you won't let it." I laughed again, for I could sense her consent very near to the surface. "I can keep on telling time by the stars for the rest of my life."

"Then I'll marry you," she said.

I got up. She rose, also, so I could put my arms around her. "Of course," I said ruefully, "no telling how long it'll be before we can get out to town and find a preacher."

She was close now, so close. She pulled away, her eyes serious on my face. "What we've just said to each other . . . will do for me."

I read her meaning. But I held back. "I can wait," I said. "If it's the right thing to wait."

She went away from me, all the way across the living room to my bedroom door. Her hand on the knob, she stopped to look back. "Come on to bed when you're ready." She went inside, closing the door behind her.

There were things to do. I went about banking the fire, checking the outside thermometer, bringing in an extra armload of wood, with a deliberate haste.

Finished, I went to her. She was in bed. The kerosene lamp was lit, showing me her face. I sat on the edge of the bed and put my hand under the covers. She was wearing the thermal underwear she had ordered from the catalogue.

I said, grinning, "I counted on finding you naked."

She made an exaggerated shiver. "Too cold! We'll make it naked sometime next spring. Late next spring."

Laughing, I stood up to unbuckle my belt. "Have it your way. I don't care."

"Hurry," she said, "or you'll freeze to death."

I stripped down to my long johns and slid in against the warmth of her body. I put a hand over her breast, one leg thrown across her fabric-smooth body, and kissed her. Her mouth was warm and fresh and lovely.

I stared into her face. The prettiest woman I'd ever seen. My woman. No bank could ever take her on a defaulted mortgage. I pressed my hand into her crotch, felt her move up against it as I pinched gently the lips of her pussy. I found a way through the fabric. She opened her legs, giving me her pussy to hold. Her mouth was warmed and softened.

"We could have loused it up so many times," I said. "But we didn't, did we?"

"Oh, Casey, I love you," she said, whispering.

I stared into her eyes. "And you'll stay with me, won't you? Here on the ranch? So nobody won't ever . . ."

"Yes," she said, still whispering. "Yes."

I'm not going to try to tell how it was that first time. You can't tell something like that, there aren't the words to make it the truth. Both clothed from neck to ankle in the body-tight underwear, we touched only in the one place that counted. But Lord, how that place did count.

Up over her, my hands holding open the unbuttoned fly of her garment so I could get inside, I waited for about two seconds, gazing into her lamplit face. Her eyes knew me. I went down into her, deeper than you could ever imagine, and it was like finding the warmest place to live during the coldest winter.

I went crazy on her there at first. I couldn't quit fucking her. Maybe it was the clothing separating our skins, leaving only my cock in her pussy. It was forever before we came to the first stopping place, both of us at the same time. She sighed, deep and heartfelt, but I was already whipping her toward the next fence. This time she was gripping my shoulders hard with clenched fists. Then there was the next fence, and the next, on and on.

I woke up in the cold morning. Maria was still in my arms. The blanket over our heads, we made a warm nest, so that when I stuck my head out the air struck frosty at my warmed face.

Maria stirred, saying. "What's the matter?"

I was listening. "It's quit snowing. I'll bet it's 20 degrees below what it was yesterday. Don't get up until I've built a fire."

She laid her hand on my belly. "We don't need a fire. Not yet."

I touched her. She was so ready I had to laugh. "Need to get the old blood stirred up? That your problem?"

"I don't think it'll start moving any other way."

I pulled the covers over our heads, taking us back into the warm cave of ourselves. Lying on her side, she lifted a leg over my hip and hitched forward to

245

absorb my cock. We fucked slowly, luxuriously, both of us moving as though we had practiced a thousand times, letting it build ever so gentle and easy, until, unable to restrain myself, I rolled on top and started banging away. I could tell, already, when she was beginning to get there; she always caught her lower lip hard between her teeth. I was crouched on her like a jockey on a horse, and she was laughing, it was so good, so right, she was so happy, and I was happy with her.

I didn't care how long the winter lasted.

It was a long season, two whole years, in which we were together night and day. We made love twice every 24 hours, at the least—on going to bed at night, again on waking up in the morning, every single day of our lives except when Maria was out of commission with the cramps.

A marvelous kind of love-making. We didn't go in for fun-and-games. I'd seen too much of that sort of thing on the dude ranch, all those strange little appetites people learn that so often become more important than the main event. We simply fucked, that was all, in the old forgotten style of sticking it in and stirring it around. You wouldn't believe the varieties of sensation we got out of it; it was like Maria was a brand-new woman every time, and I was a brand-new man.

Don't ask me why Maria began to get restless. I didn't know then, and I don't know now. God knows, I was as contented as a Brahma bull in tall clover. I thought she was, too; it hadn't occurred to me that anybody could get tired of living on the ranch. When you find the place, stay there; that's what I say.

The first signs of discontent came in bed; she began to want to experiment. I resisted, but when she insisted in those silent ways a woman knows to show her desires, I cooperated reluctantly; though when she got on top it reminded me too strongly of the blonde, when she went down on me I remembered too many other women's mouths, when she insisted I fuck her dog fashion I couldn't help thinking fondly of Two-Ton Gertie. So many other women, so many other ways, when all I wanted was my sweetheart Maria and a simple-minded straightforward fuck.

One night, out of nowhere, Maria said, "Casey, have you ever been to New York?"

"Can't say I have," I told her. "Can't say I feel like I've missed anything by it, either."

"Casey," she said, "let's go to New York."

"What's that town got that you can't get right here to home?" I said, grinning because I wanted to turn her away from this direction as quickly as possible.

"Plays," she said. "Operas. Art galleries. Restaurants." She was suddenly very excited. "We could take a suite at one of the big hotels. I could buy some good clothes, and we'd go to a different place every night. Wouldn't that be fun?"

I was watching her. "I don't run to that kind of money," I said. "If we did go, it'd be a cheap hotel, with delicatessen meals in the room."

"There's plenty of money. You know that."

"Your money. Not mine."

She put her hand on mine. "Casey, I'll bet I haven't spent two dollars since we got married. So it's my turn."

"Your turn to support us will come in about a hundred years. What's for dessert? Did you bake that apple pie?"

She left it alone for about a week. Then one night

247

—at the supper table again, just like we hadn't stopped talking about it at all—she said, "Casey, I think I'll go, then. All right?"

"For how long?" I said.

"Maybe a month," she said.

I looked across the table. "What will you be doing about your fucking?"

She tried to smile. "For a month? Just think what I'll have saved up for you when I get back."

"You've got used to it twice a day," I said reasonably. "It'll be a habit hard to break."

"Casey, don't be silly," she said. "What's a month?"

I was still looking at her. "It's forever, as far as I'm concerned. I've got the habit too, you know."

She stood up. "I'm going to New York, Casey," she said quietly. "You can come or stay. However it pleases you."

I had been hoping she wouldn't come to that. But it had been said, and I knew it was up to me now. Knowing my choices—I didn't doubt for a minute that she meant it—it didn't take no more than ten seconds to realize that I couldn't bear the thought of losing her.

"Let's get packed, then," I said. "New York, here we come." Maybe I couldn't keep her, anyway. But I had to try, didn't I?

Our suite at the Plaza was derned near as big as the whole ranch house. I spent hours at a time sitting in stores watching Maria look at dresses being paraded before her. After she was outfitted to her taste, we began going places. Just the two of us at first, plays and concerts at night, museums and art galleries in the daytime; not to mention antique auctions and horse races and night clubs. Maria wanted to outfit me, too, but I wouldn't allow it. So there I was in my

*best dude-ranch clothes, including ten-gallon hat and
cowboy boots, squiring a beautiful woman wearing a
thousand-dollar dress. It was only natural that we
caught the attention of folks, even in a place as big
as New York. Pretty soon a pleasantly hardnosed lady
came around to interview Maria and after the big
spread in the Sunday New York Times, we began to
get ass-deep in people.*

*I hadn't realized that Maria was a famous and mys-
terious woman, what with her wealth, her family
history, and the way she'd disappear out of the public
eye for years at a time. Reading that paper, I discovered things about her I had never dreamed.*

*Maria was thoroughly enjoying herself; I will ad-
mit it wholeheartedly. A week after the Times article,
she hired the largest ballroom in the hotel for a huge
dinner party. You never saw such a riot; I shudder to
think what it must have cost. The party put us on
the circuit, so every night we were booked, at the
least, for a couple of cocktail parties, and every weekend we were up the Hudson or out on Long Island.*

*I was making it one day at a time, waiting for Maria
to wear it out and come on home. We were slowly
becoming strangers—if we wanted to fuck, it had to be
about four o'clock in the morning. Even then, she
didn't put more than half her mind on it. She just
wasn't very interested in fucking; she was too busy
living some other kind of life. And almighty successful at it.*

*Of course, being a dubious quantity, I was left
pretty much to myself by those bright, clever people
who flocked around Maria. They didn't have to take
but one look to figure out that I was the current stud,
bought and paid for and costing approximately as
much to maintain as a first-class racehorse. I could*

249

have had my fun, of course, if I had wanted it. Enough pussy was shoved at me to satisfy twenty dude-ranch outfits. But I knew, in one hundred percent of the cases, that the offer didn't have a thing to do with me. Only a way for the woman to score off Maria. I was still loyal; I quickly learned how to brush them off in such a way they never tried it again. I made some high-class womenfolk pretty damn mad during that time, I can tell you.

We stayed in town through the hottest summer I've ever put in, and through the fall to catch all the new shows and exhibits, and make the opening of the opera season. When winter came, with that damp New York cold, Maria decided to accept an invitation to Palm Beach.

More of the same. Quieter, of course, with older people and scads more money. The money didn't count as much, but Maria's Florida ancestry kept her in the swim. After a month of Palm Beach, she accepted an invitation to go yachting in the Caribbean.

You never saw such a big damn boat, all brass and polish, with a professional captain and crew, including a steward at your elbow every waking minute with a drink or a bottle of suntan oil on a tray. A dozen couples were aboard as guests, and more damn high-count bridge during the afternoons and dancing under the tropic moon than you can imagine.

A few days out, the wife of our host made a dead set at me. Steven Hart was a big, florid, hearty man who was going to get it one of these days from high blood pressure. Likeable enough, because he didn't give out any more shit than he had to—which wasn't much, believe me, considering the size of his winnings at the game of life. His wife was a tiny little blonde, 20 years younger than he was, with a marvelous body and a quick, sharp mind. She was a woman you could like, all right, and I didn't have the feeling she was trying to score off Maria. She had already made her score, the only one that counted, when she had married her husband instead of becoming his mistress.

On a motor yacht, even that big, it's almost impossible to be by yourself. On this particular night, I was right up in the bow, the best place I had found. Everybody else was back on the fantail, listening to a tape concert. The bow was slicing along through the dark sea, throwing phosphorescence to each side. I had been watching a couple of porpoises having themselves a ball sporting with the bow wave. The phosphorescence, standing on their skin like luminous beads, actually outlined their bodies at times. Feeling a soft hand warm on my arm, I turned, thinking it was Maria who had come to join me.

It was Helen, the owner's wife. "Hello, Casey," she said softly. "Enjoying yourself?"

"Sure," I said. "What else?"

Though she had been pretty subtle about it— showing only a sparkle in her eye, an extra little swing of her ass when she thought I was looking, things like that—I already knew what she had in mind.

"But you're always trying to be by yourself," she said. "What do you do up here in the bow, anyway?"

"Watch porpoises," I said. "See down there?"

She leaned over the railing. Her hand still rested on my bare arm. It was the first time she had actually touched me. She straightened.

"You don't like this sort of life very much, do you?"

"It's fine with me as long as Maria enjoys it." I wasn't looking at her, but straight ahead.

251

"But you'd a lot rather be somewhere else. Right?"

"Yes, if you want to know the truth," I said.

"Anywhere in particular?"

"On my ranch," I said.

"Why?"

I looked at her. "You can't leave a ranch to be tended by a hired hand during the winter," I said. "You never know how the weather will go."

She didn't say anything, not for the longest. But she didn't quit looking at me. Then she laughed. She had a pretty laugh, light and trilling, yet with an undertone.

"It's not like everyone thinks, is it?" she said. "You didn't marry Maria for her money at all."

"No," I said.

She nodded thoughtfully. "I was beginning to think not." She went on without pause or hesitation. "How do you feel about swapping up?"

"What?" I said.

I must have sounded pretty stupid, because she became impatient. "Don't you know my husband intends to have Maria before she gets off this boat? What Steven wants, Steven finds a way to get."

"But you said . . ."

"I've got my own interests to look out for," she said. "So I made him a deal. A straight-out trade. He gets Maria. I get you. O.K.?"

"Wait a minute now," I said.

She was leaning close, her hand clasping my arm. "You might as well, Casey. He'll have her, anyway. There's nothing you or I can do to stop it. So we might as well get our kicks, too." Her breath caught. "And I . . . Jesus, Casey, I watch you walking around this ship, wearing those silly cowboy boots, and I . . ."

"Wait one damned minute," I said. "Let me get this straight. You're telling me it's all agreed-to except for me. Maria wants to get into bed with your husband, so I'm to be allowed to get in bed with you."

"I haven't talked to Maria yet. I had to make sure of you first." She grinned. "I don't intend to get left out in the cold. When he's fucking her, he's going to be knowing that I'm getting it too. That makes it all even-Steven. See?"

I was staring. "And you'll even take on the job of persuading Maria. Your husband won't have to do anything but drop his pants."

Her face turned away, though it was already shadowed by the darkness. "It's not the first time. It won't be the last."

"How can you be so sure Maria will agree? Wait a minute. You'll tell her I've already agreed, won't you?" I lifted her hand from my arm. "I don't want any part of it."

Her eyes swung back. "Are you so sure of her yourself?" she said. "Then I only ask you to do this, Casey. Go to your stateroom when it's time to turn in. If Maria comes along, you'll know she wouldn't buy it. But if I show up . . ." She put her hand on my arm again.

The hell of it was, I had liked Helen. She was my pick of all the people who had swarmed around us since we had left the sanctuary of the ranch.

So angry I couldn't see straight, I crowded her against the curve of the bow. I put one arm around her waist, feeling her body pressed hard against mine by my own strength. She didn't flinch; instead, she was giving me the shape of her pussy against my cock, in that way a woman can when she's hot to be fucked.

253

Reaching with the other hand, I pulled up her dress. I slipped two fingers beneath the flimsy strip of nylon and ripped it out, leaving her naked. In one quick move, I had my cock ready. Crouching into position, I rammed it into her steamy cunt. She gasped, taking it, and her hands on my shoulders were like claws. I pulled, shoved again as hard as I could, and then again, even harder. The breath whistled in her lungs each time I banged her against the brass rail braced across her ass.

So mad at them all—Helen, Steven, even Maria who had to have some idea, didn't she—I was not fucking for her pleasure, or for mine. I meant to tear her up. I meant to make her bleed. But it wasn't working. She was taking me, by God, taking it all and liking it, for she was struggling against my pinning grip for room in which to respond. So I let it come in one hot angry spurt and snatched it out of her.

Holding on with both hands, she moved with me as I drew away. "You can't quit me now." Her voice was like the sound of tearing cloth. "You can't leave me like this."

"The hell I can't," I said. Tucking it safely inside my fly, I turned away.

She was running after me, crying out. There on the fantail, some of the people were taking notice. She had to stop her noise and let me walk away.

Below, I stood in the middle of the stateroom and began to shake. I was helpless in the aftermath of my recent rage. And I knew why—if I hadn't done it to Helen, I would have killed some people. Starting with Maria. When I could move, I unscrewed the porthole. Even though the yacht was air-conditioned, I needed some fresh air. I was standing there, letting it blow on my face, when I heard the door open.

Thinking it was Helen, come after me and to hell with the consequences, I didn't turn around.

"Going to bed early?" Maria said. "Good idea, I guess. We'll be in Christiansted early tomorrow morning, and ashore all day."

I had to face her to say it. "Maria, this isn't our deal. I'm getting off this boat tomorrow and going home."

She knew immediately how much I meant it. "All right," she said. "If that's what you need to do. But what's happened to you tonight?"

"You don't want to know," I said. "But listen now. You can go home with me tomorrow morning. But you can't come later on if you stay on this boat after I'm gone."

"If you have to put it that way, then I have to stay," she said slowly.

I turned away. "Suit yourself. I'm going to bed."

I did sleep, oddly enough; something solid and sure was settled inside of me, where for a long time there had been only doubt and indecision. But I heard her when she came in and got into the other bunk.

She lay there for a long time. Then she said. speaking into darkness, "Casey. Will you fuck me? One more time?"

"There ain't but the one way," I said. "With the snow deep on the ground, the cold air all the way down from the North Pole, and us together in our long johns."

That was all that was said. Next morning, I caught a plane for the mainland. When I got home, the snow was so deep I had to walk the last five miles, and that night I went to bed in my winter underwear. In that cold, cold bed, thinking of my palomino mare

255

and then of Maria, I jerked off three times before I could get to sleep.

When the long telling was finished, I didn't have anything to say. Nor did Tony Two. Casey, having spoken his piece, was silent.

Maria said; "He got me, Casey. That day, right there in Christiansted. He came knocking on my door and when I opened it he told me, 'Everybody's gone ashore, Maria. We're alone.'

"I said, 'And Helen?'

"'Gone, too,' he said. 'I made her tell me. Your husband fucked the hell out of her. Now it's my turn.' And then he put his hands on me."

Her eyes were deep with memory. "He was like an old bull, Casey. I was cold at first, so cold, because I didn't want him. But he didn't stop, and he didn't stop, and when I began to get it he didn't stop then, either. He used me up, Casey, like you couldn't believe a man could use up a woman. Only after I was gone, unable to move, did he have this tight, dry little orgasm. Then he got up and went away, leaving me laying there like a rag he had used to blow his nose on."

Maria quit looking at Casey. "Fucking time," she said, rising to her feet. "Give me five minutes, then come on up to my bedroom. All of you."

Before she left, though, she went to Casey and put her arms around his head, holding his face against her body. "Casey, if it'll help any, I don't know either why I had to leave the ranch."

Without looking back, she left us.

Chapter 8

During the five minutes of waiting, no one spoke a word. Both of them, I think, knew the same conviction that possessed my soul. We had come to a certain ending. But the ending was not all, for contained within it was a new beginning.

One by one, we had told our tales; we had listened one by one to the others' telling. By this means, revealing the elements and stratagens that had brought Us to No-Name Key, we had shaped the communal history of Us. We were now brothers, yet far more than brothers could ever be, for we were all beloved of the same woman and, both all alike and all unlike, we cherished her.

We understood, in a shared understanding, the anguish, the hurts, the inadequacies that had caused us, each individually, to betray Maria; had caused Maria to betray, one by one, her three true lovers. Separately, as different manifestations of the male principle, we had been incomplete I-fragments of Us. Maria, the sole representative in Us of the female principle had been herself an I-fragment, buffeted like a piece of paper in a strong wind.

I thought I could see, dimly, what Maria's talk of the Three plus One meant, though she herself did not have the language to express it. The Trinity—Father,

Son, and Holy Ghost—were all male. In Christian dogma, the female principle, Mary, has never been admitted into the holy circle. Three plus One—my Germanic soul understood, now, that omitting the One denies wholeness.

Casey was the first to move. He went to the bar and poured a double shot of bourbon. He took it in one smooth swallowing of throat muscles. He placed the glass on the bar and slowly wiped his hand across his mouth.

"Maria is waiting," he said. "Are you coming?"

As though there might be a remaining doubt. But there was no doubt, though we knew that upon entering tonight into Maria's bedroom, we were committing ourselves to the ultimate climax. Here, tonight, we would finish. Or here, tonight, we would begin.

I led the way. As the first man, it was my rightful place. They yielded precedence, following after up the stairs. I did not knock on her door, but opened it to enter into her chamber where we—Us—had not been until now.

It was a huge bed, made of Spanish wood, its four corner posts, ornately scrolled, reaching nearly to the ceiling. Both broad and long, it was supplied with bolsters and pillows. The pristine linen, pure white and smooth with starch, waited to be rumpled and sweated by the sweaty strivings of our bodies upon the body of our woman.

Maria lay naked in the exact center of the white expanse, her long black hair spread like a magic fan. Her legs were open, showing well the thicket of her mount. Her knees were up, parted, revealing the rosy promise of her slit. She was yielding to Us the sight of her beautiful body, open, naked, unashamed, a gift of her soul.

"Let me see you."

Her voice, soft and urgent, drove Us to eager compliance. In less than a minute we stood naked before her nakedness.

"Come close," she said.

We ranged Us side by side against the bed. Gazing at our rampant cocks, eyes rapt and glistening, she sat up suddenly. She leaned her lips to my cock first, taking him into the shaping of her hand as she kissed it with a ravenous passion. My thigh muscles quivered, lusting to drive hard at her mouth. But, holding still, I took the caress as she meant it to be taken, an obeisance to her master; who yet, in full circle, she commanded utterly.

She went next to Tony Two, her eyes glowing with the enormous promise of his instrument. She measured its great length with the tip of one finger. She did not kiss it, but swallowed the bulging redness of its head, holding it warm in her mouth while Tony Two stood like a Roman statue brought to life.

She moved down to sit before Casey. Her head dipped with an avid greediness, pressing her face into his crotch. She breathed deeply, inhaling his body odor as one gulps all such brave, musky scents, horse sweat and good perfume and the smell of a man. As she did so, her nipples came slowly to their tiny erection.

In one lithe, slithering movement, she moved back on the bed. Her eyes found mine. "You first, Jerry."

Knowing what I should do as well as if she had sketched it on a drawing pad, I laid myself between her legs. My hands under her hips, I lifted her and buried my face in the thicket of her cunt, my tongue reaching first for the good sweet taste of her, then curling to flutter at her clitoris. A deep-throated moan came from her as she yielded to my mouth.

The other two were watching. I did not care. I knew that, as I tasted her funky sweetness, so were they reveling in it. Her body began a slow surge and I rode with it, as aware as if I too owned a cunt that she wanted to retreat from the delicious hurting ecstasy and, at the same time, needed more and more and more of what I was giving her . . . until she was coming, the juices gushing over my tongue as she warmed into a sweeter liquefaction.

My turn finished, I drew away. Her eyes were already on Tony Two, her arms beckoned. As I rolled to one side to make way, he came to her gently, lifting her with his hands and turning her on her belly. He began to tongue her anus, with rapid thrusts and flutterings that brought her, writhing and gasping, up on her knees. Watching, on a sudden impulse I pushed one hand between Tony Two's legs. I did not masturbate him, but simply let myself feel, so luxuriously, the shape and heft of his throbbing cock.

Casey's turn. He stood looking at Maria as she waited. "I have to do it now," he said.

Since he was the first to speak, except for Maria, his voice should have been an intrusion upon the sensuous mood we shared. But it wasn't.

"Do you want to, Casey?" she said.

"Yes."

Moving more quickly than one could believe, he was on top of her, his face between her legs, clasped tightly around his head, while her mouth opened for his cock, her hands pulling his slim buttocks down within reach. As he tongued her clitoris, he was fucking her mouth with those quick, hard, short thrusts that were his trademark. She was taking him top and

260

bottom, a sight so stirring I was suddenly on the edge of orgasm. Feeling a liberating surge of commitment to Us, I looked to Tony. Before I could censor what we meant to do, we had rolled together, taking each other simultaneously, and in me there was not the revulsion, the self-disgust, I would have expected, but only a committed joy.

His enormous cock filled my mouth. The taste was strange, like Maria's cunt yet also unlike. Neither of us strived violently to bring the other to orgasm, but dealt gently with the tender tool. We only desired to share the passionate 69 that Casey and Maria were making.

In the after hiatus, we lay resting, though both pairs had stopped short of orgasm. Each of Us touched Maria—my hand on her breast, Tony Two's hand clasped warmly between her legs, Casey's on her belly. Though breathing hard, and swarmed by residual sensation, we were content.

But it was only a moment before Maria spoke. "All right. Who's first for real fucking?"

We hesitated, each anxious to begin, but not wishing to be greedy.

"Choose," I said.

She smiled her lovely smile, even as her eyes darkened with . . . thought? . . . pain? . . . memory? All three at once?

"The way you first came into me," she said softly. "Let's live it all through one more time, in one great fucking."

"Yes," I said, speaking fully for Us.

I was not hasty. We had all the time in the world. I went into her as gently as if she were virginal, letting her soak me up inch by inch. For the first time in all the years, I was truly possessing Maria; and

Maria was truly, deeply, possessing me. A full woman now, rapt of all her powers, no longer the learning girl with raw, hungry places in her soul. I went deep, then stopped to put my mouth on her mouth. I held the kiss, feeling her vagina begin to heat and writhe under the influence of the kiss, loving every inch of my cock as he throbbed his equal love in a reciprocal rhythm. At last, so sensuously that already I was dying inside from sheer bliss, I began to fuck.

Slow, easy-riding, with long deep-thrust strokes, met each time by the perfect response of her body. Quickening, then, wholly confident she would return the accelerating rhythm without a break. I was so sensitive, her steamy vagina was like a soft hand gripping. I could even sense the minute roughness of her cervix, pressing precisely against the eye of the glans at its deepest reach.

I was coming before I was aware of it. She was coming to meet me, and I continued in a slow, molten flow that kept on and on and on, until at the end we were not simply cock and cunt but buried flesh in flesh, she one enormous pussy and me one huge penis, melted totally into each other.

In only a part of Us, there remained no need to prolong it beyond our perfect moment. Moving to one side, still lying against her, I said to Tony Two, "Take her now, Tony. Take her quick."

He did not hesitate, as I had feared he would. Wholly of Us, no longer the narcissistic lover of men, he poised his big dick for entrance. Lying so close, I felt her whole body gasp and flinch as he crammed into her depths. There was a grimace of pain on her face. But it changed as he withdrew slowly; she was waiting with delight for the following stroke. Wanting to hear her gasp again, I put one hand on his ass and pushed, shoving him deeply into her, and I was happy with her when she began immediately to come.

Tony, fucking her like a man, took her through three successive orgasms before he began to reach his own. With his mighty cock he had used her mightily and when he fell away to the other side, letting Casey come into the saddle, she lay limply, her arms thrown wide, her head back, her body open.

She lay so, a sheen of sweat showing on her skin, even after Casey was swinging fiercely upon her. He would not be denied, though; his short, hard jockey-strokes roused her slowly into a new gathering of effort, and she was swinging fervently with him when he came. She cried out for the first time, her eyes rolling back in her head as though she had fainted. But her spirit was with Us, prompting her to lift her weary arms and draw me and Tony Two closer, so that, with Casey lying spent and sprawled on top, we were huddled together in the aftermath of the first complete fuck in the life of Us.

I don't know how much time passed before Maria, first stirring tentatively to let Us know that she wanted out from under, got out of the bed. As she stood looking down, her eyes were enigmatic, yet warm with love. Before I could wonder what she meant to do, she had turned out the light. The descent of darkness, dropping Us into anonymity, altered immediately the texture of the event.

When she returned her body to our bodies, she brought with her a deeper, darker sensuousness. Our limbs began writhing a slow turmoil of voluptuous search. Remembering with anonymous joy Tony's great cock in my mouth, I found what could only be his chest; but when I moved my hand downward, it

263

encountered someone's head bent over his crotch. At
the same moment, a tongue lapped under my balls,
an excruciating sensation that drove me to a further
seeking. Finding another cock, I knew it had to be
Casey's. Half-limp, still wet from Maria's cunt, it began to rise under the palm-slick movement of my
hand. I felt the urge to go down on it, for here in
the dark everything was possible. But I was unable
to reach the lustful goal, for someone's weight was
pinning my thighs as he/she transferred the avid lick-
ing of his/her tongue to my cock.

Putting down my hands to clasp close the head in
my groin, I discovered from the long hair that it was
Maria. She shifted her body to lie full-length against
mine; I turned on my side. When I put my head between her legs, they clamped so strongly I thought
I wouldn't be able to breathe. But I didn't need to
breathe, except to snuff her deep odors.

A moment later, the magic spell was rudely shattered by a sudden squall, like that of a wildcat, ripping through the secretive darkness. The sound, so
ragged in its outraged anger, snatched me with jar-
ring abruptness out of the sensuous stupor of Us in
which we had been dwelling. I pulled myself, head
and cock, free of Maria's fleshy imprisonment, her
teeth scraping painfully on my prick as I did so, and
sprang out of bed to fumble for the light switch.

The sudden onslaught of brilliant seeing dazzled
my eyes, so that for the beat of two seconds the scene
was only a jumbled kaleidoscope of fragmented meanings. I focused on Maria. She was crouched beside
the bed, her mouth open, her face stricken. The hair-
raising sound came again. It was Casey. And no wonder; Tony Two's big dick was driven hilt-deep
into his asshole. Though Casey struggled frantically

264

to escape, Tony was holding him prisoner to his cock with both hands clutched into the tortured curve of Casey's body.

"Tony!" Maria yelled. At the sound of her voice, Tony let go. Casey dropped from him, sprawling like a broken doll. But he was up immediately, his hands darting out to push Tony off the bed. Coming after him, he stood him up with a left, then smashed a right into Tony's face. Tony's mouth opened, showing a red gash of blood. Dully, he wiped at it, then looked at his hand in disbelief.

Casey was not finished with him. As Tony retreated, ineffectual hands up, face filled with terror, he advanced in a poised crouch. Catching him in a corner, Casey pounded with short, hard blows to the body. Tony crumpled, folding into a fetal position, but Casey stooped to haul him up again, holding him with one hand and hitting him with the other. The blood sprayed with each deliberate blow.

"Casey!" Maria screamed. By the time the sound had died away, she was grabbing frantically at his arms. Casey flung her violently away and stooped after Tony, down again, his arms clasped over his head. But Maria was all over Casey now, screaming his name as though he were a killer dog to be brought to heel.

I hurried to help but Casey, insensate with rage, squared off against me. Before he could strike the first blow against his new enemy, Maria's calling had penetrated to his understanding. He stopped, his fists dangling. He was breathing hard.

"He's lucky," he said raspingly. "I meant to kill the queer son of a bitch."

Maria put her hands on his chest, then slipped her arms around his body, holding him hard. "Why did

265

you have to ruin it?" she said brokenly. "Why, Casey? Why?"

He wanted to pull away. She wouldn't let him go.

"He ain't going to fuck me. Not in this million years."

Tony was getting to his feet. His voice trembled with his quivering, bloody mouth. "But you fucked me," he said. "I thought . . . in the dark like that . . ."

Casey pulled free of Maria's restraint. Advancing on Tony, he shoved at his shoulder with his open hand. Tony Two stumbled backward onto the bed.

"Try it again. I'll cut it off and make you eat it raw," Casey said. From his anger, he should have been shouting. But his voice was low and even. "Understand me, Tony?" He slapped at Tony's shoulder. "Understand?" Coldly, he was trying to make Tony stand up and fight, so he could hit him again.

"Casey," I said quietly. "That's enough now, Casey."

He stopped. Everybody stopped. The room was suddenly still. I stared at Casey, hating him. As, I knew, he hated Tony. And—the way Maria hated Us now? I looked at Maria. Hard-eyed, glitter-eyed, she stood naked in the middle of the floor, separate from Us.

The sadness, the loss, was inevitable in my voice. "We had it, didn't we? We really had it there, for just a few minutes."

Maria's hands went up to cover her face. She was crying so hopelessly I wanted to go to her. But it would do no good. Nothing could help Us now.

Casey, physically quiet, was still glaring. "I don't know about anybody else. But I'm getting the hell out of here. I'm going home."

The risk of irreparable rupture had existed from

266

the beginning. I guess it had to be him, though, I thought, watching him stoop to gather up his clothes. He was the only one of Us who had a place where he belonged.

This, too, was a piece of the truth that had escaped me until now. Each of us had been forever alone; even Maria with her money, Tony Two with his great physical beauty, his love of self. Even me, with my talent for shaping words into larger meanings. Casey had been alone, also—but he had had a place to call his own.

I thought sadly, even if he hadn't broken it so quickly after we had got it together, how long could it have lasted, anyway? Another ten minutes, a day, a year? The miracle of Us, like any other miracle, could not be bridged across time.

Casey, already dressed, was abruptly gone. No word, and without looking back. That, of course, would be his way—a way he had followed right down to the bitter, empty end. Yet—it was a sudden, agonizing thought—how could he have driven himself to depart, now that he had known, as we had known, the glories of being Us? The I-fragment is so much more stubborn than we realize.

Maria had sat down on the bed. She held her crumpled body in an awkward, canted posture, as though it were hurting. She was weeping, the tears dropping wetly on her naked thighs.

I went to her. "Maria," I said gently.

She drew away from the nearness of my hand. "You'll have to go now," she whispered. The whisper could be heard sibilantly throughout the room.

"I'll stay, Maria. Tony, he'll stay, I know he will."

She rose. Her face was ravaged by these last minutes. Yet there showed in it a certain brave resolu-

267

tion. I thought. She has taken up again the burden of the empty life she knew before we came. Even though she knows that now she'll have to carry it to the end of her time.

"You must go," she said. Her tone was flat, finished, ended. "If one, only one, is absent from Us, there is no Us." Her voice broke on the final word, but she quickly regained control. Her hand wiped at her face, dropped to her side. "I don't want to see you. Not ever again." She was suddenly screaming. "Get out of my house! Get out of my life!"

We departed separately, as we had come, Casey first only minutes after the boat had arrived from the mainland. I had gone into Tony Two's room to see how he felt after last night's beating. We stood together without speaking, gazing down upon the thin, small-statured figure in the cowboy clothes, standing in the boat to gaze steadfastly toward the mainland, with not a single backward glance for No-Name Key. After the boat had disappeared through the mangrove passage, I glanced at Tony's bruised face. He did not say anything. I returned to my room and finished packing.

When the boat returned, I went across the hall to watch alone as Tony Two embarked for the mainland. He was, at least, different from Casey; he kept his eyes turned toward No-Name Key as far as I could see him. I wondered if he was crying.

So what does that leave me? I thought as I waited on the marble landing for my turn. Casey looks away, Tony Two looks back. And Jerry Dorn?

I remembered the strange words Maria had spoken, that eternity ago when, encapsulated in our separate states of being, we had arrived at No-Name Key. *The Axiom of Maria.* Three plus One equals Four.

268

The four is completeness, a wholeness, the symbol and sign of the universe. Why then, I wondered suddenly, do most of the spiritual disciplines use the incomplete triad instead. Must something always be left out for humankind?

I realized, suddenly, how very much I wanted to stay. Even as I listened for the boat, I was wishing desperately that Maria could appear to call me back. Once and briefly, we had found the all of Us; and I could not bear the prophetic shape of my remaining days. From here, I could see only a drab nothing. Nothing to cherish. Nothing to share. I might as well be leaving No-Name Key cold in my coffin, ready to be entered into the earth. For what is the flesh when the spirit has gone?

The boat came. I stepped aboard. I found also my manner of departure; looking neither forward nor backward, I sat with one hand covering my eyes.

At the mainland dock, I climbed out and took my bag from John Kershaw. "Goodbye, Mr. Dorn," he said, gazing up at me. The old boatman, dark-skinned and silent, had ferried us one by one across to No-Name Key. Now, one by one, he had ferried us ashore again. The boatman on the Styx, I thought, looking for an honest farewell in his old eyes; except he carries both ways, doesn't he, for we didn't get to stay.

"Goodbye," I said and turned to walk away.

There was a small grocery a mile or two up the shell road where I could call a taxi. I plodded steadily onward, the bright Florida sun beating hotly on my shoulders. I did not reach the store. Coming to a sudden halt, I declared aloud, "No. I'm going back to Maria."

I knew she would deny me. But, I told myself, I

will make her want me. I will become Us, fulfill her as Us fulfilled her. I can do it, if she'll give me the chance. Because I know her now; I know myself. I was already on my way back. Though I didn't know whether she would even send the boat in answer to my ringing of the bell, I was younger, surer, better of myself.

Tony Two was on the dock when I arrived. I stared. "Where did you come from?"

"I never left," he said defiantly. "I hid over there in the palms until you were gone." His battered face was firm with stubbornness. "I'm staying with Maria."

"What if she won't have you?"

"She'll have to let me stay. I don't have anywhere else to go." His voice cried out the desperately hopeful words. He fell silent, regarding me with suspicion. "What are you doing here?"

"I'm staying too," I said. "It just took me a while longer to make up my mind."

He grinned suddenly, coming close enough to put a hand to my shoulder. "The two of us, she can't make us go, can she? Give her time to think about it, she'll be glad we came back."

"Two out of three," I said, taking up the mutual encouragement. "It's better than nothing."

"You want to ring the bell?" Tony said happily. "Or shall I?"

Hearing the sound of a car, we both turned. A taxi. Old, battered—and bearing Casey. He got out and came toward us, limping slightly in his cowboy boots.

He stopped before Tony. "Tony Two," he said. "I'm sorry."

Tony drew back in fear and surprise. "What are you doing here?"

Casey glanced at me. "I thought about something I said while I was telling my story. *When you find the place, stay there; that's what I say.* When those words, spoken by my own mouth, came back to me, I knew I was a fool to leave No-Name Key."

"What about the ranch?" I said.

He shook his head. "It's not the place, not any more. Maria makes the place for me. That's what I didn't know before." He paused briefly, even managed a smile. "Maybe . . . maybe we can all go out there together for a visit sometime. It would make a nice change from No-Name Key for a little while." His eyes flickered rapidly from me to Tony Two. "Because you're going back, aren't you?"

"Yes," I said. "Tony Two, ring the bell."

The bell sounded across the water in quick hard certain strokes; and we stood waiting, three men together, for the boat to take us home to No-Name Key.

It came more quickly than we had expected. From a far distance, we recognized Maria at the wheel. She lifted one hand, her black hair flying, as she curved the boat in a graceful, swirling arc that ended expertly beside the dock.

So it was our Maria who ferried Us across the bay for the last time to No-Name Key. Where we—Us—would dwell forever.

HER

Anonymous

Rarely in the history of book publishing has a love story been told with the frankness and earthy honesty of *Her*, the adult love story that explores the lust, the passion, the ecstasy and the longing between a woman and a man – a book that portrays the beauty, the joy and the truth to be found in sensual love.

£1.50

HIM

Anonymous

After *Her* there could only be *Him* . . .

Every man and every woman contain two beings: the animal and the human; the spiritual and the bestial. Only when the two come together can a man or a woman experience true, sensual, ecstatic love.

Him is the story of two women and one man, who together shared a love affair that awakened them to a new world of carnality and lust – and that freed the primitive, sensual self of each.

£1.50

THEM

Anonymous

She was a sexual adventuress, an erotic explorer not of continents but of men. She yearned for them and lusted after them. She hated them and adored them. She wanted them – but most of all she wanted them to want her. She played men's games and gave them all they wanted – and more than they had even dreamed of.

More provocative than *Her*, more sensational than *Him* – this is the passionate, candid story of one woman driven by a ravenous desire for pleasure – and by her obsessive need to find the ultimate lover.

£1.60

ME

Anonymous

The millions of readers who have eagerly anticipated this new book in the world famous series of raw, candid love stories will not be disappointed. Here is all the honesty of *Her*, the power of *Him* and the natural sensuality of *Them*.

Me – where every expectation of lust and love, of dream and desire, will be met, experienced – and surpassed.

£1.60

BESTSELLING FICTION FROM ARROW

All these books are available from your bookshop or news-agent or you can order them direct. Just tick the titles you want and complete the form below.

THE HISTORY MAN	Malcolm Bradbury	£1.60
1985	Anthony Burgess	£1.50
THE BILLION DOLLAR KILLING	Paul Erdman	£1.75
THE YEAR OF THE FRENCH	Thomas Flanagan	£2.50
EMMA SPARROW	Marie Joseph	£1.50
COCKPIT	Jerzy Kosinski	£1.60
CITY OF THE DEAD	Herbert Lieberman	£1.60
STRUMPET CITY	James Plunkett	£2.50
TO GLORY WE STEER	Alexander Kent	£1.75
TORPEDO RUN	Douglas Reeman	£1.50
THE BEST MAN TO DIE	Ruth Rendell	£1.25
SCENT OF FEAR	Margaret Yorke	£1.25
2001: A SPACE ODYSSEY	Arthur C. Clarke	£1.50
	Postage	_____
	Total	_____

ARROW BOOKS, BOOKSERVICE BY POST, PO BOX 29, DOUGLAS, ISLE OF MAN, BRITISH ISLES

Please enclose a cheque or postal order made out to Arrow Books Limited for the amount due including 10p per book for postage and packing for orders within the UK and 12p for overseas orders.

Please print clearly

NAME ....

ADDRESS ....

....

Whilst every effort is made to keep prices down and to keep popular books in print, Arrow Books cannot guarantee that prices will be the same as those advertised here or that the books will be available.